NEVER AGAIN

LILLIANA ANDERSON

One heartbreak was enough...

never again

Lilliana
ANDERSON

INTERNATIONALLY BESTSELLING AUSTRALIAN AUTHOR

Edited by Making Manuscripts
Cover by Ember Designs

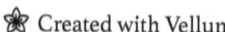 Created with Vellum

For myself. Because I'm a fucking queen.

FOREWORD

This book had been on my 'to write' list since 2012. At the time, I had the idea and even started writing a few chapters detailing Cora's relationship breakdown. But, for some reason, I put it aside and wrote a dozen other books instead.

Why did I put it down? To be honest, it was because I was afraid of the book. I wasn't emotionally mature enough at the time to deal with the themes contained within, or the kind of relationship that Cora and Bran have. But now that I'm older and more experienced as a writer, I feel that it's the perfect time to not only write this story, but release it into the world.

It isn't going to shock you. Don't worry (or perhaps, get excited) about that. What follows is a story that is funny and *very* sexy with just the right amount of angst. Bran is an alpha. Cora is a solicitor ten years his senior. If you've ever wondered what it would be like to be taken by the hottest man you can imagine, you're going to enjoy every moment of the following pages...

PLAYLIST

For a list of handpicked songs that match the feel of Never Again, visit Lilliana Anderson using the following image

1

I NEVER UNDERSTOOD the desire to put your pain on social media for everyone to see. My Facebook feed was full of people lamenting the world—fuck this, fuck that, fuck my existence—it was never ending. For me, social media was about sharing the best of my life and spying on other people's. That's why, when I found out my scumbag of a husband was cheating on me, I didn't share a single tidbit of information with the world. I quietly changed my relationship status from 'married' to 'it's complicated', then proceeded to cut the crotch out of every single pair of pants he owned.

Only my closest friends and family bore witness to my FML moments, because they were the ones who understood, the ones who mattered. Whenever my life fell apart, they picked me up and put me back together again. My mother would bake me chocolate brownies and tell me that everything was going to be OK, and my very best friend, Olivia, would shake me by the shoulders and remind me I'm a queen. "Queens don't stay down," she'd say.

All Facebook ever got was a rare photo of me looking my best. Like today, while I sat with Olivia outside a quaint Melbourne patisserie on our lunch break. My hair and makeup was on point, my lipstick a bold red, while the sun provided the lighting—a rarity on a cold day in July.

"Hashtag that one 'slaying life'," Olivia suggested. "That bastard will see how happy you look and realise how badly he fucked up." She sucked back on a cigarette then blew the smoke out in a rush. "Come to think of it. We need to go out tonight. That will *really* piss him off. You can post photos and everything."

"Go out?" The idea seemed completely insane to me.

She stubbed out her cigarette in a small aluminium ashtray. "Yes, Cora. I love you, and I think you're gorgeous, but lying on my couch for months on end, eating liqueur chocolates while watching Netflix isn't doing a thing for your figure."

"Jack always said that saying 'but' meant you could discount everything that was said before it."

She picked up her Prada handbag and slid it over her arm. "Fuck Jack. You should discount everything he ever said to you before the moment you saw *his butt* as he pumped that Sally woman from behind in your marital bed."

My stomach soured at the memory. "Don't remind me." I'd been expecting to work late on a case but was able to take some work home instead. Thinking it'd be nice to surprise Jack and have dinner together, I hadn't called ahead. I just picked up his favourite takeaway and a bottle of wine. With the word 'surprise' on the tip of my tongue, I entered the house. But the surprise was on me. The moment I walked in, I could hear them: "Harder! Harder!", coupled with the slapping of wet bodies. I knew what I was walking in on before I saw it—the sight of my partner of eleven years, my husband for one, fucking some woman from behind, slapping her arse like she was some kind of rodeo cow.

Driven by rage, I threw the food and my handbag at him, sending rice and beef in black bean sauce all over the place. Then, I smashed him in the side of the head with the only thing I had left in my hands—my laptop. The resulting injury had been enough for him to take out an intervention order against me that forced me from *my* house and almost lost me my job. Instead, I'd been taken off my cases and made the babysitter to the junior solicitors until this mess was sorted out. It made me feel sick every time I thought about it.

"Come on, stop thinking about that arsehole. We'll get your intervention order thrown out of court the moment it goes before the magistrate. Then you'll get your cases back *and* your house. Then life will start to feel normal again."

"Don't you think taking a Crown Prosecutor with me to a magistrate hearing is a bit of overkill?" Standing, I noticed my skirt *was* feeling a little tight around the midsection. Maybe I did need to lay off those chocolates...

"Considering I know every judge in the city and have slept with more than half of them, taking me is probably the best thing you could do," she assured me. "Once we're done with that bullshit order, we'll get you a quickie divorce, leave him with nothing but a set of stomped-on balls, and then *you'll* become single and amazing like me."

I couldn't help but laugh.

"And I'm serious about tonight," she added, hitting the button to activate the crosswalk. "There's nothing better in this world than having young men fall all over you. We'll pick the hottest nightclub in town and when some twenty-something picks you up, you'll forget all about Jack-Arse."

"You seem to be forgetting that I *am* a twenty-something."

She scoffed as the lights changed and we crossed. "Barely. Twenty-nine is practically thirty—which you will be in November, I might add."

"Says the woman who has been twenty-nine for eleven years."

"That's why I'm an expert on the subject."

Chuckling at her response, I shook my head, loving her candour. Olivia was over a decade older than me. We became friends when I first started working for the OPP —the Office of Public Prosecution—straight out of university. She was a barrister and had become my mentor after we worked on our first case together. Then, our personalities clicked and we became the best of friends in the years that followed.

"And I'm talking about men—well, boys, I suppose— who are barely twenty and a day. They're outstanding in the sack, super eager to please. I once had a nineteen-year-old who went all night. I was exhausted the next day but deliciously sore in all the right places. I swear they're all vying for the lover of the year award, and the best part about it is they don't want any kind of connection or relationship."

"Nineteen is a bit young for me. I don't think I could go below twenty-five."

"Don't get caught up with the numbers, darling. It's a catch, fuck, and release program. Age doesn't matter—as long as they're legal—but size definitely matters. I'm going to get you acquainted with the new way of dating."

"I thought Tinder was the new way of dating?"

"Tinder is full of false advertising and disappointing reality. *This* is Olivia's way." She pointed at herself, amusement in her eyes. "By the time I'm finished with you, you'll never, *ever* want to be married again. You'll be having far too much fun being single and free."

Olivia had been married twice. One ended when it turned out her husband preferred men, and the other ended when he wanted children and she didn't. Now, she swore that the single life was the *only* life worth living.

"Well, I kind of have to get divorced, first."

"Formalities." She waved her hand about in the air. "It takes a year of separation before you can file for divorce. You can't quit having a sex life because of that tiny technicality. Right now, you are separated, which is the same thing as being single. I was always on Ross's side; he and Rachel were definitely on a break. Besides, I doubt Jack is too concerned."

"I suppose you're right. I just feel weird about the idea of being with someone else. Eleven years with the same man is a long time."

"All the more reason to get back on that bike. It's not like you have to remember much. All the same parts go into the same holes. And when your heart is broken, the best way to feel better is to fuck someone who is so beautiful you could die."

"This doesn't feel anything like something I want to do," I responded, smiling at her advice as we headed into our building on Lonsdale Street. I hadn't been to a nightclub since my early days at university. I never dreamed I'd want to step foot inside one again. But then, I hadn't thought that I'd be single after spending eleven years of my life committed to the same man either. The fact he so easily threw that all away for a measly fuck really got my goat. I had *never* looked at another man and was bloody devastated that he thought so little of me. Worse, that he also screwed that bitch in *my bed!* I couldn't imagine he'd have the gall to take her to our home for their first time, so how many times had I slept on those sheets after he'd been fucking her on them? My stomach twisted at the thought. I was going to develop an ulcer.

"It's exactly something you *should do*," Olivia rebutted, lowering her voice once we were in the lobby so nosy ears weren't listening in. "Trust me on this, Cora. I've had more relationship breakups than you've had birthdays. And, have I ever steered you wrong?"

I thought back to the time she convinced me that I *needed* to own every colour Mac lipstick they had in store. We maxed out my credit card in about thirty minutes flat. "No. You haven't," I replied, smiling. Buying those lipsticks had been a costly venture, and I'd needed to install new cabinets to store them all. But I had zero regrets over following her advice. I loved every one of those damn things.

Scanning her ID card to open the main door, she grinned, triumphant. "Then we need to get out of here early so we can buy you a dress."

2

―――――

"I CANNOT AFFORD THIS SHOP," I stated, turning from side to side in front of the dressing room mirror. We were in Sass & Bide—not my idea—and the dress I'd tried on had a price tag that turned my face as green as the hand-sewn sequins that covered it.

"That sequined mini is gorgeous. Emerald green is your colour. It suits your dark hair and creamy skin. *And* it screams come and get me," Olivia replied, admiring herself in a fitted black mini dress that had this amazing silver embellishment curling around her waist then up around the high neck. She was made to wear designer clothes; her tall rake-thin figure was enough to make any runway model feel fat and stick their finger down their throat.

I, on the other hand, was not as *gifted*. The sequined dress barely covered my very round arse, and my enormous boobs looked like they were about to bust out of the scoop neck and take the spaghetti straps out as casualties.

"I look ridiculous. I won't be able to scratch my knee without showing arse cheek."

"Good. We're going out to get you laid."

"No." I shook my head, deciding that getting fat on too much chocolate was much better than parading around with my tits and arse on display. I didn't need a man to make me feel better. And since Jack was the only man I'd ever been with, I didn't even know if I'd know what to do. "I don't want that. I'm out." I turned around and went back inside my cubicle to change. Twenty seconds later, a familiar hand slid two more dresses over the door. One was a kimono-style silk dress in the same green as the sequined dress, and the other was black and fitted with wide shoulder straps.

"Try these, Cor," Olivia cooed, using my nickname as she wiggled the dresses to tempt me. "You look beautiful in anything, and I really think going out will do you the world of good. It's been months since you and Jack split."

Folding my arms across my middle, I looked at the dresses but didn't take them or respond to what she said, preferring to behave like a petulant child instead of the twenty-nine-year-old woman I was.

"Come on, *please*. I'll tell you what; you don't even have to pick up tonight. You can just sit back and accept the free drinks. Hell, *I'll* buy your drinks. You just need to get out of the apartment and have some fun with me." She shook the dresses again. "I'll even buy your dress for you." I reached out and grabbed the dresses before she insisted on buying shoes for me as well. "I knew you'd come around. Oh, and I'm getting you shoes too. Nothing you have at my place will do." Laughing to myself, I held both dresses against my body to decide which one I preferred while Olivia could be heard demanding that the sales assistant bring us shoes to try. There was one thing you could say about Olivia: once her mind was set on something, there was no persuading her otherwise. It was the primary reason she was one of the best prosecutors in the state.

"I think this is the one," I said, exiting the cubicle in the black embroidered dress. It held my boobs in place and enhanced my chocolate-loving curves with the addition of a very sexy centre-front split. I could see this becoming my favourite LBD.

Nodding appreciatively, Olivia gestured for me to turn around. "Yes. That's definitely the one. You're a knockout."

By the time we'd finished shopping, it was past dinner so we stopped off to grab some sushi before we went back to Olivia's to get ready for our *big night out.* She'd booked an Uber to pick us up at ten, saying that no sane person would enter a club before that time, so that gave us a couple of hours to eat and get ourselves all glammed up—although, I kind of thought of it as mutton dressing up as lamb. I couldn't imagine that I was going to feel as though I fit in to the nightclub scene any better than I did when I was eighteen. It was never my thing.

Although, I'd never had Olivia as my wing-woman before. She totally knew how to get in the mood for going out. She turned on some music, prepared vodka martinis to loosen us up, and by the time our driver arrived, I was smiling and actually looking forward to a night out on the town.

"We're going to Chaise Lounge," Olivia informed me when we slid into the back seat.

"Chaise Lounge? They named their club after furniture?"

"It's really cool, actually. The décor is red with antique-looking chairs. It's very old-theatre looking, great DJ, and lots of beautiful young men dying to get their rocks off after a tough week at work."

"Who are you to deny them that pleasure, right?"

She giggled, a throaty sound that could have also been described as a purr. "It's mutually beneficial, I assure you."

When I laughed, she reached over and gave my leg a squeeze.

"I won't ditch you," she assured me. "Tonight is about you. Bob can be my lover for tonight."

Did I miss something? Who was Bob?

Seeing my confused look, Olivia filled in the blanks for me. "B-O-B: Battery Operated Boyfriend."

I still didn't get it. Olivia laughed.

"You've been far too sheltered, Cora. I'm talking about my vibrator."

I sucked my breath back so hard that I choked on my own spit. "Olivia!"

Laughing, she patted me on the back to help me breathe. "I really have my work cut out with you, don't I? I mean, I knew you were a little straight and naïve, but I had no idea it was this bad. Do you even own a vibrator?"

Our driver cleared his throat, either getting a little hot and bothered by our conversation, or just reminding us that he was there. I caught his eyes in the rear-view mirror and felt my cheeks burn. I was so thankful when he looked away.

"No," I whispered, trying to keep this conversation as private as possible.

"No!" Olivia yelled.

I slapped her on the arm with the back of my hand. "Shhhh!" I hissed, side-eyeing the driver when Olivia frowned at me and rubbed her arm. "We have an audience."

"Oh God. Who cares? He drives an Uber on a Friday night. I assure you, this man has heard everything. Right, er"—she paused and looked at the Uber app on her phone—"Glen?"

"This is the first vibrator conversation I've been privy to," he replied.

Olivia looked momentarily dumbfounded then lifted her shoulders dismissively. "Then you need this education just as much as Cora does. Sex toys are the cornerstone of the adult relationship. Without them, life in the bedroom gets stale, bland even. Singles need them to get their rocks off when they don't score, *or worse,* when they do score and their partner fails to do their due diligence—it's always important to make sure the lady comes first, Glen. Remember that." Glen nodded, now listening eagerly. I, personally, wanted to slide down into the seat and disappear. I needed this to be over.

Of course, Olivia continued. "And couples need them to keep the interest levels up. There's only a finite number of ways you can have sex with the same person, and long-term couples get so good at getting each other off that it becomes a five-minute window of perfunctory movement that isn't satisfying *despite* the orgasm. Toys give couples something new and interesting to do together, upping the ante a little and making something old feel new again. Do you have a significant other, Glen?"

"No. I'm in between girlfriends at the moment."

"Do you have a fleshlight?"

"A...?" He let the question hang in the air. I assumed he was as clueless as I was about this fleshlight thing.

"It's a vagina in a tube that looks like a flashlight. I hear they're amazing. Do yourself a favour, Glen. Get one."

"Oh...OK," he stuttered. "Ah...we are here."

"Fantastic," Olivia replied, slipping him a fifty.

"You've already paid."

"I know. This is for you to put towards your new toy. Just promise to think of me the first time you use it." Giving him a wink and a smile, she got out of the car.

"Please don't think of me," I added, following behind, feeling a little grossed out by the whole discussion, but not enough to forget my manners. "Oh, and thanks for the lift."

"Have a good night!" Glen called after us, the sound muted as Olivia slammed the car door with a laugh.

"Wasn't he a gem?" She waved as he drove off.

"You are so embarrassing," I grumbled, beginning to wonder why on earth I thought going out with her was a good idea. While we were best friends in every other area of life, where men were concerned, we were polar opposites. Olivia went through them like Kleenex and I, well, didn't go through them at all. I kept them. *Well, I thought I did.* And the only reason I was standing in front of a nightclub, on the verge of getting a divorce was because *he couldn't keep his goddamn dick in his pants.* I wanted to scream.

"Let's get inside," Olivia said, hurriedly grabbing my arm. "You look like you're about to scream." She was as perceptive as she was ruthless.

"I am. I'm really angry all of a sudden." I was shaking. I'd spent the last few months crying and devastated, and now all of that emotion had manifested into white-hot anger. I needed to let it out.

The moment the club's music wrapped around my body in a welcomed, thick wall of sound, I tipped my head back and released, screaming into the thumping air until I was forced to take a breath.

"Now, drink this." Olivia handed me a shot glass as she yelled near my ear to be heard over the music.

"What is it?" *And where did she get it?*

"No idea. I took it from that tray over there." I glanced over to see some guy frowning at a tray of shots, now missing a couple. "Quick, before he sees." Olivia tipped the clear liquid down her throat and I followed suit. Vodka. It burned like a bitch on the way down, but sat hot in my belly with the drinks we had earlier. It made me feel instantly calmer.

"I have two words for you, Cora: revenge sex."

I nodded. A part of me agreed with her, but the rest wasn't sure sex was the answer to my problems the way it seemed to be for her. But then, the alcohol in my system was starting to make this nightclub look like a fun place to be. So, maybe, just maybe she was right?

Olivia took the shot glass from my hands and grabbed me by the shoulders. "Now, we dance."

3

I'D NEVER BEEN to a nightclub while single. Jack and I started dating in our final year of high school, and we were joined at the hip throughout university. When we'd gone clubbing with friends, it was *always* together. On the dance floor, he had been my partner. *How do I do this without him to guide me?*

Even though I was angry and hurt, I felt a pang of longing too. I missed what we once were—well, what I *thought* we were. I was single. I felt lost and unsure of my place in this world.

My self-appointed guide to singledom took hold of my hands and rolled her shoulders back in time with the music, coaxing me to move with her. She smiled encouragingly, releasing me the moment I started to move on my own. Then she turned in a circle, her arms above her head as she rocked and swayed.

Olivia had moves, her body seeming to ripple along with the beat of the music. I tried to copy what she was doing, but it felt more like a seal trying to do the caterpillar on soft sand than the lithe motions Olivia was exhibiting. I kept going though, the alcohol making its way through my veins as the lights flashed around me, pink and blue, red and white, a flashing rhythm. As each song melted into the next, the dancing bodies became an energy I could connect with, causing my movement to soften. I threw my arms in the air and let my dark hair swish from side to side, brushing against my exposed back. My skin felt alive, the thrumming beat vibrating in my chest, persuading my hips to sway and sway. I had no idea how long we'd been on that dance floor, but I was beginning to feel a freedom I'd never experienced before. I was losing myself and relaxing against the rhythm. It was...liberating.

Just as I was beginning to understand why Olivia loved coming here so much, a set of unknown hands landed on my waist and a hard, unwelcome body pressed against the back of mine. *What the hell?*

Glancing over my shoulder, I found some random guy I didn't find even remotely attractive, rubbing himself against the curve of my arse. With wide eyes, I silently begged Olivia for help. She laughed and leaned in close. "He's not hot enough for you. Let's go get a drink. My feet are killing me."

I nodded emphatically, then followed behind her when she took my hand and pulled me through the crowd. I chanced a glance back at my dance partner and saw him move on to the next poor unsuspecting girl.

"Thanks for the save," I said when we made it to the bar.

"Just make sure you do the same for me. I only want

tall and gorgeous hands touching this fine body." She ran her hands down the sides of her figure, making me laugh.

"Deal."

Seeming to know the bartender, Olivia was served quickly and came back with two vodka martinis. "Let's sit."

Finding a couch unoccupied, we sat and watched the room, taking a well-deserved breather. Seeing all the young and drunk faces that barely looked old enough to be out of high school, I suddenly felt like an imposter, a chaperone at a high school dance. I was a lawyer nearing the big three-oh. My party days were behind me. I spent my life working on cases that painted nightclubs as the starting point for dozens of assaults and drug charges. It felt almost inappropriate for me to be here—especially when I was already benched over this stupid intervention order.

"Do you come here a lot?" I asked, wondering if I looked as much of an intruder as I felt.

"Are you hitting on me?" Olivia shot back with a cheeky grin.

"No." I laughed. "Just asking a question."

"It's my favourite club." Olivia wiggled her fingers and smiled at some guy I couldn't make out in the sea of darkened faces.

"I feel old being here," I told her, leaning over to adjust the new shoes that were beginning to hurt my feet.

"That's because your perspective is messed up from being married your whole life. So, I'm not surprised."

"It was only a year. We were dating for eight years before he proposed, engaged for two years, then married for one."

"Well, that right there, should have told you something."

"What do you mean?"

"It took him *eight years* to propose. It means he was waiting to see if something better came along."

My head snapped back. Was she serious? "Maybe we were just taking it slow?"

With her eyebrows lifted, she gave me a look that told me not to be so naïve. Deep down, I knew she was right. *Did he ever really love me? Or did he just settle because I was there, available? How many other women had he 'tried out' to see if they were better than me?*

"Do you seriously think that Jack-Arse is sitting at home stuffing his face with food and feeling sorry for himself? No. He's probably fucking Slutty-Sally while searching through Tinder for his next conquest."

My stomach souring, I downed the rest of my drink. She was probably right. I hated that. "I think I need another." Standing without waiting for a response, I headed straight for the bar and pushed my way to the front, without a care for the other people waiting. "Vodka martini. Actually, no. Tequila. Four shots." I held up my fingers.

The barman nodded and got to work. I put my head in my hands and growled. Coming out was a terrible idea. It was too soon. I wasn't ready to be in public yet. How was I supposed to have revenge sex when I couldn't stop feeling angry over what my husband had done? It didn't present itself as a scintillating conversation starter.

"Shitty night?" The guy next to me spoke close to my ear, his voice deep but soft.

"Shitty life." When I turned, I was met with the most

devastatingly green eyes I'd ever seen. "Are those contacts?" I blurted, pointing like an imbecile.

He chuckled and shook his head. "All mine."

"They're super g—"

"Green, I know. I see them in the mirror every day."

"Oh, I'm sorry, I didn't mean...I've been drinking, obviously."

"I figured. It *is* a bar. Drinking is part of the package."

I smiled, suddenly feeling stupid despite my extensive schooling. "Right." My drinks were placed in front of me and I pulled out my credit card to pay for them.

"I've got it," he said, handing a fifty to the barman.

"Oh no. Don't do that."

He grinned. "I don't mind. You look like you could use a break."

"I could use a time machine," I muttered.

"What was that?"

"Nothing. Thank you for the drinks." I leaned closer so he could hear this time, I could feel the heat of his body.

"My pleasure. Enjoy your night." He winked at me then took a mouthful of the amber-coloured drink in front of him as he pocketed his change. My stomach did a strange dancey kind of thing when he looked at me—he was gorgeous with a capital G.

"Do you..." I paused, trying to figure out what the hell I was supposed to do next. It felt kind of odd accepting the drinks then walking away, and I really wanted to keep the conversation going. He was in the 'hot as hell' category with those divine eyes and full lips. His hair looked blond, or maybe light brown—I couldn't tell in the overly red lighting—and it was a little on the long side, but it suited him. When he smiled, dimples appeared in his cheeks, and his eyes creased a little at the corners, leading me to believe he wasn't quite as young as the majority of the nightclub's patrons—twenty-five, perhaps? Twenty-five and totally fuckable.

Did I seriously just think that? It sounded like Olivia was getting in my head. But it was true. He was absolutely stunning, and having him smile at me made me nervous in the best possible way.

"Do I...?" He narrowed one eye, waiting for me to fill in the blank.

"Want...one?" I pointed to the shots.

He grinned again. There were those dimples. Now my chest was dancing. "They're all yours, babe. No strings attached." With another wink, he threaded his way through the crowd until I couldn't see him anymore. *Don't go, handsome stranger. Maybe I* want *some strings attached.*

Hmm, seemed I was pretty shitty at this whole flirting thing. It wasn't something I'd practiced. Jack and I had simply clicked then settled into a relationship with each other.

Deflated, I turned back to the bar and downed two of the shots, coughed from the burn, then took the remaining two shots back to Olivia, who was engaged in a very close conversation with a dark-haired guy who had his hand on her knee. He seemed to fit her tall and gorgeous criteria.

"This is Paul," she informed me when I took a seat and handed her a shot. We clinked glasses and downed the acrid liquid. "Whoo. That one is going to go straight to my head." She turned to Paul. "Will you be a dear and get me some water?" She pouted and he was more than happy to oblige. The moment he left, she spoke in my ear. "I've slept with him before. He's returning for seconds."

"You going to oblige?" The new alcohol was mixing unkindly with my previous drinks and surging throughout my body. I was buzzing all over. *That's more like it.* A calm fell over me as my mind struggled to keep focus and all thoughts of my philandering husband were unable to take hold in my drunken mind.

"Who knows? Maybe some other time. Tonight is about you. I don't want you getting all drunkenly mopey because that arsehole broke your heart. Tonight is about you taking your life back and reclaiming your sexuality. You're a gorgeous woman with a beautiful heart and a kick-arse career. You have *everything* going for you—don't forget that."

I lifted my brows, giving her a doubtful look. She made me sound amazing. "Is this when you tell me I'm a queen?" I asked, remembering her favourite pep-talk moniker.

"You *are*," she insisted. "Just look at all those men out there. They actually think they deserve to get laid by the hottest chick they can find. Why isn't it the same for us?"

I shrugged. "Because we're women."

"No. Because we were raised to believe that being open about your desires is wrong, that being career driven is wrong. They want us to be subservient girl-friends, wives and mothers. But we don't have to fit their mould, Cora. We can do everything we want and we can have our cake too—just like the men. You need to realise how gorgeous and amazing you are. Believe it, and use that confidence the same way they do."

The way she spoke about feminine power made me want to be that amazing, confident person. Actually—and maybe it was the alcohol talking—once I thought about it, I really *was* that amazing. I *did* have all those qualities Olivia just rattled off. I wouldn't exactly call myself *gorgeous,* but I certainly wasn't ugly. I was curvy, but I had a tiny waist, and from what Instagram was telling me, that was a very fashionable quality to have these days. So, I could hold my own. "You're right," I told her, my tongue starting to feel a little thick in my mouth. "I'm a fucking *catch*. I don't have to be some guy's wife to know who I am." *Someone, please, fetch me a soapbox.*

"Right, you are. Marriage blows. Staying single is the only way a woman should be."

"Right. Relationships are for chumps."

Reaching for the martini she'd barely touched, she poured half of it in my empty glass and held it out to me. "A toast." I held my glass up with hers. "Never again," she said, a determined glint in her eyes.

I could feel that same determination surge inside me as I touched my glass to hers. "*Never* again," I echoed, feeling the power of those two simple words hitting me in the centre of my chest. Being cheated on felt like shit. I would *never* allow myself to be in that situation again. Olivia really did have the right idea. She was the happiest person I knew, and didn't apologise for anything. I needed to take a page out of her book and focus on number one for a change—myself.

"Now, tell me, who was that delicious morsel you were talking to at the bar?"

I smiled. He really was gorgeous. "You saw that?"

"He'd be the perfect man to wipe the slate clean. Did you get his name?"

I shook my head. "He paid for the drinks and said 'no strings attached' then left. I'm not even sure if he's still here."

She pressed her lips together. "Interesting."

Paul returned with two bottles of water, handed one to Olivia and one to me. I definitely needed it, my brain felt like it was being pickled from the amount of alcohol that was in my system. Once we thanked him, Paul smiled and gestured that it was no problem then sat next to Olivia and draped his arm behind her. He leaned close and murmured something in her ear that had her smiling and wriggling in her seat.

I was in awe of her ability to be so confident in her life while still oozing sex appeal. She owned her position at work, commanded respect the moment she entered a room. Olivia was a woman who knew what she wanted and wouldn't accept anything less. I could learn a lot from her.

While sipping my water, I continued scanning the crowd, quietly wondering if Green-eyes from the bar was anywhere in the room. He really was someone I could imagine myself 'wiping the slate clean' with. My attraction to him was instant, and I was in the perfect mood to explore that—drunk and needy. I *needed* the attentions of a man who could make me forget about my husband. Right now, it felt like it would fix everything.

Getting comfortable, I leaned back in the seat, admiring the young bodies as they gyrated collectively. There were so many beautiful people, and I wondered if any of them had any clue how simple their life was right now. They were in the most exciting part of their lives where the future held nothing but possibilities. Hope was abundant and fairy tales felt like they could come true. I wanted to feel that way again.

I let out a nostalgic sigh, longing to be twenty again. I would do a lot of things differently if I had the chance to relive the last decade of my life. I smiled to myself as I thought back to those years. I'd been so in love, so willing to do anything to keep my man happy. I would have gone to the ends of the earth for him if it meant he'd love me forever. If I could do it all again, I'd spend more time on my own, I'd focus solely on my career, and only spend time with men who made *me* happy. The moment they didn't, they'd be out the door, and I wouldn't say sorry, I wouldn't feel guilty. I'd be just fine because my life was all about me.

Pulling at my bottom lip with my teeth, I laughed to myself. Life really was whatever you made of it. Then I felt a delicious chill rush over my body seconds before my eyes caught with his—the guy from the bar; Green-eyes. My chest jolted. He was standing amongst a group of friends, laughing at something being said. It hurt my entire ribcage to look at him, he was so beautiful. Why he wasn't surrounded by women, I had no clue. If my reaction to him was anything to go by, he had his pick of any girl in the room. I found it curious that he wasn't using that to his benefit. *That's what guys did, right?*

About to take a mouthful of his drink, he paused before it touched his lips, smiled then tilted his glass toward me.

With a nod of my head, I smiled in return, my stomach flipping excitedly from his attention. I could see him still talking, his eyes flicking from me to the group he was in. I wanted more from him, more than a few words at the bar and smiles across the room. But...what? I'd never had to entice a stranger into wanting me. Where did I start? What did other girls do? I wanted to ask Olivia, but she was still locked in conversation with Paul. So, I looked around the room for inspiration. The most obvious answer was all around me.

"I want to dance," I said to Olivia, touching her arm to get her attention while still looking at Green-eyes. Maybe he was interested. Maybe I was just desperate. Either way, I'd drunk away my inhibitions long ago, and I was going to have the fun that Olivia had promised me earlier.

Making our way onto the dance floor with Paul in tow, I stopped in a spot that meant Green-eyes would be able to see me clearly. Then I started swinging my arse. If I was sober, I would have been embarrassed by the display; my inner stripper took hold, and I couldn't seem to stop myself. I was body rolling and running my hands through my hair, feeling like the woman Olivia kept telling me I needed to be—a Queen. A couple of guys tried to dance with me, but I pushed them away and waggled my finger at them as I shook my head. Who this woman was, I had *no* idea. But I was having fun and every time I looked in Green-eye's direction, he was looking right back. I pulled at my bottom lip with my teeth.

"What has gotten into you?" Olivia asked, her voice full of laughter.

I kept dancing as I answered. "I'm just having fun. Isn't that what you wanted?"

"Yes! I *love* this party girl." I couldn't hear her laughter, but I could see it as Paul wrapped his arms around her middle and swayed with her to the music. Then she caught me looking at Green-eyes. "Go and get him, Cor. He wants you."

"Shouldn't he come to me?" I asked, suddenly feeling out of my depth, despite the alcohol. Dancing and flirting across the room was one thing, but going up to him boldly was a whole other story.

"Games are for relationships. Do you want that, or do you want a fuck?"

My chest got tight at her blunt question. I knew I didn't want a relationship, but could I really go through with a one-night stand? Maybe... "I don't know. Maybe nothing. Maybe..." I let the word hang, running my fingers through my hair as I stopped dancing and looked around, my stomach dropping when I realised he was gone. What I would or wouldn't do didn't matter anymore. "Maybe we should just go."

Taking a step back, Olivia was grinning as she shook her head, her eyes focused over my right shoulder.

He didn't speak at first, he just slid one hand over my hip until it flattened possessively against my stomach, pulling me against him as his head lowered to the curve of my neck and he inhaled deeply. I could barely breathe. Every nerve in my body was alive and screaming for more. I had never, ever, ever, ever, *ever*, had this reaction to a man before. The question of whether or not I could go through with a one-night stand suddenly became a moot point. His touch had already melted my panties right off my body.

As his hips moved with mine to a beat that was all our own, I felt the tip of his nose brushing along my jawline as his breath caressed my neck. I let out a moan that was thankfully drowned out by the music and I curved into him, feeling the brush of his nose and lips as he travelled upward, pausing at my ear. Holding my breath, I waited for him to say something. I could feel the heat of his body as it seared through me, turning me into a desperate, quivering mess. God, I wanted him. I wanted him, and I didn't even know his name, didn't even care what it was.

"Want to get out of here?" His voice cut through every other sound in the room, so clear. It felt like a wild promise curling through my body until it pooled as a heat between my thighs.

I found myself nodding.

With a grin that curved only one side of his mouth, he wrapped his large hand around mine and led me through the crowd into the cool night air.

The change in temperature jolted me somewhat, the reality of what I was doing sinking in. I hadn't even told Olivia I was leaving.

"My friend," I said, stopping just outside the club entry.

"She knows you're with me."

"Do you know her?"

"No. She just smiled and waved as we left."

"Oh." What if he was a serial killer?

Looking down at me, those eyes searched mine with curiosity. "Changed your mind?" he asked, reaching up and running his thumb gently over the side of my face until his hand rested on my shoulder, that thumb caressing my collarbone. His touch made me feel even drunker than the alcohol had, and chased every doubt away.

I opened my mouth to speak, but all I had was a gasp

and a small shake of my head. The truth was, I didn't know what I wanted, but I didn't want this—whatever it was; a moment of insanity, a lust induced coma—to end either.

He grinned that half grin again then hooked his finger under my chin, tilting it up before he took my mouth with his, his tongue seeking entry to which I was powerless to refuse. My lips parted and he was in, taking over my mouth with skilled strokes that had my body screaming for more. *I could come from him kissing me.* I was nothing more than putty in his hands. I wanted everything he could give me and then some.

"Good," he whispered when he was done destroying my mouth. I pressed my swelling lips together, looking into those amazing eyes of his. If that's what he could do with his mouth, imagine what he could do with the rest of him. If I thought about it too intensely, I'd probably combust.

4

HAND IN HAND, we headed toward the Elizabeth Street intersection. I followed along blindly, still too drunk on tequila and hormones to spare a thought for all that could go wrong in this scenario. Olivia was right. I needed to enjoy myself. This was simply one crazy night. One crazy night where I'd let go and smile about it tomorrow. It didn't have to *mean anything*.

My heart raced faster with every step we took, even so, I smiled. This really was crazy. It was exhilarating, and it wasn't *me*. But it was *fun*. I felt alive.

We only walked for a few minutes when we turned down a small alley that had a large neon sign advertising Causeway 353 Hotel. Seeing that sign sent nerves swirling around in my stomach. This was happening. I was seriously about to go into a room and have sex with a stranger. I was...excited.

He already had a room. Doing this obviously wasn't as foreign to him as it was to me. We headed straight for the elevators where he hit the button for the top floor.

There had been no small talk, no attempt at learning anything about me. He literally didn't say *anything* the whole way here. I hadn't spoken because I didn't trust myself to speak for fear of chickening out and running the other way, or ruining this lustful feeling with silly chatter. But now, with the elevator doors closing, words seemed like such useless tools. The hunger radiated off his body, need radiated off mine. He was a lion, and I was more than happy to be his prey.

The second those doors sealed, he pulled me against him then pressed me against the metal wall, his hungry mouth wasting no time in taking mine. My hands went to his light brown hair, taking fistfuls of it and pulling while those luscious lips travelled down, his teeth grazing my chin, kissing and sucking until he reached my breasts. He took a mouthful of the abundant flesh, marking me while his hands grabbed and squeezed. It was a glorious pain that sent me into a frenzy of desire.

Inhaling deeply, I caught the scent of shampoo and a woodsy cologne, mixed with that manly smell that was different from person to person. Pheromones, I supposed, beautiful, glorious pheromones. They made me want to hit the emergency button and rip his clothes off then and there. I didn't want to wait, didn't want to waste time getting to a room when I was already dripping wet and wanting him inside me *now*.

With an electronic chime, the doors opened and we rolled out of the lift, into a hallway that could have looked like anything for all I cared. I wasn't paying attention. I was more focused on pulling his shirt from his pants and getting those buttons undone so I could get to the body underneath. It felt rock hard against me, and I knew that it would be a feast for my eyes. We landed against a door at the same time I pushed his shirt open, rewarding me with a tan, ripped torso that had me licking my lips. The tip of my tongue longed to make its way between every ridge of those perfectly sculpted muscles, and I wasn't going to waste a second worrying about what he'd think of me when we were through. This was a one-time thing.

Grabbing my arse, he held me tight as the door opened and he pulled me through. I was up against the wall and he was pulling at the straps of my dress, pushing them off my shoulders so he could get to my skin to nip and suck.

My God. I was on fire. Beautiful, skin-searing fire. My hands went to his chest and I shoved him back with a strength I didn't know I had. He landed against the opposite wall of the narrow entryway and grinned at me before he licked his lips then eye-fucked my body. *Holy crap*. Seeing that hunger caused my insides to clench and yearn. I wanted to taste him.

Stepping toward him, I did exactly what I'd wanted in the hall and pressed my lips to his chest, sucking and licking between his curved pecs, then the ridge that ran down the centre of his abs. I released a moan, feeling the hard heat of his skin, salty against the tip of my tongue. My hands worked at the waistband of his jeans, I wanted to set my eyes on the impressive cock I knew was inside. It had been pressing against me since the nightclub and I needed to see it, taste it.

When it sprang free, I gasped. It was...gorgeous, hard and thick—just like the rest of him. My mouth watered and my skin tingled with anticipation. Then I licked the head and he groaned. "Fuck me."

His head lolled back against the wall as my hand wrapped around his base before I drew him into my mouth, swallowing him back with a greed I never knew I possessed. *Who was this woman?* I was giving head like a porn star on my knees in a hotel room with a stranger.

I'd never felt so free in my entire life.

"My God. *Fuck.*" The muscles in his neck strained, and his hands went into my hair. I looked up at him, seeing the look of a man coming undone as he hissed through his teeth and tried to steady his breathing. Knowing I was doing this to him, that I was the reason he looked so completely lost in ecstasy, made me feel powerful. I hummed around his shaft, taking him in deeper, sucking him back harder. His hands tightened, pulling my hair against my scalp and I knew he was close.

With a growl, he pushed me back, lifting me so I landed against the opposite wall. I hit it with a thud, my arms flying out to catch myself. He took the opportunity to grab me by the wrists and trap me in place. "Who knew?" he murmured, then his lips crashed into mine and that cock of his pressed against my dress, probably ruining it with pre-cum forever. But I didn't care. The dress could be set on fire if it meant he'd take it off me faster.

Running his hands down my arms, he took a hold of my rib cage, his fingers digging in for a moment, grabbing. Then he spun me around so I was front against the wall and he was covering my back. That mouth of his seared a path over my skin, starting in the curve of my neck then moving over my shoulders to my exposed back.

I felt my zipper loosen and his fingers slide down, down to the waist of my panties. His mouth followed, lips skimming lightly, making faint noises of need escape my throat. Then his hands pushed and pulled at my dress until it pooled in a puddle of fabric at my feet.

He was on his knees. I was still against the wall, panting, waiting. Reaching up, he popped the clasp on my bra then dragged his fingers down the skin of my back, hooking my panties, dragging them down too. Then with a groan, he grabbed my arse cheeks, squeezing hard before he bit down. My eyes went wide and I gasped, a bolt of lust landing right in the centre of my core. *What the hell was that?*

"That arse." The words were a rumble against my skin as he stood back up, spinning me so I was facing him again. I let my bra fall down my arms and his eyes darkened. "Those tits."

I smiled, standing in front of him completely naked, completely unashamed. He made me feel like the most desirable woman on the planet. Leaning in, he buried his face in my cleavage, his hands kneading the heavy flesh of my breasts, fingers finding nipples and teasing then tasting. His mouth sucked on one and I cried out from the sensation, arching my back, and pushing that shirt off his shoulders so he was just as naked as I was. I wanted skin on skin, naked flesh on naked flesh. He was exposed, but I wanted all fabric in a pile on the floor.

With the shirt gone, my hands didn't know where they wanted to be. His chest was a smorgasbord of muscle and sinew. "That chest," I whispered, my face tilted up and pressing into the curve of his neck. I ran my teeth along his jaw, and he smiled. Then I slid my hands down those glorious muscles and pushed at the waist of his open pants. "That cock."

An erotic noise hummed in his throat, then he kicked off his shoes and got rid of the rest of his clothes, producing a condom at the same time. I stood and watched him open the foil pack with his teeth, the anticipation driving me wild when he rolled it down his shaft. I went to remove my heels.

"Leave them," he commanded, pushing the condom so it fit against his base.

"OK," I whispered, smiling as I turned away from him and walked a few steps into the room, being sure to sway 'that arse' as I did. I didn't make it far. He caught my wrist and shoved me so I was against a desk. I grinned. I was going to have bruises after this, but then at least I'd know it was real and not some crazy sex dream I'd conjured up in my drunken mind. With my arse on the cool surface, I slid back and opened my legs as wide as I could, inviting him in. His cock bounced and he growled before dropping to his knees, his face colliding with my pussy. It was a violent shock as his tongue skimmed over my clit, not in a languid suck, but a rapid flick. I grabbed his hair with one hand and used the other to support myself against the desk, my back curving as my mouth fell open, releasing a long, deep moan. It felt like he was tearing the orgasm from my body. *How the hell is he doing that with his tongue?* The build up was so sudden, so intense that my hips lifted and my body convulsed with my release. "My God," I screamed, my throat dry and hoarse as wave after wave of pleasure coursed through my body, undoing me completely.

"Fuck, you taste good." He continued to lave at my

pussy, extending that mind-altering orgasm for almost longer than I could stand. Then he licked his way up, taking a moment to pay homage to my nipples before he stood to his easily six-four of height and grinned at me wickedly. With one hand, he grabbed my hair and tipped my head back, his tongue pushing between my lips as he kissed me with force, sharing my taste. I moaned into his mouth, pulling him against me so hard that our teeth clashed. Then I felt the tip of his cock run along the inside of my thigh and land at the entrance of my pussy. He teased me with it, running it up and down, through my wetness and my over stimulated clit. I rocked my hips, whimpering in my desperation to feel him inside me. Then, answering my prayers, he pushed inside.

I saw stars.

I made keening noises.

I may have even glimpsed heaven.

Perhaps the Lord Himself.

He filled me up with one slow, controlled thrust. He *filled me.* And I stretched around his girth, my insides quivering as he pumped in and out. I held on, barely able to breathe as he drove me closer to ecstasy than I'd ever been before. Sex had always been good. Jack hadn't been a horrible lover. But this, this was the kind of sex that ruined women for other men. It was the kind of sex you thought about as you drifted off to sleep, knowing your dreams would be nothing but amazing memories. Nothing in the world was this good—not even cake and chocolate.

I wrapped my legs around his hips, pulling his thrusts even deeper. "Faster," I gasped, and he pumped with increased speed and aggression.

God, I loved it. I was being fucked, my body jostling against the desk, my hand braced above my head, while the other dug nails into his bicep, and the desk went thump, thump, thump, against the wall.

Heat pooled in my lower belly, my cries turning into low moans as he began to grunt and thrust harder. I was so close, my whole body set to burst. Then it did. My orgasm took over and I threw my head back with my release, hitting it against the wall, but not giving a shit because my body was too busy being exploded into a million tiny pieces to react.

"Fuck. Me." The words were forced between his clenched teeth as he spilled himself inside me then kissed me as he stilled, inhaling deeply like he was somehow taking some of my life force on as we both came down from that amazing high.

"Holy shit," I gasped, laughing because I'd never felt so good. "That was..." I shook my head, not even sure what I could say to do that experience justice.

He just laughed and kissed me again. "I know." Then, much to my dismay, he withdrew from my body and started to remove the condom. "How's your head?"

"It's fine. But I think I drew blood on your arm."

Tying a knot in the end of the latex sheath, he glanced at the crescent-shaped wounds on his bicep I'd inflicted with my nails and shrugged. "That's nothing compared to the marks I gave you." He gestured toward my chest and I spotted a rather large hickey making an appearance on my right breast.

"No low-cut tops for me."

He grinned. "Give me ten minutes." He leaned

forward and pressed a brief kiss to my lips. Then he headed for the bathroom.

Ten minutes for what? A shower? To go to the toilet? I hoped he wasn't planning on taking a dump in there. Because if he was, I was out of here. I didn't sign up for anything more than pure sex and fun.

I heard the bin open and close, then the sound of running water that only lasted a moment. Seconds later, he returned to the room and flopped on the bed, still naked. Everything he did took less than three minutes. What were the other seven for?

"Ten minutes for what?" I couldn't help but ask.

He'd stretched his long arms above his head and had them folded behind his head. His left leg was bent at the knee, slouching to the side and giving me an unfettered view of that beautiful cock. Even at half-mast it was impressive. I licked my lips as my eyes dragged over his tall, muscular form. I was still sated and sore, but I was fairly sure I could do it all again. Blame it on my limited experience, but I'd never wanted a man that much.

Turning his head my way, he grinned as his eyes seemed to do the same thing to me. "Round two. But, if you're going to keep looking at me like that, I could probably be persuaded to go a little sooner." His cock lifted, growing harder.

"Round two?" I squirmed where I sat. Yes. I definitely wanted round two.

"Unless you're done?"

I got off the desk and walked to the bed, trying to move as sexy as possible, which wasn't hard, because *he* made me feel like the goddess of lust. "The only thing I'm done with are these heels." I kicked them off, and before I could climb on the bed, he grabbed me around the waist and pulled me over him, flipping us so he was on top of me, one leg in between mine, his arms caged around my torso.

"Good. Because this time"—he dipped his head and brushed his lips along my collarbone, nipping my skin at the suprasternal notch—"I want to go slow." He pushed up on his hands and ran his tongue down my cleavage until he reached my belly button and licked in an unhurried circle. "Excruciatingly slow. You'll be begging me to let you come."

My breathing picked up. "You want me to beg?"

"I want to torture this luscious body of yours in the sweetest way possible."

I pulled at my lip with my teeth. That was a kind of torture I'd never known, but could totally agree to. "Do your worst," I challenged.

He settled himself between my legs and flicked his tongue over my clit, feather soft. "How about I do my best?"

My head rolled back into the soft pillow.

His *best*?

I was already ruined. God help me if his *best* was yet to come. I might not leave this bed.

5

I AWOKE SOMETIME BEFORE DAWN, my body delectably achy from the workout it had been given only hours before. Green-eyes was passed out beside me, sleeping soundly. The lights from the city illuminated the room just enough that I could make out the handsome features of his face. I felt like I should have woken him, spoken to him. I still didn't know his name, didn't know a single thing about him besides the fact that he was the kind of guy who pre-booked a hotel room and fucked like a demon. But after studying him for a while, I decided that I didn't want that. I'd done exactly what I'd set out to do —I'd slept with someone so beautiful I could die, and I felt more alive inside than I had in all the years I'd spent waiting for Jack to marry me. I didn't need to try and make it anything more than what it was.

Sliding from the bed, I padded softly about the room, collecting my things before heading for the bathroom where I quickly cleaned myself up and put my clothes back on. His toiletries were set up on the bench, so I picked up his cologne and took off the cap, scenting the fragrance. It smelled like a fresh breeze on an autumn day: subtle, earthy, manly. It was my new favourite scent. After a short internal debate, I wedged the bottle between my breasts, deciding I wanted a keepsake from my first night as a new woman. I didn't know if I'd ever sleep with a stranger again, but I always wanted to remember this feeling. I felt like I had broken out of some imaginary chains, like I could literally do *anything*.

Making sure my breasts were positioned so you couldn't see anything, I grabbed my purse and looked at myself in the mirror. My cheeks were flushed and my lips swollen. I looked exactly like someone should after the night I'd just had—fucked in the most wonderful way. Although, something about taking his cologne didn't quite sit right with me. I wasn't planning on putting it back, but I at least needed to leave him something in its place. Pulling at my lip, I grinned to myself then did yet another thing I never thought I'd do. I slipped off my underwear and left the black lacy scrap of material on the bench where the cologne had been. As far as I was concerned, it was a fair swap. *My scent for his.*

Happy with every decision I'd made over the last twelve hours, I slipped out of the bathroom and crept across the room, taking one last look at Green-eyes before I opened the door and exited the room.

"Thanks for the memories," I whispered, blowing him a kiss. Then I left, and I didn't look back. Olivia was going to be so proud of me.

THE EARLY MORNING cab ride took less than twenty minutes to Olivia's South Yarra apartment block. She lived on the third floor of a modern building that over-looked the water. The furnishing was as stylish as the woman herself, with large cream leather couches domi-nating the living area. There was modern art on the walls, and a coffee table that I had a sneaking suspicion was also some sort of sex chair because of the way it curved ergonomically. The kitchen was huge with marbled surfaces and an oven that had never been turned on— Olivia didn't like to waste time cooking and ate out or ordered in to save herself the trouble. There were two bedrooms and a study. The largest bedroom was hers with light-coloured rustic-looking furniture and artful black and white pictures of semi-naked people on the walls. The second room was her home office, and the study was her workout room. In its entirety, the apart-ment was quite small, but she'd made excellent use of the space and it was perfect for its sole occupant's purposes. However, with all the rooms taken, I was left sleeping on the couch next to the weird 'coffee table'.

The first thing I did when I got inside was take a long hot shower to work out all the aches and pains in my muscles from a night of rigorous passion. The water felt glorious over my skin, and the soap felt like a silken pillow. I couldn't stop smiling, couldn't stop thinking about the things I'd done, the way I'd reacted to his touch, the way I'd moaned without restraint. How was I ever going to top that? I could literally die a happy woman right in this moment. I didn't care about my impending divorce, or the crap going on at work. I didn't care about my homeless situation, or the court appearance scheduled for the following Wednesday. I was completely at peace.

When tiredness began to weigh down my bones, I shut off the water and exited the stall, towelling off on the mat in front of the mirror. That's when I saw the marks. He had branded me.

Everywhere.

My towel fell to the floor as I stared at my reflection. There were hickeys and bruises on my neck, my breasts, my hips, my stomach, my *arse!* I knew he'd given me a love bite or two, and I knew we'd been fairly rough, but I wasn't expecting *this.*

Wow. I was going to have to be careful how I dressed and wore my hair until they faded.

Slipping into my pyjamas, I picked up the cologne and smelled it one more time. The marks on my skin had definitely been worth it.

When I padded out to the lounge room, the sun was already above the horizon, turning the sky from pink to blue. As far as I could tell, Olivia had yet to come home. I was all alone, and for the first time since I could remember, I was comfortable with that.

"WHAT ARE YOU DOING HERE?"

Those five words jolted me from my slumber, my confusion making me worry that I was in the wrong place. Pulling the sleep mask from my eyes, I sat up and looked around, noting the familiar furniture and the bag in the corner that contained my things. Olivia was standing beside the couch, still wearing the dress she'd had on the night before, her hands on her hips.

"I'm staying here?" I answered, squinting at her with only one eye. Was she high?

"No." She took a seat on the coffee table/sex contraption. "I'm talking about right now. You left with that guy and his great thighs."

"He had a lot more than great thighs," I assured her, a grin pulling at the corners of my mouth.

Her eyes went wide. "Do tell."

I pulled myself to sitting and pushed my sleep mask to the top of my head. "We went to a hotel, and..." I paused and shook my head, finding it hard to believe last night had really happened, but unable to keep the smile from my face. "It was remarkable. He was so much more than I was expecting."

"Giant cock?" she asked, her tone completely neutral and serious.

"Definitely *well* above average. Everything about last night was above average. I think he ruined me."

"That good, huh?"

I nodded. "It really was."

She grinned broadly and let out a happy sigh. "I'm so glad you left with him. I can already see that you're a new woman. You're already sporting a couple of new fashion accessories," she said, pointing the hickey on my neck and the one on my breast that was poking out the top of my nightie.

"He was an *animal*." I laughed, getting shivers running over my body at the thought of the way he'd looked at me, the way he'd pounced.

"He sounds delicious. So what was his name? How old was he?"

I shook my head. "I honestly have no clue, but I'm guessing he was around twenty-five, maybe a little older."

Her mouth opened in happy surprise. "You *didn't* get his name?"

"Nope."

She swept me up in her arms and hugged me tight, the ache reminding me of how much exercise my body went through last night. "I'm so proud of you! The student has surpassed the master and it's only the first lesson."

"First lesson? It might have to be my last."

"No." She released me, the word drawing out as she shook her head. "This was just the beginning, my friend. There are so many fish in that sea for you to taste."

I sighed. "There might be plenty of fish, but last night, I caught a shark. How am I supposed to go back to fish after I had *shark*?"

She leaned on her hand and studied my blissful expression. "He really did fuck you senseless, didn't he?"

"Completely. I don't think I can even remember the name of that guy I married anymore."

She laughed. "Well, as long as he got you to stop thinking about what's-his-face, then whoever-he-is has my eternal gratitude. Just please don't let that experience be your last. There are so many men, and they all have their own unique skillset. This is just the tip of the iceberg, Cora."

"Just the tip, huh?"

She grinned. "Just the tip."

"Of the dickberg?"

Her grin turned into a full-blown laugh. "Get dressed," she said. "I need a good shot of coffee and some eggs over easy. We're going out to breakfast. Actually, we should make it a champagne breakfast to celebrate you taking the single life by the horns."

"More alcohol? I drank far too much of that last night. Coffee will be perfect. Bacon, even better."

6

BY THE TIME Wednesday rolled along, the weekend's bliss felt like a distant memory. If it wasn't for the fading marks on my body, I could have convinced myself that it wasn't real. The amount of briefs that had landed on my desk had me buried in a mountain of paperwork. Babysitting the new solicitors in the legal training program was not my favourite thing to do. They were all fresh out of university and most of them seriously thought they were capable of standing in a courtroom and arguing a case because they'd successfully won a mock trial at uni. I had some disappointing news for them: the courts were nowhere near as forgiving as their lecturers were.

"What is this supposed to be?" I asked Nick, a graduate who had been with us for less than a month who I'd called into my office to discuss his work.

"It's a Memorandum of Advice."

I looked at the printed page. "And what exactly are you advising that we charge them with?"

He reached over and tapped the open file. "It says

right there—two counts of sexual assault and possession of illegal substances."

"What about assault of a minor? Possession with intent to sell? Did you not pay attention to the details in the police report?"

"I did, I just thought—"

"You didn't," I snapped. Closing the file, I slapped it down in front of him. "Do it again. I want a list of every charge you can possibly think of."

There was a knock on my door and I looked up to find Olivia. "We're due at the magistrate court in an hour." My heart kicked up a notch. It was the hearing for my intervention order. I was about to go and explain why I hit my husband over the head with my laptop, knocked him out cold, then attacked his clothes instead of calling an ambulance. I really hoped the magistrate was a woman.

"I'll be right with you," I told her. Then I turned to Nick, needing to send him on his way. "Do it again, and properly this time. I want it on my desk first thing tomorrow morning." He nodded and stood to leave. "And Nick?" He paused then turned to face me. "More is better at this stage of your career."

"OK," he replied, before heading out the door. The moment he was out of earshot, I let out a sigh.

"You ready for this?"

I pressed my fingers to my forehead, my head emitting a dull throb. "Not really. I'm not particularly interested in seeing him again. Do you know who the magistrate is?"

"I've barely had a moment to scratch my own tit. We'll have to find out when we get there."

Nodding, I cleaned up my desk then took my bag out

of my bottom drawer. "OK, I'm ready," I said as I stood, smoothing my hand over the sides of my beige skirt and grabbing my jacket from the back of my chair. "Wait." I placed my handbag on my desk then dug through it, retrieving my powder compact and that magic black bullet of confidence—my Mac lipstick. I swiped an extra coat of a deep beige called Velvet Teddy over my lips and I was good to go. "*Now* I'm ready."

Olivia smiled then held her hand out to me. "Come on, let's go and get this nonsense over with."

When we arrived at the courthouse, Jack was standing in front of it smoking. The moment he saw us, he dropped his cigarette on the ground and stubbed it out with his foot, kicking it to the side with the tip of his shoe. He still cut a striking figure. He was tall; just a touch over six feet, dark-haired, olive skin thanks to his Italian heritage, and he had eyes the colour of melted chocolate. He had a classically handsome face and beautiful hands —I'd never grown tired of looking at them, they were strong but graceful. The memory of sliding his wedding ring over his finger filled my mind and made my throat tighten. *How could he do this to me?*

"Cora."

I had to look away.

"We'll see you inside, Jack-Arse," Olivia answered for me, taking my arm and guiding me up the steps.

"Can I talk to you for a second?"

I didn't answer, just kept heading for the doors.

"You're the one who took out the intervention order. She's not allowed near you," Olivia responded.

"Please, Cora," he pleaded.

Something about the gentleness in his voice made me

pause. We'd spent eleven years together. Surely it didn't all have to end so bitterly. Maybe he wanted to apologise? Maybe he wanted to end this whole intervention order ridiculousness before it went any further?

Placing my hand over Olivia's I took a deep breath. "It's all right. I'll meet you in there."

With her lips tight, she looked at me then at him before she let out her breath. "Fine. But I'll be right on the other side of that door."

"Thank you."

"Thanks," Jack said.

"I'm not doing it for you, fuck-face," Olivia spat before sauntering inside.

"She's delightful as always," Jack commented, sliding his hands into his pants pockets.

I folded my arms across my chest, and did my best not to make eye contact. The last time I saw him, he was fucking another woman. I couldn't stop the replay from looping in my head. "What do you want, Jack?"

He shrugged his suit-covered shoulders. He was dressed in a charcoal-grey suit and pale blue shirt that I'd never seen before. Although, it wasn't like he could have worn one of his old suits, given they didn't exactly allow people to enter the courthouse in crotchless pants.

"I just wanted to talk. You look good."

"I look good. That's what you wanted to talk to me about?"

He shook his head. "Like I said, I just wanted to talk. Say hi for a minute. I haven't seen you in almost three months. I used to see you all the time—at home, in court...I miss you."

"Well, I was forced to move out of our home, and

court reporters don't need to be around the Legal Trainee's Supervisor, do they? You ensured our paths wouldn't cross when you got me demoted with this." I gestured toward the court house.

"How's the new position working out for you, anyway?"

What the hell was this? I wanted to shake him. "It sucks, Jack. I didn't work my arse off to graduate with honours so I could be a glorified babysitter."

"You were working too hard before, anyway."

"That's not for you to decide." I folded my arms across my chest.

"Saw a picture of you on Facebook. You were all dressed up. Friday night, I think. You dating now?"

"Not that it's any of your business. But, I went out with Olivia for a few drinks," I told him, growing impatient because this conversation wasn't going anywhere.

"I didn't like it."

"Seeing me dressed up to go out?" I scoffed. "That's great. And how's Sally? I heard she's the newspaper's top accountant. How wonderful. Did she choose your suit today?"

A slow smile spread across his lips. "We aren't together anymore."

"Oh." I pouted mockingly. "Did she catch you cheating?"

"No. It just wasn't a long-term thing. Not like you and me."

"There is no you and me anymore, Jack. You tore my heart from my chest and stomped all over it. I trusted you, and now all I can do is look back over the last decade of my life and wonder how many times I *didn't* catch you.

How many women have I unknowingly shared you with?"

Reaching into his coat pocket, he pulled out another cigarette and slipped it between his lips. "I'm sorry," he said with a shrug as he lit up. It was the most insincere apology I'd ever heard. I'd seen sociopaths take the stand and show more remorse than he just did. Even worse, he didn't deny it. He shrugged it off. Bastard.

"What exactly are you sorry for, Jack? Sorry for cheating? Sorry because I caught you? Or, sorry for destroying my life with this stupid order?"

"All of it, I guess." He blew a stream of smoke out of his nose and squinted against the sun. *I guess? What the fuck?*

With a short huff of air, I shook my head. "You guess," I parroted, running my hand through my hair in agitation. "You know, I thought that maybe when I came over here, you wanted to truly apologise for all you'd done—for all you're putting me through. But that's not the case at all. You're still as self-obsessed as you always were."

"That's not fair, Cora. I really am sorry for everything that's happened. We were happy and I messed up."

"Then go inside and end this mess. Tell them I'm not a danger to you. Give me my life back, Jack. Everything I've worked for is on the line here."

He lifted his brow. "Who's being the selfish one now?"

My mouth opened, ready to refute that comment and remind him which one of us still had their full job and a house to live in. But I closed it again, knowing that whatever came out of my mouth next would drip in venom. Jack wasn't the man I thought he was, probably never was. I'd spent most of my adult life deluding myself. It was time to stop.

A sudden wave of exhaustion washed over me, and I looked toward the entrance. "We need to go inside, Jack." There was no point in talking to him anymore.

"Wait." He placed his hand on my arm to stop me. "I mean it, Cor...I really miss you."

I laughed a hollow laugh, my hands dropping to my sides. "You *miss* me?" Had he let me go, I could have possibly saved face. But those words, spoken as though he was some sort of victim, set off a vibration inside me that started in my chest and manifested into a red-hot ball of angry words that couldn't be swallowed down. Futility be damned, I was going to have my say. I turned on him. "You? The man who took out a fucking inter-vention order against me and got me demoted? The man who got me removed from *my* house that *I still* pay half for? The man who *fucked* another woman in my *goddamn bed*." I spat the last few words out between clenched teeth. I was shaking, my finger pointing in his face.

"Come on, Cor. Every couple goes through a rough patch. Maybe we can just put all this behind us and get on with things. We were good together." He was so calm. I wanted to punch him in the nuts. Then he reached one of those *lovely* hands out and brushed my hair back from my face as if he had the right to put his hands on me.

I flinched at his touch. I was offended by his words and pulled my hair behind my shoulders so he wouldn't be tempted to touch it again. "You think I can put this behind me?" I asked incredulously. "I saw you, Jack. Saw you *fucking another woman* on the Egyptian cotton sheets we were given as a *wedding present*. I will *never* be able to get that image out of my head."

Jack's expression darkened, his eyes focused on a spot lower than my face. "What the fuck is that?" he demanded, pointing at my neck.

"What is what?" I snapped, touching at my neck in confusion before it dawned on me. The hickey. I pulled my hair back over my shoulder to cover it again.

"Are you fucking serious? You're standing here acting all high and mighty with a fucking hickey on your neck?"

"Fuck you, Jack. Not that it's any of your business but it's not a hickey."

"Then what is it? A mouth-shaped bruise?"

I jutted out my chin. "Yes."

"You're full of shit, Cora. We've been apart, what? Three months, and you've already got some guy sucking on your neck? What else did you do together? Did you fuck him? Did you?"

"Shut up, Jack, you don't know what you're talking about."

"Poor broken-hearted Cora was so upset she went out and fucked some guy. Probably didn't even wait a month. What a slut."

I heard the slap before I felt the sting on my palm, felt the sting on my palm before I realised it was my hand that did the slapping.

A sardonic grin curved his lips as his cheek bloomed bright red from the sting.

"Good luck getting your precious life back now."

My body shaking, I looked into that handsome face of his and saw nothing but a self-centred, bitter man. *How had I ever loved him? How had I been so blind that I wasted so many years of my life on him?* I felt sick to my stomach, trapped in the middle of a nightmare I didn't know how to wake up from.

"Fuck you, Jack," I spat, turning on my heel before I lost control and hit him again.

As I headed for the front doors, I heard him call after me. "No. Fuck you, Cora. Oh, wait; some guy has already done that." Then to make matters worse, he started asking bystanders if they'd seen me hit him. Things were going from bad to worse.

Olivia was out the doors before I even got there and fell into step beside me. "What the hell just happened?"

"He taunted me. I lost control."

"What did he say to you?" She balled up her fists and headed in his direction, intent on defending me. I grabbed her arms and pulled her inside, toward the clerk to report in.

"It doesn't matter now. Let's just get through this." I was trying really hard not to cry from the stress of the situation, I didn't want her confronting him and making things any worse. I'd just guaranteed myself a life in the toilet. All those years of study. All those years of working my arse off to prove myself at the OPP were for naught. I'd never get accepted into the barrister's course. I might even lose my job at the OPP all together.

Stopping at the end of the line, I closed my eyes and shook my head slightly. "The gall of that man," I gasped. "He actually had the balls to suggest we get back together."

"Is that what the slap was for?"

I shook my head. "He saw the love bite on my neck and started making out like I was a shameless slut."

She turned for the door again. "I'll scratch his fucking eyes out."

Grabbing her, I held her by my side. "Don't, Olivia. I already lost control and now I'm fucked. He doesn't need any more ammunition."

Looking into my eyes, she relaxed her stance. "Maybe we just get in there and see what we can do? Not all is lost just yet."

"His cheek is bright red, Liv. There are witnesses." It was our turn with the clerk. I released my breath and ran my hand through my hair. "Cora Knowles," I informed her.

"Did you bring representation?"

"Ah, yes. Counsellor Olivia Beecham, um, QC."

"You brought a Queen's Council to a magistrate's court?" Scoffing, she shook her head. "She's not going to like that." She made a note next to my name then looked up and pointed down the corridor with her pen. "You'll be heard in courtroom four. Please take a seat until your name is called."

"I'm sorry, but, who isn't going to like it? Who's the magistrate for the hearing?" Olivia asked, looking concerned.

The clerk looked bored as she released a hefty sigh. "Magistrate O'Sullivan is presiding today."

Olivia's body went rigid. "Thank you," she squeaked.

"What's wrong?" I asked as we headed toward room four.

"You were right. We're fucked."

"What do you mean? A second ago you were hopeful."

"Well, I was. Until I found out who was presiding. Magistrate O'Sullivan hates me."

That was all I needed. "Hates you? But why?"

Olivia swallowed a lump in her throat before she ruefully explained herself. "Because...I fucked her husband."

I stopped walking as my jaw hit the floor. "Are you fucking *serious, Olivia*?"

She held up her hands in supplication. "I promise you I didn't know he was married."

7

"IN MY DEFENCE, he'd told me they were on a break at the time," Olivia said, stubbing out her second cigarette in half an hour. We were sitting outside a pub not far from the courthouse trying to drown our sorrows after our loss. I hated infidelity. It had never been something I had any sympathy for, and now that I was on the receiving end of such abhorrent behaviour, I hated it even more. The fact Olivia had been the other woman in some other couple's marriage was a cruel reminder that my friend had not always been the flawless, wise woman I thought her to be. Now I was paying not only for her mistake, but for Jack's as well. What was wrong with the world? It felt like I was the only one suffering here, yet *I* was the only one who hadn't done anything wrong. Well, I *did* attack my husband—twice now—but he'd totally deserved it. No one in their right mind could argue against that. Unless of course, that person happened to be a woman scorned by your legal counsel...

Olivia had been right. The magistrate did hate her.

One look at the cold stare in that woman's eyes and I knew defeat was inevitable. One would think that having been bitten by the sting of betrayal that a cheating spouse incited, she would have sided with me and understood that I was no danger to Jack as long as he kept his philandering ways out of my face. But no, the one thing she seemed to hate more than a cheater, was a cheatee. I swear I heard her cough the word 'home-wrecker' while Olivia was speaking on more than one occasion. It pissed me off that my case wasn't being heard independent to the magistrate's desire for poorly disguised revenge. But she'd seemed more intent on recording a loss on Olivia's case history than she had been on giving me a fair hearing.

Now, I was stuck with an intervention order against me for the next twelve months and was going to have to arrange for the police to be present so I could move the rest of my stuff out of the house. This was bullshit.

"I'm so sorry, Cor." Olivia's downturned mouth made her look miserable. We made the perfect pair.

"You know what?" I sighed, flicking salt off the rim of my glass. "We lost the moment I slapped him on the courthouse steps. Even you couldn't have gotten me out of that one."

Normally, Olivia could win against any odds. But, neither of us was expecting today to go down the way it did, we were both totally off our game.

"I'll probably never stand in a courtroom again," I lamented.

"Don't talk like that. We'll appeal the order, and in twelve months, they'll revoke it anyway. I'll talk to the director and make sure you don't have to worry about job security."

"I'll just have to spend a year in purgatory," I moped, slurping my margarita without bothering to lift the glass. I just stuck my tongue in the tangy liquid and curved it into a straw.

"Don't look at it like that. Consider it a gap year of sorts."

"Purgatory."

"It could be worse, you could have been charged for slapping him today."

"I know. I really messed up."

Reaching across the table, she squeezed my hand. "No. He messed up. You're just the one paying the price."

I thought about that for a moment, again hating my husband for all he'd done to me. *He wasn't sorry. He'd been gloating.* But his words. They'd stung. Like the image of him fucking his lover in my bed, his words would probably stay with me forever.

"What a slut... Good luck getting your precious life back now." God, I wanted to slap him again. I hated that he was making me feel bad about myself.

"Does this really make me look like a slut?" I asked suddenly, shifting my hair to show the semi-faded hickey on my neck.

"What? *No.* You are not a slut. He's a selfish, conceited arsehole who has manipulated you long enough. You went out that night and behaved like the queen you are. You owned that dance floor, and you turned away several interested men because you had your sights set on *only one.* You are not and will never be a slut. You are, however, paying the price for his narcissism and egotism. Fuck Jack for even suggesting such a thing."

Sitting up straighter, I shook my head and then my shoulders, wriggling to try and free myself of this crappy feeling. I needed to accept what life had thrown me, even though I hated it. "You know what? Forget all of this. I'll manage. I'll just have to start over. I'll find an apartment to rent and get used to tutoring graduates on the finer details of a succinct brief. Everything will be fine."

She shook her head. "If it had been anyone else in that court room today..."

"You know that's not true. The way Jack played up the pain he was in from my slap..." I released a heavy sigh. "It doesn't matter anymore. What's done is done, and I can't blame you. I mean, I'm the one who bashed him over the head and took to his clothes with a pair of kitchen scissors when I should have called an ambulance. I'm the one who slapped him in plain sight."

"We still should have won."

This time it was me reaching across the table to hold *her* hand. "Don't beat yourself up, Liv. I'm OK."

She let out a sigh. "I really hate losing."

"You know what? This is probably a good thing. I don't need that house back anyway. Too many shitty memories."

"We'll get him in the divorce settlement. We'll get you a gun of a divorce lawyer. The best money can buy."

"Then he'll be sorry, right?" My mouth kicked up in what was supposed to be a smile. I downed the rest of my margarita and waved at the waitress to get us another round.

"I think you need another night out," Olivia said,

nodding as she sipped at her first drink. "That cheered you up last time."

I held up my hands and shook my head. "No. No." I slapped the table in between each word. "No going out tonight. We have work tomorrow, and honestly, I'm in no mood to hook up with *anyone.*"

She leaned forward, a conspiratorial glint in her eyes. "Not even if it was Green-eyes?"

My body tingled at the mention of him, and I couldn't help but smile for real this time.

Olivia nodded, grinning broadly. "That's what I thought."

"I think *he* could cheer anybody up. That body of his." I widened my eyes and blew out my breath. "I can't even."

"Maybe you should go to that hotel of his, see if he's still staying there?"

"Surely he's moved on by now." When the waitress brought over two more margaritas, I promptly disposed of the garnish and took a sip. "He probably just rented the room for the night. Like I told you, I don't know a *single* thing about him."

"Except that he's an amazing fuck."

My cheeks heated, images of him biting and teasing flashing in my mind. "*That* he is." As much as I'd love to go back for seconds, what we'd had was a perfect night. I didn't want to alter that memory by returning to the metaphorical scene of the crime.

"Oh, that look on your face reminds me of something. I bought you a gift for today. It was meant to be a celebration, but you'll have to take it as a consolation instead."

"A gift? What is it?"

"You'll see," she said with a wink.

"WHAT IS THIS...A STYLUS?" It was pink and smooth with an ergonomic grip that fit perfectly in my hand and a long, rounded tip.

"No." Olivia laughed. "It's not a stylus."

"Then what—Oh my!" I found a button on the grip and clicked. The tip started vibrating rapidly. "Why is this happening?"

Olivia was laughing so hard that she had to hold her stomach. "It's a clitoral stimulator," she said when she got herself under control. "As soon as you told me about that tongue trick Green-eyes did, I knew you'd need this to re-live the experience. You're welcome."

"You got me a clit stimulator?" This was *not* what I'd been expecting when I opened the beautiful gift box she'd handed me. "Um...thanks, I guess?" I put the lid back on the box and set it to the side. There was no way I was going to use that thing; it would forever remind me of this awkward moment, this shitty day, and the fact Olivia gave it to me. Unlike the Uber driver from Friday night, I did *not* want to think of her while I took care of business downstairs.

Ignoring my obvious discomfort, she grinned. "They're amazing. Enjoy it in good health." Then she headed into the kitchen and poured us both a giant glass of wine. It was going to mess me up after the margaritas we'd already had. But I was seriously beyond caring. "We should toast to something," she said, handing me an overflowing glass.

I licked my hand where it dripped and gave her a vacant look. "Like what?"

"I don't know. Something positive after this god-awful day."

"OK, I've got one." I stood with her, holding my glass aloft. "To starting over."

Olivia smiled and lifted her glass to join mine. "May your future days be better than any of your past ones."

We touched glasses, causing the wine to spill a little. "Oh shit."

Olivia waved it off and took a long drink from her glass before grabbing a cloth to wipe it up. "It's a white, it won't stain. Now drink. If we kill enough brain cells we might be able to forget today ever happened."

"I am on board with that." I tipped back my glass and drained half of the dry, fruity mix.

Olivia took the cloth back to the kitchen then returned with a fresh bottle and her phone. "Now," she said, taking a seat on the couch. "We're going to get you that divorce attorney. I do have someone in mind for you. She worked on my second divorce, and Anthony didn't get a single penny more than I was willing to give him." Olivia tapped away at her phone as she spoke. "Her name is Marie Jordan, and she runs a small boutique firm specialising in family law. Divorce is her specialty."

"Is she married?"

"Happily. A surprise, right? I'm sending you her details now so you can set up an appointment. Best to be the one who files so he's forced to be the respondent."

"OK." I heard the message chime on my phone go off, signalling the text she just sent me. "I'll call tomorrow."

"Good. And we'll organise a moving van to get your stuff this weekend. We know plenty of cops who'll be willing to stand there and glare at Jack-Arse. Then, I don't know, we can put it all in storage or something—just make sure you don't leave him with much."

I drained the rest of my drink. "At this point, I really don't think I want anything."

"We can burn it if you want. The point is that he doesn't get it."

Leaning back on the couch, I groaned. "This line of conversation isn't helping me forget about today."

"I know. I'm sorry. What would you rather talk about?"

"I don't know—talk about work. Better yet, let's pull up real estate listings so I don't have to sleep on your couch anymore."

"Oh honey, you can stay here as long as you like. You know, I can clear out the study."

I laughed. "That room is no bigger than a jail cell, but thank you. I think I just need to find my own space so I start embracing this new single life—my new *normal*."

"OK. If that's what you want. Let's get drunk and shop apartments." She pulled up realestate.com, and I topped up our glasses.

8

THE NEXT WEEKEND was spent moving house. With my reduced income, coupled with the financial burden of still paying half the mortgage to a house I no longer lived in, there wasn't much in the city that worked within my budget. I found a one-bedroom apartment literally up the road from Olivia. It was shoebox tiny, but it was mine. And the complex had a rooftop pool and a big gym included in the cost, so I was pretty happy with it.

I'd hired a moving van and collected everything that was personally mine from the house—the sideboard that had been my grandmother's, my lipstick collection, and the lifetime's worth of *stuff* that seemed to pile up when you stayed in one place for too long. I'd been expecting another confrontation with Jack, but he'd been thankfully absent for the duration of my move. He was probably off staying with some new girlfriend or something... The idea of it made me feel sick to the stomach. I hated that he was the one who caused this clusterfuck and didn't seem to be facing a single repercussion. It was all on me. I was the one starting from scratch. I was the one trying to sort through my mess of a life. It just didn't seem fair. There was more than one moment during the day when I really did want to take Olivia's advice and set the whole damn house on fire. But then, I'd end up in prison for arson and Jack would look like the victim again. No thank you.

In total, I probably filled only half the moving van with my things. As much as Olivia had pleaded with me to leave him with nothing, I just couldn't do it. I honestly didn't want *stuff* that reminded me of him. And I wasn't spiteful enough to take it just for the sake of it. Instead, I took a trip to IKEA and bought myself everything I needed: a brand-new bed, dining table, lounge suite, desk, shelving, among other things. It all barely fit inside my tiny apartment, but once it was put together—an absolute marathon where I never wanted to see an IKEA Allen key again—it felt more like a home. Or at the very least, it felt like a page out of an IKEA catalogue. And that was fine with me, because the people in those pictures were always super happy with their storage choices.

"Do you know what the best part about this place is?" Olivia asked, slouching on my new sunshine-yellow couch while eating a slice of Domino's pizza.

"What's that?"

"We can still get drunk together and not have to worry about a ride home."

"We can sit on our respective building's roofs and drink while on the phone, watching each other through a set of binoculars," I joked, sitting on the chair opposite her and grabbing a slice myself. Super Supreme, deep pan crust. Each bite was pure heaven.

"You know, I think you might be onto something there." She laughed, tucking her feet up underneath herself and looking around the room. "It looks really great, Cor. It seems more like you than anywhere you've lived before."

"You think?" She nodded. "Thank you so much for all the help and support over these last few months. I know I've been a burden, but having you there has been everything to me."

"Don't even mention it. That's what best friends are for."

When Olivia went home, I spent some time unpacking boxes in my bedroom and sorting out my clothes. It was the first night in my own place. The first night I've ever *had* my own place. I'd either been at home with my family or living with Jack. I had never been by myself. The quiet was...unsettling.

I thought about Olivia and how much she loved being single and having time to herself. Then I thought about the many years I'd spent with Jack, thinking we were going to grow old together, believing I was enough for him. Pieces of our relationship started slotting together, creating a clearer picture of what we really were, well, what I was anyway. I was a cinch. I was so enamoured by the fact a beautiful man wanted me, I didn't see it, didn't see the narcissist I'd aligned myself with. It was always about him. Nothing was ever his fault. All those work trips and late-night deadlines. I couldn't question him about his whereabouts without a fight—he called me unsupportive and selfish when I did. With what I now knew, I felt sure he must have been sleeping with other women then too. Had I really been that blind? Was he deflecting his guilt onto me so I wouldn't catch him out? And, if he'd been cheating for years, why marry me? Why bother after refusing for so long?

Sitting on my bed, I ran a hand through my hair and pushed out a breath that was loaded with stress and betrayal.

Jack hurt me, used his words to poke at me until I was broken-down. Subservient. He'd focused only on his happiness. It was always 'what could I do to make Jack happy?' It was never what was Jack doing to make *me* happy? I felt stupid. Broken. I'd trusted him, loved him; I believed...

A drop of water hit my forearm before I realised I was crying. I rubbed at my eyes, angry I was wasting more tears on a man capable of treating me horribly for so long then throwing me away—*destroying me*—without a single thought for how his actions would affect me. He simply hadn't cared.

It had taken eleven years for me to see that. Eleven wasted years. Now my eyes were open and it was all I could see. Jack had never given a shit about anyone but himself, least of all me. I felt like such an idiot.

Wiping my hands over my face, I stood and shuffled into the bathroom, deciding that a hot shower would go a long way to calming my mind, along with the aches in my body from a weekend filled with lifting boxes and putting furniture together. I didn't want to think about Jack anymore, didn't want to feel the defeated and angry churning in my stomach that his actions had caused. I wanted to forget. I wanted to focus on starting again. It was time I learned how to be on my own and worry about me for a change.

As I lathered my hair, I knew I never wanted to go through that experience again. Marriage seemed like a mixed bag where you never knew what you'd get, and it didn't feel worth it to me. My parents had what seemed like an ideal yet traditional marriage. My mother stayed home to raise me and my brother—who now lived in New Zealand with his wife and three kids. And after we grew up, Mum trained to be a dental nurse. My father was an accountant, and while he wasn't the most present father in the world, he cared about us, and I'd never doubted the love between him and Mum. That was the ideal I grew up with, and I supposed that's what I'd expected from Jack as well—long-term companionship. But then, was it really that great? Mum was so much happier once she got out of the house and started earning her own income. She became a different person once we finished school... Maybe their ideal wasn't an ideal at all?

Then there was Olivia and her two failed marriages. She saw marriage as a shackle that held her back from the true life she wanted, felt that being attached to a man took away her freedom. And now as I looked back on my own marriage, I wondered if marriage was worth it for a woman at all. It seemed we always sacrificed or shelved our life goals, while the man had freedom to build a life not determined by keeping house and the idea of having children. I'd spent my twenties focused on my career, wanting to progress as far as I could, as quickly as I could, so I could build a family and return to the workforce with a good income and position waiting for me. Even working around the clock, keeping more strenuous hours than

Jack, I was *still* the one working my arse off at home, making sure there was enough food, and cleaning the fucking bathrooms. Once we had a cleaner, but she'd quit after a month. I'd bet Jack tried to fuck her too. God, that *man*! He ruined everything. I never, *never* wanted to be tied down like that again. It was freedom for me, freedom all the way.

Getting out of the shower, I dried off and headed to my drawers to get dressed feeling resolute in my decision to be a single and independent woman. I doubted I could embrace all of Olivia's lifestyle choices—I wasn't sure that I was comfortable hunting for younger men to bed on a regular basis—but I could definitely be happy with a relationship-free lifestyle.

Pulling my drawers open, the movement knocked my phone enough to activate the screen, showing me I had a missed call from my mum. She was probably calling to check that the move went OK, so I shot her off a text that said everything went well and that I'd call her after I'd had a chance to catch up on some sleep. I put my phone back on the drawers facedown so I could forget about the outside world and try to enjoy my first night alone in my own place.

Taking a moment, I looked around the small bedroom, studying the brightly coloured items I'd chosen. They were the antithesis of anything I'd chosen during my time living with Jack. Everything had been greys and neutrals. Now, everywhere had bursts of colour. From the large art print on my wall to the colourful splotches all over my quilt cover. It looked great. Even my towel was a bright orange.

This wonderful surge of happiness bubbled up inside

me and I spun around in a small circle, hugging myself because I was proud. I'd been through a harrowing weekend, and despite a tiny cry earlier, I hadn't fallen apart. I was OK. I was *more than OK*. I was an independent woman; hear me roar! Tipping my head back, I did just that, roaring into the quiet of the room then giggling at the absurdity. I was acting a little crazy, but I didn't care. There wasn't anyone around to see but me.

With a smile on my face I dropped my towel on the floor, not caring that it might bother anyone. As I lifted my gaze to the chest of drawers in search of clothes, I caught sight of myself in the mirror on top of it. More notably, I caught sight of the almost-faded love bite on my breast. It stopped me in my tracks, and I stared.

Running my fingertips over it, I had to admit that Olivia's 'catch, fuck, and release program' had its perks. That night with Green-eyes was the only positive this whole mess had amassed thus far. Every time I thought about it, I felt the stress of everything float away as my body ignited, remembering his touch, his gripping need.

I had never done anything like that before. It had taken me over a month before I felt comfortable enough to have sex with Jack. Although, back then, I'd been a virgin. But the passion, the *passion* of that night with Green-eyes was indescribable. I could write a thousand essays about it and never fully articulate that feeling I'd had inside me. I'd never felt so out of control, never been touched that fiercely. I didn't know if it was my lack of experience, or if we'd somehow ignited when we'd touched. But I did know that I would *never* stop thinking about it. That night was my new happy place.

Digging inside my drawer, I found the bottle of aftershave and held it to my nose, closing my eyes as I inhaled and conjured him up in my mind. An instant tingle rippled over my body, pebbling my nipples, swelling my core. Desire calmed my mind, and knowing I was blissfully alone, I put the bottle back in my drawers then slipped into my new bed naked. I imagined the way it felt to have his hands on my body, craving his touch inside. The throbbing between my legs grew more intense at the vividness of my thoughts, making my mind stray to that funny pink gift I'd insisted I'd never use. *Olivia* had insisted it needed to be kept in my bedside drawer 'just in case'.

Biting at my lip, it only took me a moment before I decided to give that strange contraption a try. There were speed buttons beneath the power button, and when I turned it on, I held it against my palm to test the pressure while adjusting the speed. The moment it hit something that matched the memory of what he did, I felt a bolt of desire between my thighs. I slid my hand beneath my sheets, parted my thighs, and touched the toy just near my most sensitive spot. *Holy shit.* It made my body twitch and the breath burst out of my throat. *Hello, clitoris, meet your new best friend.*

Moving it slightly, moans passed my lips as the orgasm built to a blinding height in less than sixty seconds. Then it broke loose, my back arching, my hips bucking, my whole body tingling from the intensity of it. It had taken me right back to that moment when Green-eyes had worked his magic. "Who said you couldn't get as high the second time?" I asked myself, clicking off the unassuming-looking contraption and dropping it on the bed next to me. I laughed a little, spreading out on the big bed, my body feeling soft and sated, ready for the blissful lure of sleep.

As I drifted off, taking up *all* the space on that big new bed, it was with a satisfied smile on my face, welcoming dreams of a certain someone, making it a very pleasant first night indeed.

"You look very rosy this morning," Olivia said when she met me out the front of her apartment building so we could catch the tram together to work. "If I didn't know any better I'd think you got laid last night."

I grinned a secret grin then laughed. "No. I just had a really good sleep. It's been a while since I could stretch out in a bed."

"I suppose it makes a nice change from my couch."

"It does. I think I'm going to like this living alone business."

"It certainly has its virtues. What have you got on today?" she asked as we got on the tram and tapped our Myki cards.

We moved through the peak-hour crowd and found space for us both to stand. "A bunch of new cases landed on my desk just as I was packing up on Friday. I have to hand them all out and make sure none of the junior solic-itors fuck it up. Plus, I have an intern who is still at uni coming in—God only knows how they pulled that one off."

"They aren't a part of the clerkship program?"

I shook my head. "Nope. I was told it's ongoing and was approved by the director himself."

"How very strange."

"Right? One more person with no clue what they're doing to babysit. I seriously feel like I'm dealing with children. What are they teaching at university these days? Surely we weren't that bad when we started."

"I can't really speak for myself, but you were one of the better ones. Still, you weren't without your faults. Need I remind you of that summary you wrote that was so vague I barely understood the charges?"

I winced. "I'd forgotten about that."

"So, maybe cut the newbies some slack. If you can turn them into half the solicitor you are, then the director is going to be a very happy man."

I smiled at the compliment then shifted as the tram stopped to let people on and off.

"Oh," I started when we got moving again. "I called the office for that divorce attorney you put me on to. Turns out she's retired."

Olivia looked as though I'd slapped her. "Oh God, am I that old?" She appeared stricken.

"I think her retirement has more to do with her age than yours." I laughed. "But, I do have an appointment with her replacement—some woman who's transferred from Sydney. I haven't had a chance to look into her yet."

"Send me her details. I'll check her stats while I'm at the courthouse this afternoon. I have the trial for that mugging we've been preparing for. Nasty piece of work. Stole the bag from a young mother and knocked the baby from her arms. He's just lucky the little one is OK or he'd be up for a lot more than robbery and reckless assault on a minor."

"That's bad enough. Think you have enough to put him away?"

She nodded. Then tilted her head to indicate it was our stop.

Alighting the tram, we fell into step and headed for the coffee cart outside the court. "Do you ever get depressed because of our work?" I asked.

She glanced at me as she pulled her purse from her bag. "Because we deal with the scum of the earth on a daily basis?"

"Yeah. I saw a lot in my last role, but now that I'm responsible for handing out the cases, I'm realising the sheer volume of work that comes through our office, and that's just the stuff that gets caught."

"Of course it can get depressing, but the trick is to focus on the cases you win. We can't clean up all the horror that's out there, but at least we make a difference. You've been working this job long enough to know that, Cora."

"I know. I guess it's just different now that I don't get to take part in the justice side of things. I'm only seeing the beginning of the process."

As we moved up the line, our coffees were waiting when we reached the front without us having to order. We were regular customers and Olivia has a flirt-relationship going on with the barista, so he liked to impress.

"Thank you, Antonio," she sing-songed, running her tongue along her top teeth as she handed him ten dollars and told him to keep the change. I handed over the exact amount.

"You know, you could be a little more gracious like your friend there," Antonio said.

"My friend isn't paying rent and a mortgage and makes about four times what I do," I retorted, taking my coffee with pursed lips.

Antonio held up his hands. "I meant no disrespect."

"Hmm."

With a shake of my head, I caught up with Olivia. "What was that about?" she asked.

"Nothing. I just thought I had the wrong order," I told her, not wanting to ruin her morning flirt-fest with my mini-altercation.

"That's strange. He's normally so good."

After walking the short distance to the OPP, we went our separate ways once inside, and the moment I walked into my office, Nick came sauntering in, his thumbs twiddling as he waited for me to notice him. I really wanted to ignore him until he went away, but I wasn't that mean. I just made him wait until I'd put my handbag in my bottom drawer and logged into the computer system.

"Is there something I can help you with, Nick?"

He jumped like he was about to run a race and sat in the ugly blue chair on the visitor's side of my desk. "I need to ask for something."

"Go ahead."

There was sweat beading on his top lip. "I...I need some time off."

Sighing, I started sifting through the mountain of files in my tray. "This isn't a matter for me, Nick. You apply for leave with HR like everyone else."

"I know that, I do. I just...I want to make sure it's OK with you first."

Stopping what I was doing, I looked at him carefully and laced my fingers together. "Nick, you are one of the select few graduates accepted from all over the state to be a part of the traineeship program here. It's an honour to represent the Crown, am I right?"

"Ah, yes." He nodded emphatically.

"That being said, you've been here for little more than a month. If your time off is for anything other than a family death or some sort of unforeseen emergency, I *will* hold it against you in your performance review, and take your lack of dedication into consideration when handing out cases. If you want time off for something frivolous, I suggest you wait until you've accrued holidays as per company policy."

He chewed his lip thoughtfully for a moment. "I'll wait then," he said finally, getting up to leave.

"Good choice." I smiled. Nick, like most of the juniors in my team, had decided it was a good idea to friend request me on Facebook. Because of that, I already knew he wanted time off for a music festival; the social network loved to notify you of every event your friends showed an interest in. Besides my professional reasons for keeping a vague profile, it was one of the primary reasons I kept most of my information and activity to myself.

As he stood to leave, I picked up three of the files from the pile on my desk. "Before you go, Nick. Here are two assaults and an arson for you to work on. I want a summary and presentment on my desk by midday."

"Midday?" He gulped, taking the files.

"Is that a problem?"

He shook his head.

"Then off you go." I shooed him with my hand.

With the folders clutched to his chest, he practically scurried from my office. With a sigh, I took a mouthful of my coffee, smiling to myself over the interaction while sifting through the remaining files.

"Huh. Who knew?"

That voice. It was the voice of my dreams.

When I looked up, I was met with the greenest eyes I'd ever seen, coupled with a dimpled smirk.

Coffee shot everywhere. "What...wh...what are you doing here?" I gasped, grabbing tissues and trying to clean up the mess I made while trying to wrap my head around the fact that Green-eyes was standing right in front of me, in my office, wearing a stunning fucking suit that I envisioned ripping off his body and throwing to the floor. My God, he was even more gorgeous in the daytime than he was at night.

Stepping toward me, those dimples cracking his cheeks while he chuckled at my reaction and helped me dry off the files on my desk.

"I wasn't expecting to see you here either."

Collecting all the wet tissues, I threw them in my waste paper basket and held it up so he could do the same. "I don't understand," I said, patting at my chin to make sure I didn't have any coffee dribbling down.

"Ah, I see you two have met." Adrian Sharp, Director

of Prosecutions and my boss, entered my office with a broad smile on his face.

"What? When?" I was immediately defensive. Did he know I slept with Green-eyes and this was some insane joke? I didn't think I had that kind of relationship with my boss.

"Not really," Green-eyes said. "I kind of startled her when I walked in and we've been cleaning up the coffee spray instead of introducing ourselves." He looked at me, his eyes darkening as they dropped to graze over my body, the knowledge of what I look like naked clearly at the forefront of his mind. "I'm Brandon Sharp, your intern." He held out his hand to shake mine and I took it, feeling glad I was sitting down because my knees were suddenly very weak. It wasn't just that he was in my office and my body was reacting to him, it was the fact that he just said the word 'intern' coupled with the surname 'Sharp'.

"You're, um, related?" I forced out, clearing my throat as I extricated my hand from Green-eye's, I mean, Brandon's searing grip. My hand tingled from the ghost of his touch.

The director grinned broadly. "Brandon is my son." He clapped Brandon on the shoulder.

"Your son." My voice squeaked and my eyes went wide while I forced a smile, trying not to look at Brandon as I felt his gaze burning into me. *I slept with my boss's son. Oh God, I'm fired. I'm so incredibly fired.*

"That's right. But I don't expect you to give him any preferential treatment. He can be the department lackey just like any other intern would. He's third year at ACU, so he'll juggle study with his responsibilities here. Feel free to use him in any way you see fit."

"Oh, she already has," Brandon put in, a wicked glint in his eyes.

I choked on my own spit, coughing and spluttering, almost dying, because the man I'd fucked, the man I'd done things to that would make a prostitute blush—the man I thought I'd never see again—is *my boss's goddamn son who is still at university*. To make matter's worse, the only son I was aware of the director having was only nineteen. *Nineteen*. I was the worst kind of cougar, a predator even. He was *barely an adult*.

It was getting hot. I couldn't breathe and started waving my hands at my face while pulling at my collar.

"Get Cora some water," the director instructed his son. *His son!* Oh God, I wanted to die. My life was so, so over. "Are you all right?"

He peered into my face, a worried expression on his, and I nodded, the absence of Brandon in the room giving me enough space to calm down. "I think," I said hoarsely. "I just need some air. My coffee went down the wrong way."

"Of course," he said, stepping out of my way as I stood and walked to the exit doors as fast as I could without running. When I burst out into the street, I gulped in air, running my hands through my hair as I started walking. It didn't matter what direction I was going in, just so long as it was away from that office and the glaring indiscretion in the shape of the hottest nineteen-year-old on the planet.

"Cora." A voice called after me. Brandon's.

I picked up my step. "No, no, no. This is not happening to me."

He caught up rather quickly, not surprising since he was about six four, and I was only five seven.

"That arse," he said when he fell into step beside me. "I don't mind chasing after it, but I'd rather if you stopped and actually spoke to me."

I ducked down a side street and stopped against a wall covered in graffiti. "This is a nightmare," I moaned, leaning my head back against the multi-coloured brick.

He stopped only a few inches from me. "Really? Because I think this is a dream come true." I could feel the heat of his body. "You left without a goodbye, or even giving me your name. I wasn't done with you yet." He reached forward with one finger and somehow managed to pop two buttons on my blouse, exposing my cleavage.

I gasped and he growled. I was freaked out and turned on all at the same time.

"You're my boss's son."

He moved closer. "So?"

"You're my intern."

Closer again. "And?"

"And you're only nineteen."

"Twenty, actually. I just had my birthday. You want to know what my favourite present was?" He placed his whole hand against my chest, just above my breasts. Heat seared through me as he dragged his fingers down my skin then hooked the centre of my bra, pulling until my body slammed up against his. I whimpered at the contact, my hands grabbing on the lapel of his jacket as he leaned his head down and brushed his nose against my skin. "A lacy pair of black panties."

I was melting. The heat of him too much, the closeness of him more than I could stand. I could barely hold my own weight. "This is highly inappropriate."

"Why?" he rumbled in my ear.

"Because you're so young, and because I'm now your boss."

"That just makes it more exciting." He ran his lips along my jaw, and I swear I almost came. I could barely breathe I was so turned on.

Then his large hands moved to cup either side of my face, holding me steady as he brushed his mouth against mine, teasing me. My body wanted him to kiss me more than anything in this world, wanted to find somewhere quiet and pick up right where we left off, naked and shaking. But I knew that logically it was the worst possible choice. He was too young. I was getting a divorce. I was *his boss*. There were more reasons to stop this than there were to give in. So, summoning all of my strength, I flattened my palms against his impossibly hard chest and pushed. "Stop."

He pulled back immediately, looked at me and grinned, his eyes moving between my mouth and my eyes. "Are you sure?" He let his right hand slide down my neck, his fingers brushing along my breasts.

I gulped, struggling against desire and the right thing to do. "No! I mean, yes, I'm sure. This is my livelihood we're talking about. I can't lose my job. I'm already one more incident away from dismissal."

He straightened his back, his fingers still on my skin, tracing their way to my cleavage.

"I mean it, Brandon," I said, my voice sounding more resolute than I felt.

"I know," he replied, his voice soft and intimate as he re-clasped the buttons on my blouse. "We should get back."

He stepped away, giving me the much-needed space I required to breathe in oxygen over his heady scent. "Thank you." I released a breath and straightened my blouse, running my hands through my hair in an attempt to neaten up.

Then, squaring my shoulders, I looked straight into those captivating eyes. "What happened between us can *never* happen again."

He nodded.

"OK." I was glad we'd cleared that up. Honestly, it had felt a little too easy, but I was relieved somewhat because I really wasn't sure how much longer I could keep saying no while he touched me like that.

"Do you think you can wait ten minutes?" I asked. "I'll go first and you can come back in after."

"They know I came out after you."

"I don't care. I just need a minute to myself to wrap my head around this."

He nodded his understanding. Satisfied, I turned away before stopping and turning back. "Are you seri-ously only twenty?" I asked, squinting my eyes and turning my head from side to side, studying his face.

"We hooked up the day it happened."

I shook my head. "I could have sworn you were older."

"Why does it matter?" he asked with a shrug.

"Because it does," I returned before I walked away, my head throbbing. How the hell was I supposed to work with a man—well, boy—who I not only had outrageous sex with a week ago, but also masturbated to the night before? *God, he was so amazing in bed, and he smelled soooo good. No, don't think that. He's off limits.* I shook the thoughts away as best I could. I felt like a letch. He was only twenty—nineteen the day before I met him—and he was my boss's kid. *Fuck my fucking life. Can't anything go right?*

10

"ANYTHING YOU NEED, BOSS?" Brandon poked his head through my door, leaning his tall, broad body against the frame.

I felt like sighing when I looked at him. The day had been torture. My nerve endings felt like live wires sparking aggressively from fighting to act normal when my attraction was so intense. I even had brief moments where I thought quitting my job would be a wonderful idea.

Instead, I smiled. "It's late. You should go home."

He entered my office, taking the seat opposite me and crossing his legs, ankle to knee. He obviously wasn't a good listener. "My father always taught me to be in the office before the boss and not leave until after."

"That's probably good advice for when you aren't also studying."

"I've been doing some uni work at my desk." He grinned. We were having a normal conversation, but the way his eyes kept straying from my face made his mere presence feel intimate.

Sitting back in my chair, I closed the file in front of me. "Probably not something you should be telling your boss."

He shrugged. "If I do my work and only do uni stuff in between, is it that much of a problem?"

"Considering the internship is unpaid; no, it's fine. Why are you doing it, anyway? Third year is stressful enough without adding something like this to it."

"I'm being slapped on the wrists by my father."

My brow lifted. "Care to elaborate?"

He worked his jaw from side to side then sat up a little more before he spoke. "I was up in Brisbane going to QUT."

"Queensland University of Technology? That's impressive. They have one of the best law schools in the country."

He nodded. "It's also Brisbane, or Bris-Vegas as they like to call it. There's a lot to do up there, and well, Dad decided I was having a little *too* much fun. Since he's in control of the money I get for education and living expenses, he hauled me back down here. Now I'm going to a Catholic University and working here whenever I'm not. It's his way of trying to rein me in. Possibly a little too late at this stage of my life." He met my eyes and smiled.

"That's a pretty strong reaction. What did you do?"

"Let's just say I got in some trouble and he had to bail me out."

"I see. He used his connections to help you and now you're beholden?"

"I've been beholden since I took my first breath," he muttered.

"You don't get along?"

"Only when I'm falling in line."

"And do you fall out of line often?" I had to imagine that the answer to that was a definite yes.

"What do you think?" There was something about the way he was looking at me, something about the way he smiled that told me he wasn't just talking about going against his father's wishes. I felt...undressed by him.

Taking a sobering breath, I had to look away for a moment to clear my head. I needed to address what had happened—was *happening*—between us and put the issue to rest.

"Listen, Brandon, about today. I'm sorry about the way I reacted when I saw you. I just wasn't expecting the guy, I...you know..." Putting it into words was proving more difficult than I'd thought.

"Fucked and dumped?" he offered, the corner of his mouth curving upward.

"Yes, well, no...I mean...I suppose it seemed a lot like that. It's just...if I had known who you were and exactly how young you are, I never would have done...everything we did. I was in a messed-up headspace that night, but I'm supposed to be the more mature of us both. I should have known better."

"Because you're older than me?"

"Well, yes. Almost a whole decade older than you."

"That doesn't make you more mature, Cora."

"Well, I've had a lot more life experience that you."

"Felt like we were pretty well matched when we got back to my hotel room." *He did? Wow.* He tilted his head to the side and regarded me. "How old did you think I was anyway?"

"Maybe twenty-five."

"So, five years is acceptable, but ten isn't?"

"Yes," I blurted, wishing I hadn't brought this up. "You're *so young.* I feel like I've done something terribly wrong."

His mouth kicked up at the side. "Where I was standing, you did *everything* right." He was talking about me like I was some sort of goddess in the sack. Secretly, I was loving the compliments. Jack had never been especially complimentary. "Well, except taking off while I slept. That was a pretty douche move. Oh, and stealing my cologne." He narrowed his eyes slightly, looking like he was trying to figure me out. "Why did you do that?"

"Because you smell *really* good," I responded immediately. Then I pressed my lips together to make myself shut up. This conversation wasn't going anywhere along the lines I had intended.

He chuckled. "I'll be sure to get some more so I can wear that scent every day."

"Please don't," I whispered, closing my eyes.

He released his breath, a quick burst that would have made a 'huh' sound had he given it voice. "Glad I'm not the only one."

I met his eyes again. "The only one to what?"

He placed both feet on the floor then leaned forward on his seat, placing his elbows on my desk, his voice low when he spoke. "Being around you and not being able to..." He paused and dropped his gaze to my bust, his hand closing into a fist as a grunting sound rolled through his throat. "It's torture. I've been hiding my hard-on all day."

All I could do was breathe. Even that was a struggle with the way his eyes were searing into me. This was definitely not what I'd intended when I'd brought the subject up. We were supposed to agree anything between us was a bad idea and go our separate ways.

When he sat back, my eyes dropped to his pants where a decidedly impressive bulge proved his point. I swallowed hard. I knew exactly what that bulge looked like, how it felt inside me, what his arousal tasted like...I had to press my thighs together. "You've been acting so cool since this morning, I'd begun to think it was only me who was struggling," he added.

"I'm trying to be professional." My voice was little more than a breath past my lips.

"Take off your panties and give them to me."

"What?" I shook my head, my eyes scanning the office floor to make sure no one was around to hear him. I knew the office was practically deserted at this time of day, but still. "No way."

"Take them off and give them to me." He leaned forward again and lowered his voice. "Or I'll come around there and take them off you myself." The determined look in his eyes told me he wasn't joking.

"I can't," I gasped, my body trembling with both arousal and the fear of getting caught. I'd been wrong when I'd thought of him as a boy because of his age. There was nothing boyish about him. Brandon Sharp was pure testosterone and *all man*. He was so irresistible that I was actually entertaining the idea of handing over my undergarments.

He leaned forward, his eyes locked on mine. "You can, and you will."

"Someone might see," I whispered, my heart beating wildly in my chest. I'd never done anything sexually crazy before. Never had sex anywhere daring, or even engaged in foreplay outside the privacy of a bedroom or my home. Doing anything sexual in my office made me nervous as fuck.

"Then be discreet."

My mouth fell open. My tongue went dry. Could I seriously do this?

"You've got ten seconds before I do it myself. One..."

A bolt of arousal shot between my legs.

"Two..."

He was going to come and force them off me. The idea even excited me if I was being honest, but the chances of being caught would be so much higher. While the office was mostly empty of staff, there were always a few stragglers staying behind, burning the midnight oil.

"Three..."

"OK." I shifted on my chair, my fingers pulling my skirt up my thighs until I could get hold of my panties.

"Four..."

"This is insane," I breathed as I pulled them down. Why was I doing this? It wasn't because I was afraid of him, or that I felt threatened by his words. It was completely the opposite. I was so lost in a cloud of desire that I couldn't see sense anymore. I wanted him to have them, even got off on the fear of doing something so crazy that I might get caught. I scrunched them in my hand and passed them across the desk, "You're going to get me fired," I whispered.

Taking them from me, he held them up to his nose and inhaled deeply, a low moan rumbling through his chest at my scent. Heat pooled between my legs. The way he displayed his unbridled lust curled my toes. He was so young, so incredibly gorgeous and he was sitting across from *me* unable to restrain the massive hard-on that *I caused.* My whole body quivered. "Mmm. They're soaked. Looks like you've been hiding something all day too."

He opened his suit jacket and slipped them into his inside pocket then came out with a white plastic key card. "I don't give a fuck about your age. I spent half my day trawling through the office policies to see if there was anything against inter-office relationships. There isn't." He placed the card on the desk in front of me. "I'm *very* interested in you, Cora. We can keep things professional during the day, but once the workday is over, all bets are off. You know where to find me." He tapped the card and I noticed the emblem for Causeway 353 Hotel. Huh, looked like he was still in the same room he'd taken me to that night, after all. Was he living there?

Reaching for the card, I gulped. I didn't know how to respond. He'd just taken my arguments and turned them on their head, like a true lawyer. Seemed he was a natural.

"Are you ready?" Olivia appeared at my door, shocking me out of my cloud of desire. I grabbed the key card and slipped it in the waistband of my skirt while she continued to talk, thankfully focused on whatever she was hunting for inside her bag. "I've had the most horrendously shitty day. This case is going to take all bloody week to get through. I can't wait to dive into a bottle of wine when I get home. Oh, and I heard that your intern is the director's kid?" I started shaking my head the moment she brought up the topic, but she still wasn't looking at me. "What kind of a stuck-up little brat is he? Private schooling all the way, living off Daddy's fat pay cheque? Was he as awful as the rest of those silver-spooned arseholes?" I exchanged glances with Brandon. He was smirking. "Ah ha!" Olivia looked up triumphantly, her Myki card in hand. "I knew it was in there." Then she saw Brandon sitting in the visitor chair and nearly fell over. "Who...who is that?" She pointed at him, her eyes wide.

Brandon held out his hand. "Brandon Sharp, the stuck-up brat-slash-silver-spooned arsehole."

"Oh God. You weren't supposed to hear that. I'm so sorry. I actually quite like your dad," she backpedalled.

Brandon chuckled. "It's fine. I really am a brat. Probably an arsehole too. Just don't tell the boss." He winked at her then smiled at me, running his hand over the outside of his jacket where I knew my panties were hidden. I was going to get bruises, I was pushing my knees together so hard.

Olivia dropped a hip and narrowed her eyes. "I know you from somewhere."

Brandon smiled and stood, doing up the second button on his jacket at the same time, a move that men of a certain breeding seemed to do so naturally. "Not sure where from, but I'll take your word for it. If you'll excuse me, I was actually on my way out." He looked at me and nodded politely. "Boss."

"See you tomorrow," I muttered, earning a quirked brow from him before he turned away.

I knew he wanted me to make use of that hotel room

key. Hell, *I* wanted to make use of that hotel room key. But I couldn't. It was crazy. There was no way I could have any sort of relationship with my boss's son. Regardless of office policies, it would be career suicide. And since I was already on a slippery slope thanks to one man, I couldn't afford to be reckless with another one—no matter how hot he was, or how many pairs of my panties he currently had in his possession.

Olivia shifted her position to let him past, exchanging pleasantries at the same time. The moment he left, she turned to me, a puzzled expression knotting her brow. "Is he who I think he is?" she whispered when he was out of earshot.

"Green-eyes?" I nodded.

"Holy fucking hell. You fucked the director's son?" Her mouth fell open and she sucked some air in. "This is a nightmare. What are you going to do?"

I shrugged. "Pretend it never happened. What else can I do?" The hotel key card pressed a searing rectangle of temptation against my skin. *No one would ever know if you used it...*

My God. What was I thinking? I'd just finished convincing myself that he was off limits, then a moment later I was entertaining the idea of showing up at his door in nothing but a coat and heels. I needed my head read. Or better yet, my face slapped.

Olivia placed her hands on her hips, nodding her head. "I think that's for the best. I mean, I've got nothing against a little office dalliance myself, but you have to draw a line somewhere. And your intern—who is the boss's son—would be it."

"I know. I completely agree." My mouth knew what to

say, but my mind was screaming '*But, the sex!*'. To keep my wild thoughts at bay, I was going to need to give that new toy of mine a run for its money.

"He isn't likely to say anything, is he? There's no telling what Adrian would do if he found out you banged his son on top of the whole intervention order fiasco."

"He won't say anything."

"Are you sure?"

"We talked, and we agreed to keep things professional." I neglected to tell her the part where he said that all bets were off outside office hours. "And I don't get the sense that he's the type to kiss and tell."

"That's a relief. This place would suck without you around."

"Don't worry," I assured her. "Nothing's going to happen." As the words left my lips, I tried to believe them. But deep down, I knew that the words were a lie. Where Brandon Sharp was concerned, I didn't seem to have a lot of self-control. Blame it on the hormones...

11

My new toy wasn't enough. At one o'clock in the morning, I was still awake, sitting in my bed in an oversized T-shirt and a pair of black cotton underpants, staring at the key card that assured me a trip to Blissville. Chewing on my nails anxiously, I swore it was whispering to me, tempting me to get up and go. "It'll be mind blowing," it promised in its sultry voice.

I bit my thumbnail a little too hard and caught skin. "Ow!" The pain of the bite was enough to bring me to my senses. I was acting like a hormonal teenager. This needed to stop. I was an almost-thirty-year-old woman who knew better than to play with fire.

As I sucked on the sting, I got up and tucked the card inside my handbag. I couldn't do it. As much as I wanted him, I couldn't go there. It had to remain what it was— one night of crazy, *amazing* sex. Just one. I needed to be sensible here. No more handing over my panties just because he told me to. No more lingering glances or lust-filled stares. My attraction to him had to become a thing of the past. I'd worked too hard and already lost so much. I couldn't afford to lose any more.

With that decision made, it still didn't fix the throbbing need between my legs. Still sucking the pain on my thumb, I headed over to my laptop and opened it up, pulling up a private search window then typing 'adult toys' into the search bar. A bubble of nerves landed in my stomach. *That* was something I never thought I'd do. I'd been with Jack for years and felt no need for a vibrator or a clit stimulator, or any other sort of device to fulfil my needs. It wasn't that our sex life had been amazing, but rather that it had been adequate enough that I hadn't felt the need to look for something *more*—unlike my fuckwit of a husband. If said fuckwit hadn't been available, I'd been perfectly capable of using my hands. But now, *now*, I knew there actually *was* more to experience, new heights to achieve. I had discovered what incredible sex felt like, and if I was going to stand a chance against this inappropriate attraction I had toward Brandon, I needed to make sure I was *satisfied*. With a capital S.

When the page of colourful contraptions loaded, my eyes grew wide. *What are half of these even used for?* I turned my head to the side, trying to work out what one that looked like a lotus flower was supposed to do. The scrolling bar changed to another image, showing me rabbits that I was supposed to defile, then sexy lingerie that left very little to the imagination—especially since a lot of it was crotchless or missing the bra cups. *What was the point in even wearing any?*

"Perhaps just a vibrator," I told myself, scrolling down until I found a button that said exactly that. Clicking, I waited for the page to load.

One thousand, one hundred and twenty-one items. If I'd thought there was anything simple about choosing a vibrator, I was sorely mistaken. There were colourful ones, flesh-coloured ones, ones shaped like the real thing, and others in smooth artistic shapes. Then there were the extras; ones that 'tickled' or penetrated you elsewhere, ones that moved, ones that twisted.

"I have no idea what to choose."

Biting at my bottom lip, I scrolled down the page, clicking on the items that caught my attention and opening them in new tabs. My quest for something to fill the ache I felt inside had turned into a research assignment where I took notes about size, length and features. In the end, I purchased three different types—one large realistic one, a long, stylish-looking G-spot one, and one that massaged back and forth with an attachment to tease my clit.

Satisfied with my choices, I selected the same-day dispatch option—I needed those things here as fast as possible. I couldn't be held responsible for what I'd do if I had to spend another night on edge and unable to sleep because my intern was hotter than sin, and I had the literal key to his bedroom.

With my purchase complete, I headed back to bed, yawning as I crawled over the thick duvet and got inside. I was exhausted, but my brain was a slush pile of mixed emotions. It sucked that my life was so messed up. Thirty was supposed to be the age where you had all your shit together. But, my life was the exact opposite of that. Nothing seemed to be going my way. And the one thing that had been good about it was now another problem on top of a shit pile I couldn't even see over. To think, it was only a few months ago that I'd been lying in bed in my own house, talking to my husband about a good time to start a family. Jack had held my hand and kissed my knuckles softly. "We'll start the moment you turn thirty," he'd said. Even with my career aspirations, that declaration had made me so happy. While I was none the wiser at the time, it turned out that the same hand holding mine was the one I'd witnessed slapping another woman's arse only days later. My whole life had changed in the blink of an eye.

Rolling on my side, I closed my eyes against the wave of emotion that threatened to leak out. Damn that man. This entire mess was because of him. If he'd just kept his dick in his pants, I'd be lying beside him, peacefully asleep and dreaming about babies. *Fuck that man.*

Reaching over to my bedside drawers, I grabbed my phone and typed out a message, needing to get it out before I could even consider sleeping.

Me: Did you ever really love me?

I looked at the screen for a few moments, watching the message change from *sending* to *received.* It was 2:58 a.m. I put my phone down and rolled over, my eyes heavy and my soul confused as I drifted off to sleep.

12

Jack: Of course. I still do.

I WOKE up to find the incoming message, sent to me at 5:00 a.m. I stared at it, disbelieving, my eyes burning as I typed my reply.

Me: Then, why?

One thing Jack and I didn't get to do was have a screaming fight, not even a heated discussion about his infidelity. I had been blissfully unaware until that can't-un-see-balls-deep-in-another-woman moment. But I had questions that needed answers. At first I was so upset that I couldn't even think about him or take his calls. Then I was so angry after the intervention order came down that if he were paper, I would have scrunched him into a tiny ball and set it on fire. I suppose I was going through those stages of grief, because I'd finally come to a point where I accepted it, accepted that my life had irrevocably changed and there was nothing I could do about it. I simply wanted to know why.

Jack: Meet me for lunch

Me: I'm not allowed around you, remember?

Jack: Forget the intervention order. We should talk.

Me: We can talk over the phone. I don't want a criminal record

Jack: Face-to-face

I stared at his words, wondering if I truly was accepting enough to be able to sit down and have a conversation with him. We'd been separated for three months. So much had happened in that short period that it felt like a lifetime. We were different people now.

Jack: Please. I'll beg if I have to

Closing my eyes, I shook my head and bit into my lip. What if this was this some kind of trap? He could completely destroy me if he made it look like I was the one to break the intervention order. Did he *really* want to talk this time? I honestly wasn't sure about his motives anymore. His actions of late had made me question everything I'd thought true about him. But then, he *had* texted his invitation. I would have physical proof should our meeting be contested. I quickly screen-shotted our conversation to be on the safe side. I'd like to think he was ready to be an adult and talk. But I wasn't that naïve girl anymore.

Taking a deep breath, my thumbs moved over the keypad on the screen.

Me: Fine

Jack: Sezar. 12:30?

Sezar was an Armenian restaurant that he loved, not far from my work and generally quiet during lunchtime. My heart hammered against my chest, my thumbs hovering as I hesitated over my reply. Was I ready for this?

Before I could give it any more thought, I quickly tapped out my reply and hit *send*.

Me: See you then.

Dropping my phone face down on my bed, I got up and took a long sobering shower. My brain was foggy from lack of sleep, and the mess of thoughts that flipped between misery over Jack and anxiety over Brandon. It was like I was two different versions of myself: one was the broken-hearted woman of an unfaithful spouse; the other was an unburdened woman in the epicentre of her sexual awakening. With frayed nerves, I felt a little crazy.

To get through this day, I needed coffee and lots of it. I also needed a ridiculous amount of concealer to hide my under-eye bags. Spending a night horny then melancholy didn't do a thing for my complexion. And as much as I hated myself for even thinking it, I didn't want Jack to look at me and be thankful he no longer had to look at me every day.

If I was going to survive this next year of my life, I needed to get my shit together. The first step was convincing Jack to revoke the intervention order so I could go back to being a solicitor advocate. The next step would be making sure that Brandon was under no impression that any sort of out-of-the-office activities would be happening between us. It didn't matter how attracted to him I was. I couldn't afford to jump from an eleven-year relationship into a complicated office romance with a man almost ten years my junior. I was supposed to be this empowered single woman. Losing sleep agonising over two different men wasn't the way to do that.

With my long hair wrapped into a tight bun on top of my head, I put on a neutral-coloured suit with a soft mauve blouse that tied at my neck instead of a collar. Then I slipped my feet into a pair of black court shoes and pulled a piece of paper and an envelope out of my desk drawer. Taking the key card from my bag, I wrote a simple note to take care of my twenty-year-old problem: *I'm sorry. But it won't work.* Then I folded the paper around the card and sealed it inside the envelope, dropping it on Brandon's desk on my way through the office. He'd find it there when he came in after university later in the day. The relief I felt was insurmountable. Today was going to be business as usual. I'd said it before, but this time I meant it—I was reclaiming my life.

"Off to court?" I said, asking an obvious question when Olivia leaned against the door of my office wearing her barrister's gown and wig.

She nodded glumly. "We're starting at ten, but I wanted to tell you not to wait for me tonight. My cases are piling up so I'm going to work late once today's hearing wraps."

"Anything I can do to help?"

With her lips pressed together, she shook her head.

"We have one of the other solicitor advocates working on it."

"I understand." With my recent demotion, it meant that I wasn't allowed to be associated with any OPP cases in an official capacity. I'd not only lost my position, but also lost my credibility with my fellow solicitors. It had been explained away as a 'shift in priorities'. But no one took a demotion with a bigger workload because of a priority change. Everyone knew that. They just hadn't said anything directly to my face, preferring to whisper and make assumptions behind my back instead.

"I do want to hang out with you, though. Promise me you'll come clubbing on Friday? I'm going to need it after this week is over, and I really want my bestie by my side."

Smiling, I nodded. "Sure. Although I'm going home alone this time."

"That might be a good idea." She laughed. "I'll see you tomorrow morning."

When she left, I sorted through some new cases and handed them out to my solicitors. Despite feeling a little dejected about not being able to work on any high-profile cases, I did it all with a bounce in my step and a sense that everything was going to be OK. I'd made up my mind about what had to happen with Brandon, and I wasn't even dreading my lunch date with Jack. I felt cool, calm and capable.

"You seem chirpy today," Penny observed when I handed her a pile of charges to summarise. She was a tiny girl with a small voice who was probably the most capable junior solicitor in a group of ten.

"Just in a good mood," I responded, moving to the

next cubicle to hand Nick his daily cases. "Are we going to have any trouble with these today?"

He shook his head and smiled. "A complete summary of all the issues. No cut corners."

"You're learning." I grinned in return, feeling like the fairy of human depravity as I floated around the office handing out files detailing assaults, rape, robbery and drug deals like they were candy. Perhaps the lack of sleep had done something to my brain. But it was the first day since I'd been demoted to this role that I got through my morning's work without hating every moment of it. This wasn't forever.

Before I knew it, it was time to meet with Jack. Nerves danced about in my stomach as I pulled my bag from my drawer in preparation to head out. It made me realise what my good mood had been based on. *Hope.* Hope that this meeting with Jack would mean the end of that damned intervention order. Having the weight of that thing lifted from my shoulders would mean *everything*. *Please let something go right for once,* I begged the universe as I touched up my lipstick and slid my jacket over my blouse.

When I headed outside, the bite of the cool air cut straight through the material of my jacket, causing me to wrap my arms around myself and lean into the breeze.

When I paused to cross the street, I honestly hadn't seen him.

"Trying to avoid me?" I jumped with a start when Brandon appeared by my side. He must have been walking in the opposite direction to where I'd come from.

"No. I just have somewhere I need to be. You coming from uni?" I tried to keep the conversation as neutral as possible even though I was already feeling a fire in my belly with him so near. *What was it about this guy?*

"I am. Do you want company?" His scent drifted my way on the breeze. That cologne. He was wearing it. He'd bloody gone and bought some more just to tease me. It was so bloody intoxicating. My resolve was slipping and I had only been a minute in his presence.

"I don't think that's appropriate."

He shifted a little closer, leaning down to speak near my ear. "Do you know what's inappropriate? Taking a man's room key then leaving him with nothing but your panties and his own hand to keep him company. I was disappointed last night, Cora. I hope you're not planning on letting me down again."

Sucking in my breath as my whole body caught alight, I had glorious visions of his strong arm stroking that giant cock. I wanted to drop to my knees in front of him and take my turn. But, I forced myself to keep my calm and meet his eyes. "I'll see you at work, Brandon."

He smirked, obviously not buying my indifferent act for a second. Then, as I stepped away to cross the street, his large hand wrapped around my upper arm.

I gasped as he pulled me against him in a discreet move that wouldn't be perceptible unless someone was specifically watching us. Then he dipped his head and inhaled deeply, scenting me while also filling my head with his overwhelming heat and smell. He was too close. I couldn't think with him this near. "Don't fight this, Cora. You and I, we're inevitable."

Then he released me, and I stepped away, the chill air frigid against my skin after the heated reaction he'd caused. The distance between us was just enough that I could breathe, could think. I straightened my jacket and set my jaw. "Not if I have a say in it," I responded as I caught a break in the traffic and crossed away from him.

"You don't," he called after me, a grin on that handsome face of his. God, he looked amazing in a suit. Even from my viewpoint, I could see how taut he was beneath the fabric. My tongue tingled at the memory.

Why did the Trainee Supervisor cross the road?

To stop herself from dry-humping her intern on the other side.

Walking away, I shook my head, more at myself than him. How did he have some crazy power over me that I struggled to control? I needed to work that shit out. But first, I needed to keep my appointment with the other complication in my life. More so, I could do with a cold bucket of water tipped over me, but the cool Melbourne air would have to do.

"Thanks for coming," Jack said when I arrived. He'd stood to kiss, or perhaps just hug me in greeting, but I'd held up my hand to refuse. I needed my space from him for a very different reason.

"You understand what a risk this is for me, don't you?" I asked as I took my seat across from him.

"I do. That's why I really appreciate you coming."

It was a huge risk, and the only reason I took it was because I hoped the benefits would outweigh those risks.

"Well, I appreciate your willingness to talk. I think it's long overdue," I said.

"I agree."

Unsure how to begin the exchange without launching into a diatribe starting with 'how could you do this to me' I clasped my hands on the table, looking around the quiet restaurant. It was strange sitting across from my husband, doing something we'd done many times before. Now, it felt like we were strangers. The past months had changed everything—my feelings, my outlook, my ability to trust. I found myself fidgeting, twirling my thumbs. I felt so out of place across from him.

"Hey. It's OK. It's just you and me here." He placed his hands over mine. For a moment I closed my eyes, feeling a familiar touch that should've been so comforting. Instead it felt like an intrusion. With a sharp inhale, I pulled my hands away, placing them in my lap. Suddenly I knew exactly how to begin.

"I need to know why," I said to my hands, my voice lacking emotion. "I need to know how long." Sucking the air in through my nose, I looked up to meet his gaze. "I need to know how many."

His expression closed over and he looked away. There were only a couple of other tables occupied around us. The restaurant was so quiet that it felt like everyone was listening.

A waiter came over and offered us drinks. Jack ordered a beer, while I ordered a water with lemon; I didn't need any sort of narcotic dulling my senses. I wanted to go through this with a completely sober mind.

Jack wiped his hands over his face then leant back on his chair. "Because I'm a dickhead," he stated simply. "I've had the perfect woman standing in front of me all my adult life, and I was too much of an arse to appreciate it, and too proud to admit I was wrong. I messed up and I've made you pay because of it. I'm sorry for that."

Nodding slowly, I let that bit of information sink in, weighing it against his actions of late. They didn't fit together. Then I waited as our drinks were delivered and Jack asked our server to give us a few more minutes to order.

Once we were alone again, I spoke. "That touches on the why. But I'm still waiting to hear the how long and how many."

His fingers toyed with the label on his beer. "Do you really want to hurt yourself with that information?" *Hurt myself?* That question turned my stomach. It insinuated that the number was going to be far greater than I'd anticipated. I'd really been hoping Sally was the only one...

I met his eyes and steeled my heart against any further pain. "I think I need it if I'm ever going to move on from this."

He stared at me for a moment, his dark eyes clouded. "Move on how?"

I shook my head. "I don't have the answer to that question."

Nodding, he wiped at his mouth then glanced toward the waiter, signalling for him to return. "We should order."

The questions I'd asked hung in the air unanswered as we ordered meals we probably wouldn't be finishing. I wasn't even sure if I could sit there until they were made. The question of numbers felt heavier on my mind with every passing moment.

"I'm going to revoke the intervention order," he announced when the waiter left. I held my breath, keeping my excitement at bay, because Jack was known for adding the word 'but'. He rarely did anything out of the kindness of his heart. "But first"—there it was—"I want you to seriously consider working through this with me. I love you, Cor. I always have, and these past few months without you have been...a wake-up call."

No. This wasn't why I'd come.

I was there because I wanted the order revoked and answers for closure, not a new beginning. There were some things in life you just couldn't un-see, some things that were simply unforgivable.

"How are we to do that, Jack? How do we move past everything that's happened between us? You cheated, I attacked you, then you intentionally and viciously took my life's dreams away from me. How do we move beyond that?"

"We talk. Perhaps even go to marriage counselling. I made a terrible mistake and the situation we're in right now is all on me. You aren't to blame. I know that. I just want to do everything in my power to make things right again. We've been together so long that you're my *family*. I know I fucked it up. I reacted like a cunt and I'm asking you for—no, hoping to *earn*—your forgiveness."

I wanted to open my mouth and say no. I wanted to tell him he was insane and that he'd ruined any love I had for him by banging God knew how many women while we'd been a couple. But I stopped myself, kept my tongue firmly in my mouth. He was effectively holding the intervention order as ransom. If I said no to any sort of reconciliation attempt I could be assured he'd keep it in place. I had to be smart. If I agreed to counselling, perhaps I'd get everything I wanted: answers *and* the end of the order.

It was worth a shot.

"I can agree to counselling," I told him, just as our food was delivered to our table.

Jack's lips curved until he was beaming. "We'll make this right again, Cor. You and me, we belong together."

No. We don't.

I took two tiny bites of my food, tasting nothing. He tried to make small talk as if everything was suddenly going to be fine between us. He rambled on about a story he was working on then even had the audacity to probe me for leads on anything juicy that had crossed my desk at the OPP.

"I don't work on high-profile cases anymore, Jack," I reminded him. He did have the decency to look contrite. But still, I couldn't sit across from him any longer, preferring to lie about a message on my phone advising I was needed back at the office immediately. I didn't care if he believed me. I just needed to get out of there.

We parted ways with a brief hug that he instigated and I hated, along with a promise he'd contact me with details about our first counselling session.

"You'll need to revoke that order first," I reminded him.

"Absolutely," he said, dropping an unwanted kiss on my right cheek. "I was an arsehole for taking it out in the first place."

"I won't argue with that." My skin felt *wrong* from his touch.

By the time I returned to the office, I felt marginally better. My heart was still bruised, and I still didn't have any answers. But I had a tiny morsel of hope that out of basic human decency, Jack would do as he'd promised. That intervention order felt like a noose around my neck with Jack in control of the other end of the rope. He knew I needed it revoked, and he was more than happy to exploit that for his own end. But what exactly was that? The fact that he cheated, and probably more than once, told me that he didn't believe in the institution and sanctity of marriage. Why go to so much effort to force me back to him? I struggled to believe he truly missed me. Perhaps he missed the things I *did* for him, but I couldn't imagine he had any real feelings for me, because if he did, he never would have cheated in the first place. I would have been enough.

That was a depressing thought, knowing you weren't enough for someone. I'd lived my life for Jack, made all my plans with him in mind, yet he'd enjoyed an alternate life in *spite* of me. How had I not known?

Pulling my phone out of my bag, I dialled my mum. I needed to hear her calming voice and wise words if I was going to even think about getting through the rest of the work day. Besides, I still owed her a phone call from the weekend.

"She's alive!" Mum crowed the moment we connected.

"I'm sorry, Mummy. I've been busy." I sounded like a little girl.

"Uh oh, you only call me that when you're upset. What's going on?"

I sighed. "Nothing. Everything. Tell me about life in Warrnambool. Have the whales come past yet?" Warrnambool was down the bottom of the state, a few hours' drive from Melbourne. It was a popular tourist destination due to the seaside location and the fact that humpback whales migrated by the coast every year. It had been a wonderful place to grow up, and when I was feeling down, I missed it dearly.

"Yes. Your father has his binoculars and his camera out on the deck to watch them. I'll get him to email you pictures. But, you really have to take some time off one year and come down here to see them again. They're always gone by Christmas." The week between Christmas and New Year had been the only time I'd managed to make the trek back home for years. That seemed absurd. I'd had time off work other than then. *Why hadn't I gone to see them more regularly?* I loved my parents fiercely, so it—

Oh.

Fuck. Me.

Year after year Jack had begged me to go anywhere but Warrnambool. He'd wanted seaside resorts to *unwind.* God, how many nights had I lain in our resort suite waiting for him to get back from hanging with some *new mates he'd met at the bar*? How the fuck had I missed so many hints?

I should have insisted on going home to see my parents.

"I will, Mum. I promise. Next year, perhaps."

"I'd love that. How is the new apartment? Are you all settled in? Did that man give you any trouble when you went to collect your things?" That was a lot of questions in one sitting. I tried to answer them all in order.

"It's small, but I really like it. And it's starting to feel like home. I've put a lot of colour around it to liven up the space."

"Sounds wonderful. Did you get your grandmother's sideboard?"

"I did," I assured her. "It has pride of place in my living area. Jack wasn't even there when I collected my things."

"You should have burnt the house down and left him nothing to come back to," she muttered, making me smile. She sounded just like Olivia.

"You're not the only one to suggest that."

"It's what he deserves, that miserable excuse for a man."

"Mum," I interrupted before she went off on a rant. It was understandable that she was angry for me, but I needed her to dial it back so I didn't get flustered again.

"How's work?" she asked, changing tack.

"Busy. I'm on the tail end of my lunch break right now. I just wanted to hear your voice before I got back to it."

"OK, I'll let you go. I'm glad you called. I miss you, honey."

"Miss you too, Mum." With that, I disconnected the call, feeling slightly better after hearing her voice. My emotions were so up and down these days that it was hard to stay grounded. I had this hope that once the intervention order was gone, everything would start to fall into place. There'd be no more marking other's work. I'd be back in the trenches untangling cases, interviewing witnesses, attending bail hearings, and doing any number of things that actually mattered. I'd be relevant again. I smiled at the thought.

"Thinking about me?" Brandon entered my office with a stack of new case files in his arms.

I was in no mood to scold him over being inappropriate, and truthfully, seeing him caused a fair amount of the day's stress to fall from my shoulders. He was a welcome interruption. "I was actually thinking about getting my old job back."

"What was your old job?" He placed the files in my tray.

"Solicitor advocate to Olivia, the barrister you met last night."

"Your friend, the blonde?"

"That's her." I tapped the pile of briefs that had been checked over to indicate he could hand them back to the junior solicitors. They'd either correct their mistakes or send them up the chain.

"And why aren't you still working with her?" he asked as he lifted the pile with those strong arms of his. He'd removed his jacket and rolled his sleeves halfway up his forearms. I wanted to bite his skin.

Instead, I looked up at him and smiled. "Let's just say that you aren't the only one who gets in trouble at times."

He grinned. "Now I'm intrigued."

"Be intrigued while you hand those back. When you're done, sit with Penny while she does the preliminary workup on the drunk driving case I handed her this morning. She can take you through the issues." I could see a lot of potential in Penny and knew that having her teach someone else would be a great way to reiterate her own learning. I could see her being able to work autonomously soon.

"Sure thing, boss," Brandon said, turning to head out. Before he got out the door, I called his name.

"Did you get the envelope I put on your desk?"

"I did." His lips quirked as he shifted the weight of the files to one arm. *Did he think this was funny?*

"And you understand where I'm coming from? We're cool?"

He chuckled a little. "I'd better hand these out." And then he was gone.

Confused by his response, I started on the pile he'd left for me and found the envelope beneath the first file. The card was gone, but inside was another note: *Not if I have a say in it.*

13

SINCE I DIDN'T HAVE to wait for Olivia, I managed to get out of work early, needing to avoid any sort of alone time with Brandon. That cologne of his was simply too much for my senses. By the time five o'clock rolled on, I was biting my lip to stop myself from burying my nose in his chest and biting his delicious skin. His effect was so... carnal. I couldn't explain it. My brain was resolute in the morning, but by the afternoon I was squirming in my chair and daydreaming about his violent thrusts.

Please be there, I silently begged as I entered the mail-room, finding my parcel sitting on the ground beneath the letterboxes.

"Oh, thank fuck," I said as I leaned over to pick it up, then rushed for the elevator so I could get inside my apartment and try my *toys* out.

Excitement thrummed below the surface of my skin knowing that a sated evening was in my near future.

The moment I got inside, I placed the box on the

small white coffee table and dropped to my knees in front of it.

"Who needs the complication of a man when you can buy all the fulfilment you need?" Using my keys to cut the tape, I flipped the box open with grand plans of wine, bubble baths and battery-operated boyfriends. But my expression dropped along with my hopes when the box contained nothing I ordered.

"What the hell is this?" I pulled out a contraption that looked like it should be used for abseiling that I discovered from the packing slip was a sex swing, along with silk rope, a blindfold and gag, and some padded handcuffs. "The fuck?"

Flipping the lid on the box, I double-checked the address. They got that right. It was just the contents they got wrong. How obscenely disappointing.

Digging through my bag, I pulled out my phone and found their website, logging in to double-check my order. It was right on the screen. I found their customer service number and put through a call. This was a life and death emergency. If I didn't get off properly and soon, I was going be wired all night. I didn't care if they needed to hire an emergency courier—I *needed those sex toys.*

Just as I was cursing while listening to a recorded message telling me their operating hours, there was a knock on my door.

"This had better be a parcel delivery," I muttered, stomping over to the door and flinging it open.

What was waiting for me had a sexy grin, amazing green eyes, and a bag of takeout dangling from his index finger. "I brought dinner."

Brandon Sharp.

"What the hell are you doing here?"

He pushed past me into my apartment. "I figure if I'm going to fuck you, I should at least feed you first."

My vagina jumped for joy.

My head had alarm bells going off inside it.

"You shouldn't be here. How do you even know where I live?"

He stopped in front of my coffee table and put down the bag of food, picking up the padded cuffs. "I see you were expecting me."

Rushing over, I shoved everything back into the box. "Those aren't mine."

"Cora Knowles. Invoice number 21563. One Sex Swing-black. One silk play t—"

I snatched the packing slip from his hands and shoved that in the box too. "Yes. It's under my name. But they got my order wrong."

That just made his grin even broader. "Now I'm really intrigued. What was your real order?" He advanced on me, his arms going around my waist, pulling me against him, his hands sliding to my arse. "I have ways to make you confess," he rumbled against my ear, his teeth biting my lobe.

I melted against that taut body of his, my own buzzing with need. How did he do this to me? I felt drunk and willing, ready to do anything he wanted.

Then he stole my phone from my hand.

"What are you doing?"

He moved away from me swiftly, pressing the home button to open the password-protected screen. "What's your password?"

Ha! I had him there. There was no way I'd give him

that information. I shook my head and took a step backward.

"That's fine. Don't tell me. It's Touch ID. Give me your thumb."

"No!" I hid my hands behind my back, and lifted my chin in defiance.

The moment I saw the glint in his eyes, I knew I was in trouble. The corner of his mouth twitched then his upper body hunched. He was ready to pounce.

A squeal burst from my lips when he shifted, and I turned tail and sprinted to the other side of the couch, putting a barrier between us.

"That's not going to stop me."

I bit my lip, the smile too hard to fight as I watched him like a hawk, moving in the opposite direction to him, a game of cat and mouse.

He laughed, and I taunted him by wriggling my thumb in the air, daring him to come and get me.

He didn't fail to meet my challenge.

With one swift movement, he leapt over the couch and caught me. I shrieked with laughter as he lifted me off the floor and dumped me on the couch cushions, my body bouncing for less than a second before he climbed over the back and pinned my body beneath his.

He grabbed me by the wrist. "Let's get this phone open, shall we?"

"Not if I can help it." I grinned, trying to make a fist to thwart him further.

"I have other ways to make you talk," he murmured, wickedness in his eyes as he kept me pinned, his legs mixed with mine, his chest weighing me down in the most magnificent way.

Suddenly, I was very aware of how close he was, how vulnerable I was in this position. Screw the sex toys. I had the real, live man on top of me and my resolve didn't give a fuck about the implications when he was this close. *No one had to know.*

My smile dropped from my face. I pulled my lip with my teeth, while rampant dirty thoughts filled my mind.

"I love the way you do this," he murmured, bringing his thumb to my mouth and freeing my bottom lip. "It means you have nothing but filth going through that sexy mind of yours." With enough pressure to wipe away my lipstick, he ran the pad of his thumb against that same lip, his eyes darkening as he watched intensely.

The action and the expression on his face tipped me over the edge of indecision. I wanted him, and no amount of logic was going to change that.

Shifting slightly, I caught his thumb between my teeth, biting gently before sucking back, laving the pad with my tongue. My eyes dropped closed and I moaned at the taste of his skin. I'd missed that.

His chest made a long deep, resonant sound as he withdrew from my mouth, dragging his fingers down my chin to my neck where he pulled at the tie of my blouse. "I've been dying to tug on this all day. It's the sexiest damn blouse I've ever seen." When he exposed my neck, he ran his fingers over the soft skin before wrapping his whole hand around it, fingers pressing into flesh as he lowered his head and placed his forehead against mine.

His breath washed over me, minty and warm, my lips burned with need, wanting the sweet torture of his nearness to end. "Fuck me, Brandon," I whispered.

"Call me Bran," he responded, his lips at the edge of

mine, his erection pressing forcefully against my hip. "Brandon at the office. Bran when we're alone. Understood?"

"Yes," I whispered, moving my mouth to try and catch his. My body was screaming. I needed to taste him. "Please, Bran." I moved beneath him, pressing against his erection, pushing my swollen breasts against his chest.

The hand at my throat shifted and he swept his thumb along my jaw. "I like it when you beg."

Then he kissed me.

That mouth.

That tongue.

My body thought it was New Year's Eve, with an array of fireworks going off behind my eyes, causing my desire for him to treble.

I whimpered beneath him, my body coiling into an intense ball of need as his hand glided up my arm, his fingers entwining with mine.

Then it was over. And the stark realisation of what just happened hit me when my thumb was pressed against the home button on my iPhone.

He played me.

Like a fiddle.

"Bran!"

He sat back, his thighs straddling my waist so I couldn't get up. "Let's see what kind of toys Cora Knowles likes to play with." His thumb moved over the screen while his free hand fended off my flailing arms as I tried to get it back.

"You don't play fair."

He grinned. "No. I don't."

Then I folded my arms and pouted, trying to hide my humiliation with anger. "You're an arsehole."

Ignoring me, he kept his focus on my phone. I wanted to curl up in a ball and die. Once he saw what, and how much I'd ordered, he was going to think I was some sort of oversexed nympho.

When his brow lifted, I knew he'd found it. *Please Lord, open the ground and swallow me now.*

He took a moment, studying the list quietly before he shut off my phone and placed it on the coffee table without a word.

The suspense was killing me. "Well?" Now he'd seen it, I needed to know what he thought.

Leaning back over me, he took a hold of my wrists and pinned my hands above my head. "I think the box delivered was much better."

"You do?"

"Uh-huh." He kissed and bit at my neck. "You don't need a big thick vibrator when you have your very own big thick cock right here." He pressed said cock against my thigh.

"My very own?"

He nodded. "On call. Twenty-four-seven."

"That sounds a lot like a relationship."

"Or a very dutiful fuck buddy. Take your pick, feisty. Whatever name you give it, it's still going to be you and me fucking each other's brains out. Now"—he reached an arm out and rummaged around in the box, withdrawing the silk rope—"let me show you how much fun this box of goodies is while I remind you why a giant vibrator isn't as good as the real thing."

As he wound the rope around my wrists, I grinned up

at him. "It might take some convincing. I was really looking forward to those toys."

He fastened the knot around my wrists then anchored it to the lamp table.

"They were a poor substitute for me and you know it."

"Someone's arrogant."

One side of his mouth tilted upwards. "Maybe. But I'm still right. You were worked up after our meeting in your office and instead of coming to me last night, you ordered all those toys to fill the void my cock should have been filling. It's simple maths." He barely knew me but was completely right in judging my actions. What was he, a spy?

"And what did you do to fill the void?" I hoped I wasn't the only one in a sexual frenzy last night.

He pulled the blindfold from the box and ran the silk through his hands, wrapping it around his fists before pulling it taut then placing it over my eyes. "I jacked off a thousand times, imagining I was spraying my cum all over your tits and arse. But it wasn't enough. I *need* the real thing." His voice gruff, he lifted my head and tied a knot. With my world ensconced in darkness, all I could do was feel him. His lips pressed against my ear. "Just like you need the real thing, Cora. What's going on between us is more than just wanting to fuck. It's about the desire and anticipation when we're around each other. You can't synthesise that." *What was going on between us was more?* The idea made me nervous. Bran was young and beautiful. He was part of a powerful family and had the world at his feet. How long would it take before his desire waned and he got bored of basic me, deciding he needed his fulfilment elsewhere, just like Jack did? It wasn't outside the realm of possibility. What did I possibly have to offer him that he couldn't get from a much younger woman?

"So, what do we do?" I asked, breathless and shrouded in dark. Not being able to see his eyes made it easier to ask questions. "Screw each other until this desire and anticipation is out of our systems?"

"If that's what you want." His tongue drew a trail down my chest as his fingers undid the buttons of my blouse and pushed it aside. "But I expect it's going to take a *very* long time. I can't stop thinking about this body of yours."

My breath quivered in my throat as my skin bumped, excited. With my sight gone, my hands tied above my head, I could hear every movement, sense his touch before his fingers met my skin. He was gentle yet rough, each grab of my flesh firm while he also ran feather-light fingers along the skin of my heaving breasts. He collected them in his hands and pressed them together, growling at what he saw.

"I've been dreaming about these tits since I first saw them. They're magnificent." His hand worked the lace cup of my bra down freeing the mound of flesh to be worshipped by his hands and mouth. He sucked on my nipple, pinching me between his teeth. Then he squeezed and teased, releasing my nipple with a pop before I felt his teeth against my skin. "I'm going to have to mark them to make sure they're mine."

With a firm suck and swirl of his tongue, he took my flesh in his mouth again. I moaned as he placed his mark on my body, arching against him and writhing for more. I didn't know why I liked it so much, and as long as he kept the love bites to places I could hide beneath my clothes, I was more than happy to accept them. It was possibly the domination, the arrogance, or the possessiveness of the act. I liked that he took what he wanted from me and willingly gave what I wanted in return. That first night with him felt like freedom, and this was no different. Despite being tied up, I knew his touch was a promise I was free to take, free to respond to. *And would absolutely and thoroughly enjoy.*

Then his fingers sank into my skin and dragged down my abdomen to the waist of my skirt. Gripping my hips, he flipped me over to my stomach, the silk rope twisting above my wrists. I felt the button to my skirt release then the zip open. He pulled the fabric down my legs, his hands covering my arse cheeks and squeezing through my black lace panties. "And that arse. I just about blow in my pants every time I see you lean over." He slapped the left cheek, hard. Then he rubbed away the sting and pulled my panties aside, his hand running over the smooth skin. "This arse is mine too." His teeth bit into my skin before he sucked back, marking me again.

"Bran," I moaned, my core aching for more. I wanted every-*fucking*-thing he had to give.

His hand ran over my arse cheeks then slipped between my thighs, staying on the outside of my panties. This was torture. Sweet, sweet torture. If I didn't come soon, I might die. "Those lips are mine too. The way they say my name, they shouldn't be speaking another man's name in the same tone. Not until I'm done with you."

Pressing his fingertips against my clit, he massaged me through my panties, getting me to gasp and curve back into him as my senses started to spin out of control.

"Bran," I moaned again, so close.

"Mmm, say it again." His fingers slipped beneath the fabric and plunged into my depths. He released an erotic growl.

"*Bran.*"

"Tell me you aren't going to fight this anymore." He worked his fingers in an out, in and out, pressing against my G-spot and sending me into a frenzy.

"I won't," I gasped, my head spinning, my body on fire.

"Promise me that no other man will touch you." His fingers moved faster.

"They won't." I loved the way he demanded. I felt claimed. *Wanted.* In that moment, there was no doubt in my mind that I was the only woman Bran was thinking about.

"Promise me."

"I..." My mouth fell open, my orgasm at breaking point as his fingers moved inside me.

"Say it, Cora."

"*I promise,*" I shrieked as I exploded around his hand, my body bucking as his fingers kept working me, pushing my orgasm as far as it could go.

"I'm a selfish man, Cora." He spoke close to my ear as my moans turned into screams of ecstasy. This was almost more than I could stand. "I take what I want, and I don't share."

With those words, the weight of his body left mine, leaving me whimpering at the loss while feeling full from his proclamation. It was just what I needed. My ego had taken such a hit from Jack's infidelities. Having a man as sensual as Bran demand that I be only his stirred something primal inside me. I felt...desirable, powerful even. This man was relentless in his pursuit of me and unforgiving in his taking.

I loved it.

When I heard the zip on his pants and his belt hit the floor, anticipation ached within me. Then I heard the telltale sound of a condom wrapper opening. Moments later, his hands were at my hips, removing my panties by breaking them at the seams, tilting me upwards. Then, I felt his cock press into my entrance.

"Ohhhhh." There it was, the feeling I'd been seeking. *Needing.* The sensation of being so full that my mind couldn't function. My eyes rolled back in my head when he began to move, working my insides as his fingers dug into the flesh at my hips.

Another orgasm built to a tremulous conclusion. My moans akin to an animal in pain, but I couldn't stop them or give a second thought to what my neighbours might think. I was too far gone. Too lost as his glorious cock speared me from behind and altered my perception of reality.

His pace quickened and I gripped the edge of the couch, the only thing I could reach with my bound hands. Each time we collided, I let out a gasping yelp until my body stiffened and I exploded once more—reality disintegrating—with me floating somewhere in the middle of it all.

"Fuck, Cora." His voice was strained as he thrust once more, pulling out of me quickly. I heard the snapping sound of latex then a thud on my arse that could only be the weight of his enormous cock. Then a pool of heat landed at the apex of my seam, running between my cheeks. *Did he just cum on my arse?*

With a sound coming out of him that could only be described as pure ecstasy, he placed his hand against my cheek and rubbed the hot cum into my skin. "Now it's definitely mine," he growled, leaning down and biting my skin gently.

I gasped. *Holy fuck. That. Was. Hot.* I wasn't sure I'd ever wanted a guy to come on my skin before, but *that* and the way he did it was...my God...it was orgasmic— twice. I'd been branded—Bran-ded—and it was glorious.

Reaching his body over mine, he kissed and sucked at the back of my neck, untying the silk and releasing my hands. The sex swing and the gag could go back to the store, but the blindfold and silk rope were staying. I would happily let Brandon Sharp tie me up any time.

I was limp in his arms when he pulled me to standing and slid the blindfold from my eyes. "Feeling good?" he asked with a grin.

"Uh-huh." I nodded, leaning my half-naked body against him.

He pushed my blouse off my shoulders and removed my bra. "Already?" I asked, thinking he was going for round two.

"First we shower. Then we eat." He lifted me so he was cradling me in his arms. "Then we have dessert."

"Am I dessert?" I asked with a sigh.

He smiled. "Yeah. You're dessert."

14

"I THINK we need to make one thing abundantly clear," I said as I sat on the bench the next morning, Bran caging me with his body as he fed me toast and coffee. We'd barely slept all night, and my body was achy all over. But I had more energy that morning than I ever remembered having before.

"And what precisely is that?" His eyes dropped from mine as he took a mouthful of his own coffee. Just watching him swallow turned me on. I reached out and ran my thumb across his full lips. He smiled then bit the pad of my thumb playfully.

"This thing," I started when our gazes locked again. "It's not a relationship. We work together and we fuck when the urge arises. That's it. I can't offer you any more than that." In some respects, I felt I was giving him an out. But to have anything more complex would probably put more strain on myself than I could handle.

He smiled, seemingly unfazed. "Understood. My only condition, as stated previously, is that I don't share. I'm an only child so I've never been very good at it. Plus, it's rare to find a woman so willing to take all I give without flinching." He pinched me playfully on the outside of my thigh and I liked it, especially when his hand then covered the sore spot.

"You mean the marks you like to leave behind or the rough manhandling you're so fond of?" I took a bite of the toast he held out to me.

"All of it. Most girls"—he took a breath, as if he wasn't sure he should speak up—"don't take too kindly to being marked. They find my brand of fucking a little too rough and intense." It was rough and intense. But that was what made it so delectable for me. He kept me riding that fine line with expert hands.

"Most girls? You're only twenty. How many could you have possibly gone through?"

He grinned. "You'd be surprised. I've quite the appetite, and I like to dominate. In the bedroom, of course. At work, you're one hundred per cent the boss."

I liked his brand of dominance. What was it about him that made me accept his commanding behaviour in the bedroom? Was it because *I* was angry? Angry at my life and my husband? Or did I have something inside me, a dormant desire to be manhandled and marked that I'd never explored before?

"You can just switch it off like that, can you?" I snapped my fingers, imagining that a man like Bran would prefer to always be in control.

"What happens in the bedroom stays in the bedroom." He smiled, a mischievous glint in his eyes. "Or on the couch, the shower, the kitchen..."

I studied his expression, feeling slightly lost in those

jade-green eyes of his. "That's exactly how it has to be. I need your word that this arrangement between us stays just that—between us. I will not be the subject of office gossip, Bran. I don't even want Olivia to know."

"I won't breathe a word."

"OK. So, we do this, and when we've gotten to the point where we can be in a room together without wanting to tear each other's clothes off, we'll end it and no one's job has to suffer because of it."

"I love it when you talk dirty to me." He grinned and leaned forward to kiss me. I placed my hand on his chest and stayed out of reach.

"I'm serious, Bran. These are my terms. This is all too problematic to be anything else, and I want to make sure we're on the same page before this goes any further."

With his hand gripping the back of my head, he pulled me forward, despite my protest, so his lips pressed against my ear. "I will fuck you in the shadows of every place you hold dear so that even when we're finished with each other, you'll get excited just walking through the door, remembering what it feels like to have my cock inside you." My entire body quivered at the thought of everything he could *and would* do to me. I knew we had an expiration date, and surprisingly I was OK with that. There was no way a ten-year age gap coupled with a complex work situation could result in any more than a fling, and that was discounting the whole Jack debacle. Yes, a fling would do me just fine. Bran might never become my happily ever after, but he could certainly be my happy for now. No worrying about the future, or wandering eyes, we'd do this until it wasn't fun anymore.

It was the perfect setup, and I was going to enjoy every moment of it.

"As long as no one finds out, you can fuck me anywhere you like." I threaded my fingers through his hair, holding tight as he worked his magic at the nape of my neck.

"Is that an invitation?"

"It's a demand."

"Hmm. I'm going to enjoy being your dirty little secret." He parted my thighs, his fingers sliding through my arousal.

"Emphasis on the *dirty.*"

A devilish grin took over his features. "How long do we have?"

Based on the time on the microwave, there was about half an hour before I was due to meet Olivia.

I groaned. "Not long enough."

He dropped to his knees. "You'd better hold on," he warned me, right before his mouth clamped over my clit. My hands flew out and gripped the edge of the bench.

My God.

That tongue!

"What blush is that you're wearing? I could use something that colour this morning. I look like death," Olivia said while we walked to the tram stop. Brandon had walked in the opposite direction and caught a cab to his hotel so he could change into a fresh shirt and suit before heading to the office.

"How late did you work last night?" I asked, avoiding

the question. I couldn't exactly tell her I was wearing the shade *just fucked by a twenty-year-old.* As open-minded as Olivia was, I knew she wouldn't be on board with what I was doing with Bran for a second. She'd already made it clear that she thought having anything with him was a bad idea. Her mindset was generally career first, men later. She'd think I was insane.

And maybe I was insane. Who knew? The only thing that was abundantly clear was that I couldn't resist him. I honestly felt that I had no choice but to give in to the desire or combust from the heat. Our attraction was that intense. The way I saw it, this spark between us would eventually fizzle out and we'd part ways with great memories. But until then, we were going to have a lot of fun working that excess energy out. And I was going to have a wonderful time receiving all those multiple orgasms he seemed so intent on providing.

"I left the office at one. Then I worked at home until four. I'm in court again at ten. When that wraps up, I have a pre-trial conference for that guy who ploughed his car into those pedestrians. His lawyers are trying to claim that he couldn't help it because on a genetic level, he's predisposed to violent outbursts."

"That just gives you cause to ask for the maximum sentence without the chance of parole due to his likelihood to re-offend. What a joke. Can't you send your solicitor to deal with it instead?"

She shook her head. "She's good. But she isn't quite up to your standard. One needs to be ruthless with those bastard defence attorneys, and she's too soft."

"I'm sorry I can't be of help."

Lifting one shoulder, she twisted one side of her lips downward. "Jack-Arse is the one who should be sorry."

"Speaking of. I kind of had lunch with him yesterday."

Her eyes grew large. "You *what?* Did anyone see you?"

"He asked me and no, no one who mattered saw. It was as amicable as it could possibly be."

"So, you didn't slap him or knock him unconscious this time?"

"No. He wants to go to counselling."

"Marriage counselling?"

I nodded.

"Do you want that?"

"Not particularly. But he says he'll revoke the order if I go with him. I think it's worth going just for that. Plus, I want answers, Liv. I want to understand why he cheated and why he intentionally ruined my life when I left him because of it."

"You don't need a counsellor for that. He did it because he's a tantrum-throwing cunt. Plain and simple."

"I'm sure there's more to it than that."

"Why the about-face all of a sudden? What's his angle?"

I shrugged. "He says he misses me."

"He misses what you did for him." She snorted. "Taking care of him, doing his laundry and cooking his food. Must be hard having to look after himself for a change. Poor baby boy."

"I'm not doing this to reconcile, Olivia. I'm doing it to get my life back. That's all."

"Thank God. I'd have to rescind our friendship if you let that cretin back in your life again."

I laughed. "Seriously?"

She met my eyes and shook her head. "Of course not. But I felt there needed to be some sort of a threat over your head to make sure you see sense. Relationships are terrible things and cheaters always cheat. Those kinds of leopards never change their spots."

"Don't worry. There's no way Jack and I are getting back together. Understanding why he felt the need to cheat will be a happy by-product."

"Oh, that reminds me. I checked into that divorce attorney. She seems good. Young, but good. She generally ties everything up in mediation."

"Is that a good thing?" I had only touched on the legalities of divorce at university since I specialised in criminal law over family.

"Yes. It means everything gets sorted quickly and amicably. It's rare that judges get involved."

"OK. I'll set up the meeting then."

"Maybe wait until Jack gets rid of the order. You don't want to risk him catching wind of this and changing his mind."

"Good point," I said, stepping off the tram outside the court.

As per usual, we lined up for coffee before heading into the OPP.

"Speaking of male complications, how goes your new intern?" Olivia glanced toward the office building where Brandon could be seen walking up the stairs. With each step, the pants of his grey suit tightened against that taut arse. I could feel myself getting warmer. That arse currently had my fingernail imprints in it.

"Monday was weird, but yesterday was fine," I said,

keeping my voice even while being sure not to make eye contact.

"*He's* fine. How *that* came from the loins of Adrian Sharp I'll never know; must take after the mother. If he was working for me, I'd have to take masturbation breaks just to get through the day. And it's worse for you because you already"—she looked around to make sure no one we knew was in earshot—"fucked the boy to oblivion."

With a laugh, I glanced to the office doors he'd just walked through. "Technically, it was the other way around, and I assure you, he was no boy."

She lifted her brow. "All man? It's a pity he is who he is. You could have gone back for seconds. But never thirds." She held up her finger in warning.

Taking a deep breath to stop the satisfied smile from creeping across my face, I lifted my shoulders. "There's so much going on in my life right now, I can't even consider that," I assured her, lying to her face.

"You're a fucking saint. You don't really have much choice in the matter, but still, you're a saint."

If only she knew...

15

"Morning, boss. Here are some new case files." Bran placed the piles on my desk then added my mail on top. "And your correspondence."

"Thank you." I grinned, pulling the mail off the top and flicking through it. I'd had most of my personal mail redirected to the office while I was between homes, but now I was starting to update my contact details everywhere so it went to the apartment instead. Looking at the redirection labels, I furrowed my brow, remembering an unanswered question from the night before. "You never told me how you got my address," I said quietly, my eyes meeting his.

Grinning, he picked up the files he needed to hand back out. "I followed you, of course."

"Excuse me?" As much as I admired his pursuing tactics, that was possibly going a little too far for me.

He chuckled at my obvious shock. "I'm joking. I saw your change of address form when I took my paperwork to HR on Monday."

"So you memorised it?"

His eyes darkened. "I think you'll find I memorise a lot of things." The way he looked at me told me he was remembering every naked curve of my body.

My cheeks flushed slightly. "I bet you do," I replied, shifting in my seat while reminding myself to keep this conversation office-friendly in case the wrong person walked in and noticed the sexual charge in the air. "Are you at university today?"

"I leave here at three. A lecture then a tutorial. I finish around six."

"Then you have coursework to do, right?" I knew I was fishing for information about his whereabouts that evening. I needed to know if he'd be visiting. Last night only served to feed my hunger for more of him.

He grinned. "I actually have an essay to finish for my legal ethics class."

There was a knock on my open door. Nick popped his head around the corner of the glass wall that separated my office from the bull pen. "Are you busy? I have some questions about the charges on this police report. They don't make a lot of sense."

"Of course," I told him. Then I turned back to Bran, placing a mask of calm over my face. "Well, good luck with your paper. If you get stuck, I'm sure one of the juniors will be more than willing to help you out."

"I'll be sure to ask." When he left, I had to fight with my eyeballs to make them look at Nick instead of Bran's arse as he walked through the door. I was disappointed I wouldn't have him in my bed again that night. But I supposed my body could probably do with the rest and a long bubble bath in preparation for the next time...

"So, what's this problem you're having?" I asked Nick as he slid into the seat across from me, handing me his file.

"If he asks Penny to help him, she'll be useless for the rest of the day," Nick said instead of answering my question.

I opened the file anyway, trying to put my head into the work at hand instead of worrying about the next time I'd get to see Bran naked. "What do you mean?"

"She's got a massive lady boner for him. I've never heard her giggle before. Yesterday, when he sat with her to work on whatever case you said he could look in on, that's all she could do. I had to put on headphones."

"Was he flirting with her?" The question jumped out of my mouth before I had the chance to stop it. The idea of him flirting with the other solicitors placed a lead weight in the centre of my chest.

Nick shrugged. "Does a guy like that even have to?"

I smiled at the off-handed comment. He was right. Bran didn't have to flirt at all. All he had to do was look at a woman and she'd turn to mush. "So, this case?" I started again, shaking off my Bran-brain.

"Yeah." He leaned on my desk and pointed to the police report. "It says they arrested him for possession and intent to sell, but the volume of the drug isn't enough for the second charge."

"Then you charge him with something less," I responded.

"Like what? Public intoxication?"

"Is that in the report?"

"His blood alcohol level was point one six."

As I sat with Nick and worked through the charges he

would recommend, I couldn't stop my eyes from wandering to where I could see Bran chatting to Penny. He was smiling about something and she was looking at him in absolute wonder. A knot formed in my stomach. He'd said *he* didn't share, but did that rule apply to him too? It grew increasingly difficult to focus as my mind ran off on its own. Would I have to watch him act like that with every female here? Nick had been right. All he had to do was *look* at a woman and she was putty in his hands. Worse was the fact he was *smiling*. Dimples on a regular guy were distracting enough, but on an Adonis like Bran, they caused women's ovaries to cry out from the agony of wanting to have his babies. Our office didn't have a shortage of attractive single women either. Fling or no fling, I didn't know if I could handle watching him peruse the office for his next conquest after me. *Or, maybe I was being hypersensitive?*

Calm the fuck down, Cora.

When I sent Nick back to his desk, I jumped from task to task, unable to focus on anything for more than a few minutes at a time.

Did it really matter if he was flirting with the female solicitors? It wasn't as if we were in a committed relationship, or anything. We'd just made it clear that we were fucking. *He'd* made it clear that he didn't want to share *me*. But I hadn't exactly made it clear I didn't want to share either. Considering what I'd just gone through with Jack, I probably should have made sure he understood that. My foot tapped anxiously as I tried to think of a way to speak to him without anyone listening in.

When an email came through requiring evidence boxes from the archive, I saw the perfect excuse to get him alone. I wouldn't be able to focus on work until I made my side clear as well.

I walked out of my office and approached his desk with the printed instructions in my hands. "I need you to go to the archive and collect these boxes."

He took the paper from me and frowned at the list. "The archive?"

"It's downstairs."

"I'll show him," Penny piped up, a little too enthusiastically. She was so tiny and perfect. *Everything I wasn't.* Up until today, I'd liked her. But suddenly, I couldn't look at her without feeling threatened by her perkiness *and* youth. Ten years felt enormous.

Eyeing her carefully, I plastered a smile on my face. "You have more than enough work to get through, Penny. I'll show him."

Her smile dropped as she slumped down in her chair. Bran grinned. "Lead the way, boss."

Heading toward the lift, I could feel him watching my arse as he stayed a step behind me. I kept my head up and focused on needing to hit the call button so I didn't turn around and throw him a coquettish grin. Remembering his earlier promise, *every* surface looked like a good place to fuck.

"Hit the basement," I told him once we were on board. It was difficult standing in a confined space with him and not recalling the last time we were in a lift, preparing to tear each other's clothes off.

"You seem pissed," he said, clasping his hands in front of him, mindful of the cameras watching us even though we were technically alone.

"Not pissed. Just...I don't know what I am."

"I'm hoping it's turned on. Because my dick is aching for you right now." My knees almost gave way. He said all of this with a straight face. If someone were watching the monitors, they'd have no idea what he just said, unless of course, they could read lips.

When the doors opened, I headed to the archive room, opened it with my employee key card, and pushed open the door. I didn't speak again until I'd walked the length of the room to make sure we were alone.

"What's this about? Are there actually files to get?" Bran asked, watching me with a careful eye. "Something is going on, isn't it?"

"I don't like you flirting with the girls in the office," I blurted, crossing my arms in front of my chest protectively. "I know this is just an arrangement between us, and that I asked for it to be that way. But you said no sharing, and I want to make sure you understand that extends to you as well. No sharing—ever. That also encompasses flirting and leading other women on with that...*face* of yours."

"My face?"

"Yes. I get that there are girls out there who are closer to your age and prettier than I could ever be, and if they turn your head, that's fine. Just end this...*thing* between us before you start with all your smiles and meaningful looks."

By the time I finished, he also had his arms folded, his eyes full of mirth.

I released my breath. "Great. Now you're just going to laugh at me. I must sound like some psycho."

Glancing around the room, he turned away from me then walked to the end of a storage row. "You coming?"

"Why?" I followed him anyway, waiting for his response while he continued to look around. "What are you doing?"

"Stand here." He pointed to a shelving unit packed full with archive boxes.

I did as he asked even though I didn't understand. "I'm serious, Bran. Just tell me you understand I won't share either. Then we get the damn boxes and go upstairs."

He stood in front of me and looked around again, before reaching over my head and pushing against the shelving like he was checking to see if he could move it.

"What the hell are you doing?"

Seeming satisfied, his hands grabbed my hips and dug in. "This," he said, a moment before he crashed his lips against mine and kissed the absolute living shit out of me. I melted against him, my arms wrapping around his neck as his fingers worked, pulling my skirt up until it was bunched around my hips. Lifting me off the ground as if my weight was nothing to him, he pushed my panties to the side, freed himself, and plunged into me bare.

He filled me violently and I moaned at his intrusion, my mind reeling as he worked his hips back and forth, fucking me so hard that the shelving rattled. My moans echoed, each thrust causing a clang that punctuated the otherwise silent room. What the fuck was going on? How had I—a normally sensible person— managed to get myself into the situation where I was having sex in the archive room with the intern? This was crazy, beyond crazy, it was *insane*. Anyone could walk through that door, either searching for files or looking for us. But as he pumped into me, my body pushing against shelving and shifting boxes, I didn't give a flying fuck. The only thing that mattered was that orgasm building inside me, my desire for it, and the man causing it.

"Oh God, *Bran!*" My words got lost in his palm as he clapped his hand over my mouth, quieting my moans as I came.

"Shhh," he whispered. "Someone just came in."

My eyes went wide as I heard it too—a shuffle of a foot then words.

"I thought you said they came down here."

"That's what Cora said. They needed files or something."

The second voice was Penny. The first was Adrian Sharp, the director of public prosecutions—my boss and Bran's *father*. We were dead. Deader than dead. Finished.

This was a stupid decision. I never should have trusted myself to speak to him alone at work. We're going to get caught and this is all going to be— Ohhh

Brandon started moving inside me again, painfully slow, his hand still over my mouth as his intense eyes bore into mine. I could barely focus. The fear of getting caught in the act, coupled with the act itself was undoing me. I wanted to flee, but I wanted to stay. I wanted to tell him to stop, but I wanted him to keep going.

I wanted him to keep going.

I had completely lost my mind.

My heart pounded against my ribcage as footfalls sounded at the front of the enormous room. They were looking up the aisles, the director's voice ringing out, "Brandon?"

This was messed up. It was even more messed up that I was getting off on it.

"Maybe they left already?" Penny suggested. Followed by a scuffing sound, then footsteps receding until the door clicked open then shut.

Bran's hips immediately picked up speed, his hand dropped from my mouth as he plunged back and forth, his pelvic bone rubbing against my clit as he drove me home once more.

This time I came without sound, my mouth open and my fingers pulling tight against his shirt. God, this man needed to start holding mandatory classes on how to be a good lover. No woman would ever have a bad day again. Archive rooms would never be safe.

With one more thrust, a quiet groan escaped his lips and he kissed me hard, spilling inside me. Once spent, he cradled the side of my face in his hand. "I am fucking one woman, and one woman only. I think about, dream of, and get hard for one woman only. As my cum runs out of your pussy today, let that be a reminder. That woman is *you*. Only you." He pulled out of me and straightened my panties, tucked himself away before he pulled my skirt back down and fixed the buttons he'd managed to pop open on my blouse. "I don't want you to question my loyalty to you again."

"OK," I whispered, feeling too drunk on pheromones to do anything much more than support my own weight and nod. He was a drug. That was it. He was some new designer drug that came in the shape of a hot-as-sin man and made intelligent women senseless. It was the only way to explain what was happening. I couldn't be held responsible.

"Glad we had this talk," he said, pressing a brief kiss against my lips. Then he pulled the printed page from his back pocket and held it up. "I suppose we'd better get these boxes."

"They're um..." I was struggling to speak after... after...*that*. God, how to describe the workout my body just had. "They should be down here. Grab the trolley." I pointed to the trolley against the wall, leading him to the section we needed and showing him where the boxes were.

"So, who exactly did you think I was flirting with?" he asked, stacking the boxes on the trolley, one on top of the other.

I looked at the floor, feeling silly for getting jealous just because a tiny girl was giggling over him. "Penny," I mumbled.

"Penny?" He laughed. "I did *not* flirt with Penny. For the record, I don't flirt at all. You should know that better than anyone. If I'm interested in someone, I don't waste my time flirting. I take."

I shrugged. "She was giggling and she's so small and adorable."

"Not my type."

"Penny is everyone's type."

"Not mine. I like curves and flesh. I want to hear a satisfying slap when my hand collides with your arse." A thrilling shudder rolled over me. I hated the insecurity I felt because of Jack. Bran had pursued *me*. He was the one who had insisted on monogamy in the first place. I was being too sensitive.

"I'm sorry. I obviously have trust issues, and I got

stupid jealous. I was out of line. Especially when I'm the one putting all the restrictions on this thing."

Finishing with the boxes, he tipped the trolley back and grinned at me. "It's OK. I kind of like you jealous."

My teeth pulled my lip into my mouth, biting back the smile that was too eager. He shook his head and let out his breath. "Please don't do that when we're being watched by cameras, because all I want to do is pull that lip out and bite it myself. And where you're concerned, I don't have a lot of control." I couldn't even begin to express how good his words made me feel. Even better, his actions backed them up.

"Something tells me we're both having that problem."

"It's fun to be bad though, right?" He leaned on the trolley, bringing his face level with mine. My heart sighed at his smile. He was so damn beautiful to look at that it hurt.

Where was he eleven years ago? He could have saved me from making a terrible mistake with Jack if I'd met him sooner. No sooner than the thought entered my mind, the answer to it slapped me in the proverbial face and took my smile with it. Eleven years ago, Bran was a nine-year-old boy. *What the fuck was I doing?*

"Everything OK?" He narrowed his eyes, obviously noting my shift in demeanour. "If you're worried about the absence of a condom, I'm clean, OK?"

"It's not that—although you could have asked me first. You don't even know if I'm on the pill."

"I do know. I saw the packet in your bathroom." He tapped his head. "Good memory, remember?"

"Of course." *He was only nine when I was eighteen!* "Listen, um…I think it's best if you go up there without me.

Tell them I left you here alone to get a coffee or something."

Nodding his understanding, he turned the trolley toward the door. "I'll say I was slacking off in the loading dock if I get asked why I wasn't in here when they came looking. My father won't be surprised to hear that."

"Good idea," I said in a rush. "I'll be up in about ten minutes." I glanced at my watch. "Actually, you'll be gone by then." It was nearing three.

His expression clouded. "I suppose I will."

I held the door open for him then turned toward the loading dock to exit. "I'll see you tomorrow."

"Sure thing," I heard him say as I walked away quickly. Once outside, I pressed the palms of my hands against my face, the reality of the mathematics assaulting my brain.

When I was old enough to drive, he was only seven.

When I started high school, he was a toddler.

When I started school *he wasn't even born*.

What was I doing?

What was I *thinking*?

I was turning *thirty*. I was too young for a midlife crisis but it sure felt like I was having one.

I was being reckless.

I needed to stop.

16

"Do you think we can go somewhere a little quieter this time? I'm in the mood for cocktails and girl talk," I said to Olivia at her place on Friday night. I'd promised her I'd go clubbing after the tough week she'd had at work, but after successfully dodging Bran since our tryst in the archive room on Wednesday, I really needed to unwind somewhere I didn't think he could possibly be.

"Sure. Did you have anywhere in mind?"

Not that avoiding him had been easy. He'd turned up at my place on Wednesday night, hitting the buzzer for a good five minutes straight before he started ringing my phone. I didn't even remember giving him my number, but like a lot of things, he seemed to get that information on his own.

Eventually, he settled for a text.

Bran: What's going on?

I didn't answer.

The next day, he'd tried to get me alone so we could talk. It was exhausting trying to avoid him when I was his boss, but it needed to be done. I gave him tasks that kept him busy in other departments—research with paralegals, filing with witness support. I could tell he was pissed and the text I got from him at the end of the day was proof of that.

Bran: This isn't over

Once again, I ignored it.

Friday was a little easier because he had classes for most of the day and was only in for a couple of hours in the morning. I'd organised to have him sit in on a deposition that would keep him locked in a conference room until just before it was time for him to leave. Then I scheduled a team meeting that backed right onto that so the only time he was near me was in the company of ten junior solicitors.

Now, I was ignoring my phone and getting ready at Olivia's to make sure I wouldn't be home if he decided to turn up and wait me out. I didn't know if my resolve was strong enough for another night knowing he was within my reach. *I also didn't know how I'd react if he gave up too...*

Leaning forward to apply a fresh coat of mascara, I answered Olivia's question. "I had a look online before I left work. There's a place setup as a speakeasy. It's hidden high in a building and they have a saxophone player and a blues band. The reviews say the cocktails are to die for."

"I think I've heard of the place. It's not my usual relaxation spot, but honey, I can pickup anywhere." Olivia turned to me and winked, licking her bright red lips. "Oh,

I cannot wait to work out this stress in some guy's bed tonight. Preferably a brunette, I think. I haven't been with a Greek boy in a while. And you know what they say about the Greeks?"

I shrugged. "That they like anal?"

She burst out laughing. "Well, yes, all men are obsessed with anal. But I was referring to the fact that they like to conquer."

"Oh, I get you," I responded, putting on a smile. The word 'conquer' had given me flashes of Bran and the way he conquered every part of me with such skill. My whole body sighed with longing.

It had been difficult saying no to him. My attraction to him felt like a tangible thing that could be held in my hands and examined up close. Not that it would make any sense to the human eye, because something like that could only be deciphered by the eyes of the gods.

Wearing a blue satin kimono-style cocktail dress, I sauntered into the bar on a pair of dangerously high iron-fist heels covered in butterflies and skulls. One look at the various ages of the clientele had me smiling and relaxing as I dragged Olivia to the bar to get the ball rolling on our cocktail-induced buzz.

A blues band played in the corner of the room, the rhythmic beat of the snare drum causing me to bounce my hip as we waited for our drinks to be mixed.

"I think I love this place," I said once we'd collected our drinks and found seats. "The music and atmosphere is great, and we can actually hear each other speak."

"I admit to liking it as well. The buffet is pretty good too." Olivia smiled her I-will-suck-your-cock-and-fuck-you-till-morning smile at a dark-haired guy at the bar. He lifted his glass to her and I wondered how long it would be before I was flying solo.

"How did your trial end up?" I asked, sipping the extremely strong but delicious cocktail.

"The jury came back within half an hour. Unanimous guilty verdict."

"Congratulations. Another scumbag in the lockup thanks to Olivia Beecham, QC."

She bowed her head dramatically. "I'm just doing my duty to society."

I laughed and drank some more, relaxing into the ambience.

"Have you heard from Jack?" she asked.

"Oh, yes. A letter came to the office today. It was a confirmation of our appointments—every second Wednesday for a minimum of three months."

"Fortnightly appointments for three months? And you were informed by letter at *work?*"

"I thought the time and frequency were a bit much, but he doesn't know my new address, so it makes sense that he sent it to the office."

"But *three months'* worth of therapy? That's ridiculous. When do you start?"

"Wednesday at six. I figure I'll discuss the schedule during that first meeting. I'm not interested in that big a commitment, either. I just want out of my marriage, Liv."

"I'll drink to that." Olivia held up her glass then drained it. "Hmmm, look at that tall drink of water over there." She nodded toward a blond guy wearing a blue-grey suit.

"He looks too young," I responded, having learned my lesson. I needed to stay away from the male species all together, especially until I got past my attraction to Bran.

"What about him?"

The next guy she pointed at was barely a day older. "Seriously, I'm not interested. They're all yours."

Leaning forward, she eyed me carefully. "Having the director's kid working for you has really messed with your head, hasn't it? Did something happen?"

Staring into my drink, everything that had gone on was on the tip of my tongue. But instead of speaking up and telling her what I was dealing with, I shook my head. "It's just awkward. I don't think I'm made for one-night stands—especially when they come back to haunt me. I don't think I can hook-up with younger guys. I keep looking at him and thinking how he wasn't even born when I started school. I was old enough to drink before he even hit puberty."

She threw her head back and laughed. "So? It's not like you were trying to sleep with him back then. He's a twenty-year-old *man*. You are a stunning twenty-nine-year-old woman."

"Almost thirty," I pointed out.

"Semantics." She rolled her eyes. "My point is that there's nothing wrong with it. Men get divorced and fuck twenty-somethings all the time, no regrets. Why should it be any different for us?"

Picking up my stirrer, I swirled it through my drink. "It just feels wrong."

"Because of the math or because you're still into your intern?"

"The math. I'm *not* into him," I responded a little too quickly.

She grinned. "Sure you aren't." Then she leaned forward, lowering her voice conspiratorially. "You obviously need another good fucking, Cor. You can't just stop at one mind-blowing night. If you don't want to go for the young and energetic ones, how about a little silver fox?"

"Silver what?"

She shifted her eyes to the side. "Ten o'clock. He's been watching you since we walked in."

I turned my head, trying to see who she was talking about.

"That's two o'clock."

I adjusted my gaze.

"That's nine."

"Oh my God, I'm shit at this game. Just point him out."

"I can do better than that." She smiled in the direction of a guy with dark salt-and-pepper hair who looked closer to her age than mine. He was certainly attractive. When he smiled back, his dark eyes creased at the sides. He had a strong jaw, excellent dress sense, and when Olivia beckoned him over, I noticed an air about him that looked as though he ate women for breakfast—in a good way.

"No. Don't call him *over*. What is with you and needing to pimp me out every chance you get? Sex isn't the solution to everything. In fact, it's created pretty much every single one of my problems of late."

Looking at me, she grinned. "But it's *so* much fun."

I couldn't argue with that. "He was probably looking at you anyway," I hissed.

"Ladies." The silver fox—as Olivia called him—said

when he arrived at our table, his eyes hungry. "Can I interest you in a drink?"

I opened my mouth, ready to say 'no thank you.' When Olivia jumped in and spoke ahead of me.

"She'll have a vodka martini. I, on the other hand, already have a drink waiting for me at the bar. I'll leave you two to get acquainted."

Giving me a wink, she stood and sauntered to the bar where the guy she'd been eyeing off earlier was waiting. Sure enough, he handed her a drink the moment she stepped into his space. *How the hell did she do that?* There must have been signals. I didn't even see it happen.

I turned back to my new 'friend', who had slipped into Olivia's newly vacated seat. "I'm really sorry about her. I hope you don't mind getting stuck with me instead."

He smiled and signalled for the waitress. "I'm sure your friend is lovely, but it isn't her I'm interested in."

"OK." I smiled in return. "Although, I'll warn you, I'm not much company tonight."

"Rough week at work?" He placed our order with the waitress and asked for it to be put on his tab: a vodka martini for me and a Scotch on the rocks for himself. *Macallan. Hmmm, top shelf.*

"Isn't every week a rough week when it comes to work?" I responded.

"I suppose it depends on the work. I'm Tim." He held out his hand, palm up. When I took it, he gave my hand a gentle squeeze.

"Cora." His hands were really soft. Softer-than-mine soft. And this close up, I could see that he was probably even older than Olivia, which meant he was over a decade older than me and didn't seem to give a fuck that he was. He was hitting on me like he deserved it.

I glanced to where Olivia sat at the bar, laughing up a storm while flirting wildly with her new plaything. *Touché, Olivia, touché.* She'd turned the tables on me to make a point. And it worked.

"What do you do for a living, Cora?"

As I began my answer, my eyes drifted to the entrance where a rather large and familiar figure stood, dressed in thigh-hugging dark jeans and a royal-blue dress shirt, tucked in at the waist, cuffs rolled to his elbows. Seeing him caused my heart to squeeze in my chest. *How did he know I was here?*

I stumbled over my words, struggling to form complete sentences until our drinks were delivered and I summarised with, "It's really boring actually. Why don't you tell me what you do?"

Tim launched into a speech about logistics and supply chains that I tried my best to listen to, but ultimately didn't hear because my attention couldn't break away from those intense green eyes, watching me from across the room. Just his presence stole my breath and made my whole body tingle. Based on his stance and tense body language, he was pissed. I knew without a doubt that he would cause a scene if I didn't get to him fast.

"I'm sorry, Tim." I interrupted him and stood, touching my head to feign an ailment of some sort. "I'm actually feeling really unwell. I need to go."

He seemed legitimately concerned. "Can I do something to help you? Call a cab or something?"

"No. I'm fine. I'm sorry I have to cut this short. It was really lovely meeting you."

"Perhaps we can do this another time then?" He reached into his jacket pocket and pulled out a business card.

Taking it, I thanked him. "Of course," I lied. Then, with my eyes on Bran, silently warning him not to approach, I made my way over to Olivia and touched her shoulder.

"Is something wrong?" she asked, her smile dropping slightly from her lips.

I shook my head. "I'm fine. I have an awful headache all of a sudden. Are you fine to get home on your own?"

She stepped away from her date for a moment. "Not feeling the silver fox?"

I shook my head. "It's not that. I just don't feel well. Will you be okay?"

"Of course I will." She waved her hand dismissively. "I've been doing this solo for years, honey. I know how to take care of myself. Besides, I don't think I'm going home tonight if you get what I mean." She grinned and gave me a wink.

I laughed. "Well, you have fun and call me tomorrow?"

Leaning in, she gave me a hug and kissed my cheek. "We'll have lunch. Make sure you look after yourself."

"You too."

Once she returned her attention to her dark-haired conquest, I headed for the lifts and got on, my eyes still filled with warning as I shot a look in Bran's direction. What the hell was he doing here? Couldn't he take a hint?

He slipped into the elevator a few seconds behind me.

"Are you following me?" I hissed when the doors closed.

"Were you just on a fucking date?" he demanded in return.

I stared up at him, refusing to answer until he answered me. We glared at each other, travelling to the ground level in static silence, attraction and frustration crackling in the air between us.

"Fuck," he growled, snapping to action. His hands slid into my hair on either side of my head as his mouth collided with mine. I fell against the wall of the elevator, feeling it rock slightly as my hands twisted in the fabric of his shirt. His tongue took control of mine, turning me into that woman who was incapable of controlling herself after the simplest touch. He had a power over me I couldn't describe. I could tell myself that we were bad for each other, I could understand the reasons and take steps to make it a reality, but the moment he touched me, I was gone. It didn't make sense.

Stopping with a jar, the lift chimed then opened, giving us that injection of reality we needed to break apart. "Get off me." I pushed against his chest and stormed off the elevator. He caught me by the arm and I spun around to confront him. "You don't get to bully me into being with you, Bran. You don't get to follow me around and force whatever this is to happen."

"I didn't follow you. I'm not a fucking stalker. Although you're making me feel like one. I went to the office after class to see if you were still there. The name of this place was written on your notepad. I didn't need to be Sherlock Holmes to figure out you'd be here." He stood a little straighter, his height slightly intimidating when combined with his anger. "What the fuck happened, Cora? One minute you're yelling at me for talking to some girl, and the next you're trying to ghost me and hook-up with some guy who's way too old for you."

A burst of laughter escaped my chest and I turned away, evading his grip and making it out onto the street. He followed hot on my heels and grabbed my arm again, spinning me to face him.

"Talk to me," he demanded.

"Talk to you? About what? The ridiculousness of what you just said? Or the insanity of this whole situation?" I raked my hands through my hair then held up my fingers, counting off items as I spoke. "First of all, if that guy up there is too old for me, then by that same reasoning, I'm too old for you. Secondly, this thing going on between us...it's mental. I'm your boss. There might not be a policy against inter-office relationships, but there is an ethical reason why people in a position of power shouldn't date their subordinates. Thirdly, you and I obviously can't separate what's going on between us and our work. We fucked in the archive room, Brandon. Even worse than that, we almost got caught—*by your father,* no less. And to put the cherry of insanity on top of the crazy cake, we just. Kept. *Fucking.*"

He reached out to me, and I nearly melted as I noticed his eyes softening. But I flinched out of the way.

"No. Don't touch me. I can't think when you touch me."

"Doesn't that tell you something?"

"Yes. It tells me that I need to stay *away* from you."

"You want this to be over?" His eyes twitched slightly, but he kept his voice even.

"Yes! It needs to be over. I've worked too long and too hard to lose my job, my career prospects. I want to be a barrister, Bran. I'm never going to get accepted into the bar course if my reputation is screwed because I got caught screwing *you*."

Inhaling through his nose, he straightened up then looked down the street. There were people milling about, some eyeing us carefully as if they were worried we were about to throw down.

"You want us to be over," he repeated. And I nodded, my stomach a tight ball of emotion as I forced the movement.

"We don't work."

His arm shot out, and he grabbed my hand and pulled. "Come with me."

"No, Bran." I tried to pull back, but his grip was too strong. I was almost running to keep up with him. "Let go."

"You want us over? Fine. But there's something you need to witness first."

Pulling me along with long angry strides, he walked me almost a full city block before finding his destination.

"A strip club?" I asked. *What the hell?*

"Keep walking." He tugged my arm.

When we walked through the door, a dark blanket of heat and sound wrapped around our heads. The lights were low with a slight red hue to them, making the whole room feel much more surreal than it would otherwise be. There were men everywhere: in groups, alone. There were women too, some watching the show, some sitting within the groups of men. But there were no women alone. Well, besides the strippers. But they were easy to spot because they were wearing underwear that barely covered their assets. The girl flicking her hair on stage wasn't even wearing that much. She was completely naked, holding on to the pole as she lifted her legs into the shape of a V, showing everyone exactly what she ate for breakfast.

I looked away. *I hated this.*

Just as I was about to demand an answer to why he brought me here, Bran touched one of the working girls on the arm. She turned, and the moment she spotted him, she grinned and wrapped her arms around his neck. The way she lingered while he spoke into her ear, her arms still resting over his shoulders, I assumed the knowledge between them was intimate. My stomach twisted and my eyes burned. *Is this what he wanted me to see? That he didn't need me to get laid? I already fucking knew that.* I tugged my arm free. I wanted to get out of there. *I needed to go.*

No farther than two steps to freedom, his strong arm wrapped around my waist and pulled me against his chest. When his mouth touched against my ear, my brain fogged. I needed this to stop. He couldn't keep touching me when I was trying to do what was right.

"Don't go running now. This is what you want, Cora."

"I didn't ask to come here."

Pulling back, his eyes met mine, full of dark determination that frankly scared the life out of me. I didn't think he was going to hurt me physically, but I had a terrible feeling that whatever was about to happen would hurt a hell of a lot more than anything physical could.

"Let me go."

He shook his head, then turned and pulled me through the crowd until we came to a door where the stripper he spoke to waited. She looked at me with a lustful grin then beckoned us inside.

"I don't want whatever this is," I yelled, shoving against his immoveable side.

Using both hands on either side of me, he pushed me until I was sitting on a couch. Then he took my bag and opened it up, pulling out Tim's business card and tearing it in half. He threw the torn pieces on the floor. "We had an agreement," he spat, dropping my bag on the couch next to me. "Tonight, with that guy, you broke it." He pointed to the torn pieces on the floor. "If you want us over, sit and watch."

"What?"

"Sit and watch," he snapped, taking a seat across from me. "If you make it to the end, I'll let you go. Hell, I'll even quit the internship. You'll never see me again."

"And if I don't?"

"Then our arrangement stands, and this ends when we're *both* done. Not with you trying to force me away before I've had my fill. Not with you deciding to go on a date with some other guy when you promised yourself *to me*." The volume of his voice rose, his eyes a furious storm that had me close the tears.

"It wasn't a date," I argued.

"Then what was it?" he bellowed.

"None of your business," I shouted back. "I don't want you."

"Then this won't bother you a bit."

He was playing with me, trying to make me jealous by

bringing me here and paying a stripper to give him a lap dance. If there was a time when our age difference was so glaring, this childish act was it.

"Go on then," I spat, folding my arms across my chest as I sat back, challenging him.

As the stripper moved over to him and climbed on his lap, I began to shake. Just seeing her young, tight, and impossibly slim body moving over him was hard enough. But I forced myself to watch, knowing I needed to make him understand that I was serious—he and I couldn't work. We couldn't exist as fuck buddies. Things were too intense for that. If we continued with this, we'd mess up our lives and each other. Then at the end of it, I'd be the one left alone and jobless; ruined and bitter. After the mess my marriage had become, I couldn't do that to myself. I needed to walk away to protect myself, to protect my heart. One heartbreak was enough for me.

She removed her bra. Her body rolled as she pressed her perfect tits against his face. His hands came up and took a hold of her hips. *That was how he held me.* As I watched his fingers dig in, my heart jumped into my throat and my eyes burned. *Why was he touching her?*

With my heart hammering, I tightened my arms, my fingers digging into my flesh to try and stop myself from crying. *Why was he doing this?* What was he trying to prove? That I wanted him so much it was a sickness? He was only proving he could be callous and spiteful. *But why was he hurting me?* Why was I letting him? This was even worse than walking in on Jack and Sally. In contrast, this was intentional. Acted out in front of me to cause the maximum amount of pain. *Why did I deserve that? Why?* I wanted to be sick. I couldn't watch. But I had to. I needed this to be over.

Then she slid from his lap to the floor on her knees and my chest gripped tight in a blind panic. I couldn't watch. *I couldn't watch. No. no. no. no. This was not happening.* Her hands ran down his chest, landing on his belt. I closed my eyes, turning away.

"Watch!" Bran bellowed.

I pressed my eyes tighter, tears streaking down my cheeks as I shook my head. Then I heard a zip. *"Enough,"* I shrieked, my tears wracking my body. "Enough!"

Shaking my head faster, I covered my face with my hands. Rocking back and forth, crying violently. The door opened and closed with a burst of sound then silence, and for a second I thought I was alone. But then large arms wrapped around me and Bran dragged me onto his lap, his mouth pressing kisses against the top of my head. I buried my face in his neck to avoid the reality of another woman's scent on his clothes.

"Why would you do that to me?" I wailed, pushing my fists against his chest, still wanting to get away while also craving the strength of those arms wrapped around me. *"Why?"* It was more than I could bear. *I can't...*

He pulled me closer, held me tighter, rocking me until I started to calm down. Then he placed his hands on either side of my face and lifted my head so I met his eyes. "The idea of you with any other man makes me *insane.* And seeing you with that guy tonight"—he shook his head—"it felt like someone shot an arrow of fire into my heart. I don't know what's going on between us, Cora, but I know it's something I can't walk away from. Judging by your reaction just now, I'm guessing it's the same for you too."

Closing my eyes, I felt tears splash down my cheeks and onto my chest. But I nodded, because he was right. Fuck him. He was a bastard. But he was right. I couldn't walk away, couldn't even run. I was his. God, help me.

17

THE CAB RIDE to my place was silent. I couldn't speak to him. Perhaps he couldn't speak to me either. We'd both done things over the past few days that we couldn't be proud of. The push and pull had become so intense that it detonated appallingly in a strip club's private room. Now we somehow had to deal with that reality on top of the insanity of our bodies calling to each other. I had no idea what I'd gotten myself into.

With a sigh that felt more like pain than breath, I rested my head on his shoulder. I needed to be close to him despite all the crazy. Why couldn't I be more like Olivia? Or even Jack? It seemed they could take bed partners without it turning into something more. And it seemed neither of them ever had any regrets. How did one manage to live life like that? Was I incapable of being anything but a monogamous one-man, long-term relationship girl?

Maybe I had an obsessive personality. That would make sense, would even explain the reason behind me waiting around for Jack all those years. But then, I'd never felt the way around him that I did with Brandon. If Jack had pulled the shit Brandon pulled tonight, I probably would have attacked him and run the other way. But with Bran, our connection was...more than I could explain.

"We're here." Bran's voice was gentle as he roused me from my thoughts and paid the driver. "Wait there."

Too tired to argue, I stayed put as he got out of the cab and walked around to open my door. The moment my feet hit concrete, he scooped me up into his arms and climbed the steps of my building.

"You really don't need to carry me," I told him, little fight to my voice as my head rested against his chest.

"Yes, I do," he said, using my key fob to get through the main entry, heading straight for the lifts. "I've got a lot to make up for."

My hand tightened, holding on to the fabric against his chest as I buried my face deeper, tears falling as I inhaled that scent so indescribably his.

"Who was she?" I whispered, the images of the smiling girl and the familiar way she touched him assaulting my mind.

"She's no one."

I lifted my head to watch his expression. "Did you date her?"

"No."

"Fuck her?"

It took a beat for him to answer, but I knew it would be in the affirmative based on the flicker of his eyes and the tension in his jaw. "Once."

"When?"

"Does it matter?"

"*Yes.*" I couldn't handle the way I was feeling. I felt broken and repaired with a meagre paste of flour and water. At any moment, I could fall apart and shatter completely. But the only thing stopping that from happening were his hands holding me together while I dried. I needed him to reassure me and tell me he wasn't going to let go, drop me, destroy me. My heart couldn't take it if it turned out he was lying to me too. I'd had enough of that with Jack.

"A couple of months ago when I came back from Queensland."

"Did you pay her?"

"No."

"Then why only once?"

"She wasn't what I wanted."

"What exactly do you want?"

He stared at me for a long time. "You."

The intensity of his eyes and that single word brought tears to my eyes. "Then why did you do that to me?" My chest ached an impossible hurt. I'd been so angry with Jack when I found out he'd cheated, but even then, I hadn't felt like *this*. This level of pain was something much deeper, like my soul had been torn and was bleeding pain.

"Because I'm an arsehole who was losing his mind at the thought of not having you."

I dropped my head so it was once again resting against his chest while he opened my apartment door. "The idea of us is completely crazy. *We're* crazy."

He carried me to my room and set me on my feet. "I'm not sorry for wanting you, Cora. But I am sorry for the way I treated you tonight." His fingers worked down the zipper at my back, undressing me slowly. "Forgive me." He laid me on the bed, climbing on top of me while teasing my body ever so gently. "I lost my mind."

"I hated you touching her." My voice broke.

"I'm sorry," he whispered as his lips brushed along my jaw, kissing away my tears.

"I hated that you let her."

"I'm sorry." His hands slid over my curves, and I kept crying, clinging to him, begging him to make it up to me. *To heal me.*

"I hate that you make me feel like this."

"Forgive me," he whispered, when he slipped his fingers between my legs and brought me to climax. I cried while it happened, wanting him and hating him at the same time. It was a mess, a seriously fucked-up mess. I barely recognised myself.

"Forgive me, baby," he whispered when he pushed inside me, kissing me gently, his tongue making sweeping strokes as he moved his hips torturously slow. I clung to him, my emotions intensifying with each languid stroke. He played my body like a finely tuned instrument, bringing me to the brink again, coming with me when I shuddered around him. "Don't turn me away."

His words hit me in the chest—vulnerability I hadn't caught before. He seemed so sure of himself, so in control. But at the core of it, he was just like the rest of us —scared to be alone. Afraid of rejection.

"Bran." My hands lifted and ran through his hair, fingertips tracing over his features as he looked down at me, his eyes questioning and unsure while our bodies remained joined. He pressed a soft kiss to my lips.

"I'm sorry too," I whispered, because I was. I was sorry for trying to ghost him. I was sorry for my lack of control. I was sorry for listening to the advice of others. I was sorry for existing within an obviously shitty marriage. I was glad it was over, but I was now sorry that Bran was left with such a mess because of it. The only thing I wasn't sorry for was going home with him that night. Despite the complications it had caused, being with him was the only thing that felt right. *He* felt right.

———

"I've been cheated on before," I said into the dark, our bodies wrapped together in a tight cocoon after making love more than a couple of times. "I came home from work and they were fucking in my bed."

"I'm sorry," he whispered, the theme word of the night, as he pressed his lips against my bare shoulder.

"At the time, I thought I'd never get over it. Then you happened and I experienced something so powerful that I stopped being sad. I stopped being angry. But now, with everything that's happened in such a short time and the risks involved...I'm scared. Not only do you have the power to hurt me, somehow, you also have the power to completely destroy me."

He wrapped me tighter in his arms, releasing a long, pained sigh. "I'm so sorry, baby."

Baby. I liked it when he called me that. It made me feel cared for, protected...

"Would you have gone through with it? If I hadn't yelled enough? Would you have let her—" I choked back a sob, unable to say the words.

"No," he whispered, his lips against my hair. "I couldn't. She wasn't you." He rolled with me, covering me with his body as he buried his face into my neck. "The way I feel about you, need you; it's an insanity. It's no excuse, I know, but it's how I feel around you. I need you to forgive me."

With my arms wrapped around his neck, my fingers digging in hair, I drew a stuttered breath. "I can forgive you, Bran. Just promise me you'll never do something like that again. I'm not blameless here. I treated you badly this past few days too. But no more using people against each other. No more getting mad and acting recklessly. Just because this feels crazy, doesn't mean *we* have to be."

Pulling his head up from its resting place, he looked down at me. "I can promise not to use other people, Cora. But I can't promise not to act crazy. I mean, this thing between us, it's not normal, right? Nothing about this is normal."

I reached up and brushed my fingers through his silky hair. "Maybe we should both be committed?"

He rolled off me, landing on his back with a soft thud, one arm still around me. "What happens if this feeling gets worse instead of better? How do we even begin to control something like that?"

I shook my head. "I don't know. But all relationships lose their intensity eventually. I suppose we just wait it out."

"And what happens if it never dies down?"

"Then I guess we're stuck with each other."

"Would that be such a bad thing?"

I looked at him for a long time. *Could I see this man becoming a part of my future? Could I handle feeling this sick with need long-term? And what would happen when I got old before him? Would he turn into every other man and start looking for the next pretty young thing?* There were so many questions, none of which I had an answer to.

"I don't know, Bran. Maybe we'll get better at handling it. Maybe we'll just end up destroying each other. Either way, you scare the fuck out of me."

Lying beside me in the dark, I heard his breath moving in and out of his body. For a moment, I thought he was asleep. Until he turned to me and kissed me as though his very life depended on it. "For the record, Cora, you scare the shit out of me too."

18

WE SPENT the weekend in bed, spent every night after that too. At work, the archive room was avoided, and we did everything we could to behave normally. But there was a daytime tryst during lunch on Tuesday when a supply closet in a busy eatery offered too good a chance to be missed. Our appetites were insatiable.

By the time Wednesday rolled around, he was all I could think about, knocking off work early to sneak in an on-campus visit. He'd walked out of his ethics class to find me leaning against the opposite wall, hunger burning in my eyes. I'd never seen a man so happy to see me.

"Tell me you know of a dark corner somewhere," I'd said after his mouth had finished his hello. He'd grinned, pushed those epic dimples into his cheeks, then dragged me down the hall and into an empty lecture hall where we fucked against the wall in the back corner.

By the time we were done, he was late to his next class

and I was late to my first marriage counselling appointment. But at least I arrived with a smile on my face.

"Sorry I'm late. Crazy day," I said, breezing in, still feeling Bran's presence between my thighs.

"I was just about to call," Jack said, eyeing me carefully.

"No need." I smiled. "I'm here now."

The counsellor ushered us into his office where we were directed to sit on a mottled-grey couch.

"As I'm sure you're both aware, counselling can be a great way for couples to work through their troubles and find a new common ground that they can use to rebuild their relationship." Our counsellor was a short, stout man, with a rather bulbous nose and squinty eyes. He kind of reminded me of Mr. Magoo. Actually, once I saw that similarity, I couldn't get past it. A smile stayed glued to my face.

"You seem happy to be here today, Cora. How about you let us know what you're hoping to get out of our sessions."

That wiped the smile from my face. There was nothing like getting called out by the teacher on the first day to take the fun out of something.

I looked at Jack, who seemed very serious, and nodded for me to give my answer.

"Well...I um...I'm hoping to get some clarity." *Clarity*. That was the nice way of expressing it. Having spent the last four nights with Bran, I was learning more about myself sexually, but also emotionally. I wanted Bran in so many ways, *needed* him. I had *never* needed Jack in that way. We had simply become...comfortable, used to each other. But at the time, I had no idea about this other level of feeling. When I was with Jack, I believed that was how long-term relationships were supposed to feel. It hurt that he hadn't been fulfilled enough by me and what we had to stay true. Why wasn't I enough for him? At what point did his respect for me decline to a point that he was comfortable bringing another woman into my bed? I felt overwhelmed and took a deep breath, ready to attempt putting my thoughts into words. "I suppose I want to understand what it was about me that wasn't good enough for Jack. I also want to know exactly how long it had been going on for and how many affairs he had. Was he using protection with them? Or was he recklessly fucking them and me without a thought of spreading disease?" I knew I hadn't caught any STDs from him— Olivia had made sure I got tested as soon as I found out he'd strayed—but I still wanted to know if he'd thought to protect me, or if he'd just been focused on pleasuring himself.

"That's quite a list." Mr Magoo smiled, showing no teeth. *Did he have any teeth?* Odd. "I think we'll also take the time to explore your anger issues. It's my under-standing that you have an intervention order in place with a proviso added to allow you to attend these sessions without penalty."

Whatever was left of my composure dropped completely as his words sunk in.

"Excuse me?" I looked at Jack, my eyes wide in ques-tion. He lifted his hand to rub at the back of his neck.

"My attorney didn't think it was a good idea to revoke it completely. Not until we knew if this was going to work out."

"You have an *attorney*?

He had the decency to look sheepish as he nodded.

"And the intervention order still stands?"

He nodded slowly.

I stood and shook my head, my anger levels rising. "You," I blustered, searching for the word. "You arsehole!"

"Now, calm down, Cora," Mr. Magoo started, holding his hands up pleadingly.

I turned my anger on him. "I *will not* calm down. This man lured me here with the promise that that order would be revoked. If he's keeping it over my head, then I have no reason to be here." Turning on my heel, I headed for the door.

"These sessions are court ordered, Mrs Knowles. As an officer of the court, I'd have thought you understood that."

Stopping with my hand resting on the handle, I turned back around. "*Former* officer of the court. That intervention order has prohibited me from practising."

Mr. Magoo gestured for me to take a seat. "Then you have even more reason to be here. I'm not saying that you and your husband need to reconcile, but you need to attend and participate in these therapy sessions for me to make a recommendation to the court to get that order revoked early. You walk out that door and you'll have to wait the entire twelve months."

Holding my chin up—tamping down the rage bristling beneath the surface—I returned to the couch and sat. Mr. Magoo smiled. "Perhaps we can continue by having you turn to your husband and tell him how you feel towards him right now."

That wasn't going to be a problem. "Right now," I said,

looking Jack dead in the eye. "All I want from you is a divorce and to *never* have to see you again."

Jack's mouth dropped open and Mr. Magoo jotted something down on his notepad. "And Jack, what about you?"

"A DIVORCE?" Jack ran after me when I stormed out of the office as soon as the hour was up. I'd barely spoken the whole time, feeling furious that once again, Jack was getting his way.

"You're the one with a lawyer, Jack."

"You don't?"

I spun around and faced him, my finger pointing in his face. "No, as a matter of fact, I don't."

"Come on," he scoffed. "Your best friend is a barrister."

"She's a *Crown Prosecutor. Not* a divorce attorney." I took a few steps then stopped and turned back to face him. "I cannot believe I was stupid enough to fall for this, that I thought *you* would actually do something to *help me.*" I turned away again and growled. "I can't even look at you right now." Pacing back and forth, my fists tight by my sides, I tried to get a handle on my emotions.

"Cor," he started, using that tone of voice he always used when he belittled my feelings and told me I was acting crazy—that I didn't understand a situation. I'd been so stupid for so long. Allowed him to pull the wool over my eyes and dazzle me with his charm. No more.

"Don't speak to me. I don't want to hear your lies and bullshit. You can't even answer a simple question without some sort of guarantee that you'll get something out of it. How dare you treat me this way? You know how hard I worked to get where I was. You took that order out to purposely spite me for leaving you, and now you're using it to manipulate me into giving you another chance. Here's a newsflash for you, Jack. I will *never* give you another chance. You disgust me. I want a divorce. I want a divorce. *I want a divorce!*"

Spinning on my heel, I stomped down the street, ignoring him calling my name. I'd wasted eleven years of my life on that man. I was done listening to him.

19

Sitting forward in the warm bath, I closed my eyes and hummed pleasurably as Bran's nimble fingers massaged shampoo in my hair. He'd arrived not long after I got home from the counselling session, and helped me work out a lot of the frustration when I jumped him at the door. Still, I couldn't stop the anger simmering under the surface. Jack was such a fucking bastard.

I sighed, running my hands over the long legs that extended out either side of me. Never was I gladder of the fact my apartment had a large spa bath that could fit two people.

"You seem distracted tonight," Bran said, getting me to tilt my head back as he rinsed out the shampoo.

When he was done, I leaned against his chest and closed my eyes, feeling at home when his arms wrapped around me and he pressed a kiss against my temple.

"Remember how I told you I got into some trouble that affected my standing at work?"

"I do." He picked up the bath sponge and squeezed

water all over my chest, washing my skin with gentle strokes. He was a rough lover, but a gentle carer; the perfect mix of soft and hard.

"I thought it was over, but it isn't. I feel like I'm caught in career limbo and I'm powerless to change it."

"Want to tell me what happened?"

Frowning, I took one of his hands and pressed mine against it, noting how large it was by comparison. "Not particularly."

He released his breath slowly and hooked a finger under my chin, tilting my head so we were looking at each other. "I know you don't want this to be a traditional kind of relationship, but that doesn't mean you can't talk to me."

"I know that." I smiled briefly then turned my head away. "I just don't want to get into it. It depresses me and I don't want to be depressed with you." In fact, I didn't want any part of my life with Jack intersecting with Bran and me. They were two different worlds with very different emotions. Bran was my happy place and Jack was my mountain of regret. The two didn't mix.

"OK," he said, running his nose along the shell of my ear. "I suppose if you don't want to talk, then I can at least take your mind off things." His hand slid over my stomach suggestively.

Shifting slightly, I parted my thighs, giving him access to the place he sought.

"Does it help when I do this?" he asked, his fingertips playing with my clit in circular motions.

"Mm-hmm."

"How about when I do this?" He pushed two fingers

inside me, angling his thumb to continue his stimulation of my clit.

"Yes."

"And this?" His other hand slid underneath my breast, his fingers finding and twisting my nipple.

"Uh-huh," I gasped, my hips rocking with the perfect movement of his hand.

Lifting my arms out of the water, I threaded my fingers into his damp hair, pulling at his head as I twisted and found his mouth.

Our lips brushed, but I didn't find the connection I craved. "Kiss me," I whimpered, trying in vain to pull him closer. I wanted his tongue in my mouth and his teeth on my lips. Opening my eyes, I looked straight at him. I wasn't above begging. "Please."

I was met with dark pools of mossy green, watching me intently as his slid the tip of his nose against mine. "Not until I see you come."

He was so close, his lips mere millimetres away, torturing my desire as his hands worked their magic. Our eyes locked, but I struggled to maintain focus. He was so beautiful. What he saw in me, I didn't quite understand. There was just something there, something so huge that it filled the world around us and made what was happening between us feel like the only thing that mattered. Everything else fell away when we were alone.

"Bran." My body tightened, preparing to fall.

"Don't look away," he murmured, adding a third finger, filling me further. It tipped me over.

"*Bran*." His name. It was a sound that came out as a moan that he caught in his throat when his mouth covered mine, and my body shook and shattered against his hand. When he released me, I turned in his arms, keeping our mouths together as I deepened the kiss and wrapped myself around his waist, taking his length inside. I shook against him, moaning and kissing, rocking and gasping. He took handfuls of my flesh, pushing and pulling as he claimed my mouth, my skin, my body, until we both exploded, our shattered pieces mixing together, entwining us even further.

He was becoming a part of me, a part of this new life I was carving for myself. It was still early days, but I couldn't imagine growing tired of his presence or his touch. Or his mind. And I wasn't sure if I wanted to. In these moments of bliss, the idea of keeping this intensity seemed like heaven. But in reality, when the endorphins had settled, my hunger for Bran was more like hell— needing to be hidden in the shadows instead of celebrated in the light. A dirty little secret. Would it be possible to make this last when the odds were so obviously against us?

20

"Why didn't you read this properly? I cannot believe you didn't realise this was court ordered. We could have appealed the decision." Disappointed, Olivia stubbed out her cigarette as she handed me the letter I'd received detailing my counselling sessions. I felt like the dunce of the legal profession. "What a bloody nightmare." She lifted a hand and adjusted her oversized sunglasses, leaning back in the chair at our favourite café. Well, it was her favourite because it was one of the few that still allowed smoking.

"I know. I was stupid and didn't read the whole thing." Folding the pages, I slid them into the envelope and tucked it away in my bag. "I should have known it was too good to be true." I'd been too distracted by a certain twenty-year-old office hottie to pay much attention to anything.

"That attorney of his is a snake. I'll bet he's forcing all this on you while still fucking some plaything on the side."

I shrugged. "He said he wasn't, but I don't put a lot of stock in what Jack says. Lying seems to be his default setting."

She lit up another cigarette. "Let's not forget manipulation, philandering, duplicity, as well as general cuntiness. I swear, I never understood what you saw in that man. I've always felt he was a snake-eyed devil."

"Don't hide your feelings," I stated, sticking my finger into the side of my apple turnover and licking off the cream.

"It's better than eating them," she said, her eyes falling to my sugar-coated pastry.

Bunching my brow together, I glared at her. "Fuck you, Liv. What's up your butt today?"

She shook her head and stubbed out her half-finished cigarette, blowing out a lungful of smoke as she did. "I'm sorry," she said, looking genuinely regretful for her misplaced comment. "I'm just really stressed right now. What with work and worrying about you...and my missed period, I'm not getting a ton of sleep lately."

I choked on a flake of pastry. *Did I just hear that right?* "You missed *a period*?" My eyes bugged out of my head as I tried to react and have a drink of water so I could breathe.

"I'm hoping it's menopause," she replied, reaching for her cigarettes and pulling another one out halfway then sliding it straight back in the packet.

"You're only forty. It's a bit early, isn't it?"

She lifted her hand to her head. "God. What if it's not?"

"You mean, what if you're pregnant?"

She worried her lips together and nodded.

"Then we deal with it." I reached across the table and took her hand. "I'll support whatever decision you make. Have you taken a test yet?"

She shook her head. "I am literally too scared to."

"OK. How late are you?"

"Two weeks. Normally, I'd put it down to stress, but I'm never this late and that Paul"—she shook her head —"he keeps coming back. *I* keep letting him through my door—I'm not supposed to do that. Bringing them to my place is against my rules."

"What about that guy you were with last Friday?"

"I'm *two weeks* late, Cora. Even if I had gone home with him, that would be an impossibility."

"*If* you went home with him?"

She avoided eye contact by fidgeting with the mug in front of her. "It's possible that Paul called me and I ditched the guy at the bar and met up with him instead."

My eyes widened. "You're in a *relationship,*" I gasped.

"No." She was in complete denial. "*No.* I don't do those."

I fought a smile. A small part of me felt glad that Olivia wasn't infallible when it came to men either. But mostly, I worried for my friend. "You aren't on the pill?"

"I'm late for my depo shot because I've been so busy with these trials. And we got carried away one night and the condom broke... The timing fits."

"OK. Then we go and get you a test. We can do it tonight. I'll come to your place and hold your hand while you wait."

She released a small laugh. "Could you take the test for me too?"

"Sorry, doll. I'm not the one who might be pregnant."

Clapping her hand against her face, she moaned. "God, what if I am? I'm not responsible enough to have a baby. I'm selfish and conceited and I don't love anything other than my own reflection."

"That's not true at all. You love money too."

She laughed. "That's true."

"But seriously, Liv. This is going to be fine. I'll be here for you every step of the way."

Nodding, she straightened her back and took a sobering breath. "Well, now that that bombshell is out of the way, we should probably get back to work. Meet you out front at six?"

"Absolutely," I replied, plastering a smile over my face as I secretly texted Bran underneath the table.

Me: emergency best friend duty tonight. Don't come

As we headed back to the OPP, I felt the vibration of his reply in my bag.

Bran: I'm probably going to jerk off thinking about your tits, so I can't promise

that 🐷

I had to fight the smile that threatened to overtake my mouth.

"What are you acting all coquettish about?" Olivia asked. She *never* missed a thing.

I stopped walking. "Nothing. I just thought of a funny movie. I'll get it for tonight to help lighten the mood. Why don't you go ahead of me?"

"Sure," she said, flipping her hand. "Why don't you get some of those chocolates you like so much too? And if you don't mind..." Her eyes pleaded with me.

"Of course, I'll get the test too."

"Thank you," she mouthed, hugging me. "You're a gem."

Turning around, I headed to the nearest store, typing a text as I walked. Grinning at my teasing words.

Me: maybe you can imagine giving me a pearl necklace?

The dots immediately danced.

Bran: you're making me hard. Now I want to fuck your tits

Me: I'm already wet thinking about it

Bran: fuck. My dick is aching. Where are you?

Me: tut tut. You'll have to wait

Bran: I want to fuck you. NOW

Me: I'll come to you when I'm done tonight. Leave your room key in my desk

drawer.

Bran: Don't make me wait. I want you now.

Me: tonight

Bran: now

Me: tonight

Bran: fine. Leave your panties at home

Me: who says I'm wearing any now? 🐻

Bran: you're killing me 😵

Pulling at my lip with my teeth, I smiled to myself as I tucked my phone away. It buzzed one more time.

Bran: seriously, tell me where you are

WHEN I MADE it to the office with a bag of purchases on my arm, I was surprised to see Bran's desk empty. A quick question to my team members told me they weren't sure where he was either.

Figuring he'd been borrowed by one of the other departments, I went into my office and closed the door slightly to hang the grocery bag containing Olivia's comfort food and pregnancy test out of sight.

It was then that a familiar arm reached over my shoulder and pressed the door closed with a gentle click.

His lips rested against my ear. "Just a taste." Soft kisses and tiny licks travelled down my neck as his hands slid over my curves.

"You're crazy," I whispered, smiling even though this was the riskiest thing he could have done. While we were out of sight behind my door, the front wall of my office was made with a mix of frosted and plain glass. The frosting provided a modicum of privacy, but still, you could see inside. All it would take is one person pressing their face up against my window and we'd be caught. "Just wait until tonight. I promise I'll make it worth your while."

A groan laced with need and discontent emanated out of his chest. "Fine. I'll be patient. The rest of me though"—he pressed his formidable length against my backside—"is going to wait *im*patiently."

He stepped away and I turned to face him, smiling as

I prepared to tell him to pick up some files and get back out there. Instead I was met with a stark expression.

"What is that?" he asked, staring over my shoulder.

"What is what?"

"Holy shit." His face went white, and he stumbled backward. "I need to sit down." He dropped into the visitor's seat.

Confused by his reaction, I turned my head, the box for the pregnancy test staring me straight in the face through the plastic bag. *I'd thought I hid it better than that.*

"Oh shit. That's not mine." I moved toward him, pausing to open my door so no one would question what we were doing in there together.

He looked at me, one eyebrow frowning. "Yeah, and when I was caught smoking in year eight, I really was holding it for Nick Butler."

I moved to stand at the end of my desk, folding my arms across my middle as I spoke quietly.

"I promise you it isn't mine."

"Then whose could it possibly be? How long have you been thinking this was a possibility?"

"Jesus. Would you just listen to me? It isn't mine. It's what the best friend emergency is about."

"Olivia?"

"*Yes.* And if you dare breathe a word, I will never do that thing that made your eyes roll back in your head again."

Relief relaxed his features as he let go of his breath. "Thank fuck. And you don't need to threaten me, baby. Not my news to tell."

"Good. Now pick up this stack of files and get back to work before people start asking questions."

He grinned and did what I said with a small salute. "Yes, boss. Oh, and you'll find that card you asked for in your top drawer." With a wink, he walked out the door.

Taking a seat at my desk, I pulled open the drawer and found the hotel key card inside with a sticky note attached: *No underwear!*

21

"I NEED WINE FOR THIS. We should have brought wine." Olivia sat on the floor of her bathroom with her back against the wall, the offending stick sitting across the room on the vanity.

"That wouldn't be very good for the baby," I soothed, rubbing her arm as she hugged her legs against her chest.

"How did this happen to me? Forty years and not a single scare. I didn't have a scare in my first marriage, or in my second. Then I let one twenty-six-year-old worm his way into my life and suddenly I'm pregnant. Oh, why couldn't it have been menopause?" Her wide eyes locked with mine. "I can't have a *baby*. What would I do with it?"

I lifted a shoulder. "Love it."

She looked at the ceiling, blowing air forcefully through her lips. "I was put on this earth to be a fantastic lay and to put criminals behind bars. I can't be responsible for a child. I can't be the objective person I am if my emotions get in the way. Do you know how many paedophiles I've put away?

How many aggravated assaults against a minor? This world isn't fit to bring children into, and if it's a girl then it's so much worse. How do I do this, knowing what I know?" In all the years I'd known Olivia, I'd never seen her cry. Now, tears rolled down her cheeks, dark from her mascara.

"Oh Liv, we see the absolute worst of humanity come through those doors. We chose to work there because we believe justice can be served, and we can make a difference while doing it. The average person doesn't have even a sliver of that shit affect them. Your child will experience even less than that because they'll have you to protect them. Big bad Olivia Beecham. You are the strongest woman I know. You can do absolutely anything." I grabbed a box of tissues and handed them to her. "Including have a baby."

Wiping her eyes and nose, she relaxed her legs in front of her and let her head drop against the wall. "I really can't. I can't make any relationship work."

"Of course you can. You and I have been friends for years."

"Plus, I'll be stuck with Paul in my life forever. He's amazing in the sack, but even he'll get boring at some point. And nappies and breastfeeding are *not* sexy."

I brushed her hair out of her face. "You'll make them sexy."

"I'm going to ruin this kid. I'll have to start saving for the therapy bills the moment it comes wailing out of my vagina."

"Stop, Liv. You're going to be great."

She twisted the tissue between her fingers. "He's fifteen years younger than me. *Fifteen.* You freaked out over a ten-year age difference, I'm having a baby with a guy young enough to be my teen pregnancy."

"Does he know anything about this?"

She shook her head. "I've been ignoring his calls."

"Perhaps you should call him? This affects him too. It's something you need to talk through together."

She closed her eyes. "I hate that you're so right about all this."

Twenty minutes later, she was still talking to Paul on the phone in the other room. I could hear the soft murmur of her voice, but ultimately, I was sitting alone in the quiet with my thumb in my arse—metaphorically, not literally.

Pulling my phone from my bag, I went through my Facebook notifications to keep myself from eavesdropping. It never ceased to amaze me how vacuous this whole social media thing was. No one spoke about anything important. There were random posts about food, children and the usual 'my life is worse than your life' posts, I scrolled past most of them, noting that Nick's girlfriend was way out of his league. Then a message popped up.

> Bran: best friend duty involves FB stalking?
>
> Me: how do you even know I'm on here?
>
> Bran: there's a green dot next to your name
>
> Me: huh. So there is. What are you doing?

A shot came through of papers and his laptop lying on the bed.

Bran: how are things your end?

Me: she's on the phone with the father now

Bran: yikes. Positive test, hey?

Me: she's freaking out

Bran: I would be too

Reading Bran's reaction, I thought about *my* desire to start a family. While I was glad I found out about Jack's infidelities before we had kids, pregnancy—being a mum —had been relegated to a dream that would gather dust along with my eggs. By the time Bran was ready for kids, I'd be going through menopause.

I stopped myself from continuing that train of thought. Bran and I were intense, but we probably weren't long-term. I was logical enough to understand that. There were simply too many obstacles for a future to be a *real* consideration. When we were together, it felt like nothing in the world mattered, but apart, without the pheromones clouding my judgement, I understood that relationships like ours rarely lasted. They simply ran their course and died out like a too-bright star with no gas left to burn.

Me: I'm always careful. Don't want to ruin the girls with all those hormones.

I sent him a shot of my cleavage.

Bran: you're killing me

He followed that message with a picture of his giant bulge.

Me: That's not going to help you study

Bran: I'd rather be studying you

Just as I was about to respond, Olivia walked in the room, looking like she'd been dragged through the emotional wringer.

"How'd it go?" I asked, slipping my phone into the waistband of my skirt.

She rubbed her palms against her thighs. "He's coming over."

"How'd he react?"

Meeting my eyes, she shrugged. "Same as me. He's petrified." Sitting on the arm of her sofa, my old bed, she gestured toward the phone at my hip. "Who were you texting?"

"No one important," I lied, trying to sound flippant. "How far away does Paul live?"

A slow smile spread across her lips, but it wasn't a happy one. It was the smile of a person who knows they're being lied to. "You're fucking him, aren't you?"

"What?" It was a classic avoidance tactic—act dumb, maybe they'll believe you.

"The intern. You're fucking him."

I laughed and shook my head. "No." The word became elongated as I went through the same tactics we'd seen criminals use over and over again. First, act dumb. Second, deny everything. "That would be crazy."

"And yet you're still doing it. I can see it in the way you're behaving. Plus, I'm pretty sure that's a hickey I see peeking out at the neck of your blouse."

I immediately moved my neckline, causing her to smile knowingly. "You don't know what you're talking about." Third, anger and misdirection. "Maybe you should be focusing on your own mess instead of making up shit about me to get your mind off it. I came here to support you, not to be a victim of your Spanish Inquisition."

She held up her hands, her voice calm. "I was simply making an observation, Cora. What you do and with whom you do it is your business. I just want you to be careful. I don't need to remind you what's at stake." Her blue eyes held mine solemnly. Then there was a buzz on the intercom.

"I should go. Let you two talk."

She nodded. "Just please be careful," she whispered, giving me a long hug.

"I will," I whispered back. Fourth, when it's obvious you've been caught, drop all pretence. "Good luck with Paul. Call me if you need me."

"Say hi to Brandon for me."

I nodded. "And it's Bran. He prefers to be called Bran."

22

WITH AN OVERNIGHT BAG on my arm, I used the key card to access the lifts at Bran's hotel, preferring to knock at his door so we both got the full effect of my arrival. Nerves were dancing inside my stomach the entire journey over. One false move and the entire city of Melbourne would cop an eyeful of flailing breasts and lady parts.

That's right, I was doing the time-honoured visit to my lover wearing nothing but an overcoat and heels.

With a light tap on his door, I waited, listening to his footsteps on the other side. He took my breath away when the door creaked open. He was wearing nothing but a pair of pants unbuttoned at the waist. No shirt. All I could see were rippling muscles and a giant V that fit perfectly within the open fly. I could even see a light trail of hair... *God, I loved that body.* I licked my lips. "Been doing a little prep work while waiting for me?" I asked, my eyes falling to his open pants.

One side of his mouth pulled up as his darkening

eyes met mine. "I have a beautiful brunette on the brain." His hand slid inside his pants as his gaze moved down my body. "Please tell me you're making my dreams come true and there's nothing underneath that coat." When he removed his hand, there was a decidedly large bulge waiting for me.

"Why don't you open it up and find out?" I stepped in and dropped my bag, holding out the sash.

Tugging it, he slid it out from around me with a *whoosh*, throwing it over his left shoulder. The coat fell open, breezing against my skin to reveal me in nothing but a pair of electric-blue heels. His smile widened, turning salacious as he pushed the coat off my shoulders. "Nice shoes. Wanna fuck?" he asked, grabbing me by the thighs and lifting me until he threw me onto the bed. I landed with a bounce and a burst of laughter as he discarded his pants and climbed on top of me, his throbbing cock trailing along my legs.

"I worship you," he murmured, lifting my right leg as his lips moved against my smooth skin, planting soft kisses before he playfully bit my calf. I giggled. And he smiled at me wickedly, placing my ankle on his shoulder as he reached his free hand forward and ran his fingers over my mound.

"I've been known to pray at the altar of Bran myself," I responded, gasping when the tips of his fingers slid through my arousal then pushed inside.

"You feel too good." He slid another finger inside, using his thumb to massage my throbbing clit. "Too good."

"Inside, Bran," I gasped, wanting to come with his

length inside me, my desire to shudder while wrapped around his girth mounting. I used my legs and reached for his arm, pulling him toward me. "Please."

With a growl, he grabbed my hips and flipped me onto my stomach, pulling back until I was on my knees. His hand collided with my arse, sending a loud slap, and a yelp from me into the room. Then he evened out the sting by clapping his hand against my other cheek before sliding his hand up the centre of my back and winding my long hair around his hand. I made a small helpless sound as he pulled my hair and pushed inside me at the same time. Pleasure and pain, joining together in one harmonious movement. *God, he was so good at this.*

"You're like a vice," he grunted, his hips swivelling as he slid back and forth, gliding through my arousal, pushing deep inside, a glorious feeling that was almost too much. "You grip me so hard that it almost hurts to come."

I hoped that was a good thing, but I was too far gone to make any other sound that wasn't a moan. The animal side of me took control whenever he was inside me and all I could do was experience his movement and take from his body. I felt transported to another plane of existence.

"Oh God." My voice tore out of my throat in a harsh cry, my back arching as I pushed against him, taking him as deep as I could while I came.

"Fuck." His hand released my hair then his fingers dug into my hips as he pulled out of me, flipping me over to my back.

Grabbing my legs, he forced them straight then climbed

on top of me, his knees over my waist, his slick wet cock slotting in between my breasts. "Those tits." With a squeeze, he pressed the mounds of flesh around his length, thrusting back and forth between them until he erupted, spurting hot cum in a pool across my collarbone. I felt the fluid run to my neck as he pulled back, out of breath, but smiling.

"There's your pearl necklace," he said, using his fingers to trace the shape around my neck then spread his cum across my chest. I laughed then reached up, tugging against the silken strands of his light hair, guiding his mouth to mine.

"My favourite piece of jewellery."

Pulling back, he looked down at me, his dark eyes softening. "You are so fucking beautiful."

"So are you." I smiled, feeling a little too exposed at his compliment. He saw me raw. In our short time together, I'd exposed some of the best and worst of myself in his presence, and still he found me enticing. *How long could that possibly last?*

Leaning down, Bran kissed me, his tongue, tasting me in long leisurely licks. I sighed against his skilled mouth, my body feeling sated and soft beneath his contrasting hard. Breaking away, he rolled off the bed and scooped me up.

"I can walk." I laughed, even though I loved the way he fucked me hard and dirty then tenderly cleaned me up.

"Don't question it. This is how I take care of my woman. I fuck you, I bathe you, and I feed you."

"Then we do it all over again." I smiled, holding on to his broad shoulders.

"Fuck yeah," he said with a smile. "Once is never enough."

No. It wasn't. And to be honest, I already hated the day when once *would* be enough for him, because that would probably be the day before he said goodbye.

23

"Your birthday is coming up next week?" The counsellor posed it as a question, but he knew it for a fact considering my birthday was on the file he had in front of him. It was the beginning of November. Spring was in the air with the sun pushing out the winter clouds that took up residence in Melbourne each winter. Bran and I were still devouring each other most nights with no sign of stopping. When my birthday arrived, it would be four months together—not that I was counting. On top of that, in only one more session, Jack's and my three months of therapy would be over. I was almost free from having to see him. My thirtieth birthday would certainly be a memorable one.

"That's right," I replied, doing my best to *not* look at Jack. In fact, I was sitting as far away from him on the couch as I possibly could. After weeks of these sessions, I was still no closer to getting any answers. All we'd spoken about was my anger towards Jack, and the reasons he felt the need to find fulfilment in the arms of another woman. Shockingly, all ten of his stupidly pretty fingers seemed to point at me because I 'worked so much'. It was a total cop-out. The counsellor seemed to provide little help as far as I was concerned. He was so infuriatingly neutral that I never knew if he sided more with Jack's version of events or mine. He simply sat there every session, asking stupid questions and taking notes. I hated it, hated coming to these fucking sessions for no real reason other than getting that order revoked. *I swear, if Jack finds a way to keep it in place after this, I'll do more than hit him. The police would never find the body.*

"It's her big three-oh," Jack said proudly, reaching over and patting my leg. I shot him a warning look, my eyes screaming, *don't touch me.* I somehow managed to squish even closer to the opposite side of the couch to evade any further contact. We weren't there yet. Not even close. Never would be.

Mr. Magoo noted the exchange and surprise, surprise, jotted something in his notes. "How are you feeling about hitting that milestone considering the state of your marriage?"

"If you're asking me if I feel like a failure because my husband is a liar, a cheat and a manipulator, the answer is no. In fact, I feel relieved. Jack and I had spoken about starting a family when I turned thirty. So I'm happy because I didn't tie myself to him with a child. Lord only knows what having a lying cheat for a father would do to the poor thing."

Mr. Magoo nodded and made a few notes before turning his attention to Jack. "How do you feel after listening to Cora's comments?" The man seriously had zero personality.

Jack pressed his lips together, looking like the wounded party. "It hurts," he said. "It hurts me knowing how much I've hurt her. I keep looking back on our life together, and I've done nothing but screw up. I kept looking to other people—other women's attraction to me —to validate my self worth."

"You say 'women' and yet you still won't admit to a number," I retorted, getting fed up with him forever evading that simple question I felt I had the right to have answered.

He looked at Mr Magoo, then down at his hands. I felt I wasn't going to get an answer today either. Would I ever?

Shaking my head, I turned away, playing with my earring and looking at a landscape of the Australian bush on the wall. There was a kangaroo and her joey drinking from a billabong. Little did they know but there was probably a crocodile hiding in there, ready to grab them. Predators were like that. You'd think you were safe then they tore your reality to shreds. Jack would know. He was good at fucking with reality.

The room had grown very quiet and I wondered if perhaps I'd said all that stuff about predators out loud. Jack picked at the skin on his palms, the callouses he'd earned from lifting weights. I hated when he did that. No one wanted someone else's dead skin on their floor.

"The first time was during our first semester at uni. My media class had a group assignment due," he started, causing my chest to tighten and my stomach to twist. We'd barely been dating a year. *What the actual fuck?* A sudden surge of panic surprised me by breaking out into a cold sweat all over my body. *Do I really want to hear this? Do I really want to understand the depths of his betrayal?*

I had to swallow the bile that rose in my throat before I could manage to speak. "The...the one where you compared the movie and the book?" I remembered it because they'd gone to see the movie in a group and he made a bunch of excuses why I couldn't join in. Then he didn't get home until nearly 3 a.m. I'd been beside myself with worry.

He nodded. "I didn't have car trouble."

Somehow I knew that. Even at the time I think I knew, but I chose to ignore it. I was too *in love*. I wanted to believe him. And he'd become so doting and attentive afterward that I felt bad for doubting him.

I clasped my hands on my knees, my fingers pinching. "Go on," I urged, keeping the feeling out of my voice.

"I felt awful afterward," he confessed. "I stayed true to you for the next two years. But then you got busy with your traineeship on top of school, and I started feeling...unimportant."

"So it was *my* fault for not paying you enough attention?" I snapped, hating that he was still putting any part of his actions on me.

"I'm not saying that," he returned. "I'm just trying to explain and give you the answers you want. This is what you want, right? All the gory details?"

"No! Not the gory details. Just the facts. *How many* and *how long* were you cheating?"

"Nine," he admitted, closing his eyes as the number fell from his lips. "It happened on and off for ten years."

Nine. "Did you love any of them?"

"No. Maybe. I don't know. But I loved you more. It's why I stayed."

I bit back a laugh. "And I should be grateful for that?

You robbed me of a decade of my life, Jack!" *Nine.* "How dare you sit there and say you loved me when you didn't even care enough to not screw other women."

"I tried. Every time I tried. But I kept getting drawn back in. I was addicted to the chase."

Nine.

"Addicted? You're blaming this on a disease, Jack? As far as I know there is no legitimate disease that causes accidental dick insertion. Did you use protection?"

"Yes," he replied, looking at his hands again.

The moment his nail found the edge of a callous I snapped.

Nine.

"Quit picking at your fucking hands!"

"I'm sorry," he said, tucking his hands between his thighs to stop himself.

"No, Jack, I'm sorry. I'm sorry I was so stupid and so naïve that I put up with your bullshit for *so long*." I stood up and started pacing the room. "Nine women, Jack. *Nine.* That isn't an accident or an inability to control yourself. That's one hundred per cent premeditated screwing on the side. The fact you even had protection on you shows you made conscious decisions to stick your dick in the body of other women then come home and do exactly the same thing to me. Or did you fuck all of them in our bed?" I shook my head, raking my hands through my hair to try and shake that sickening feeling away. "What kind of a man *does that*? And what if I hadn't found out, Jack? Would you still be fucking Sally or would you be into someone new? Someone called Sandra perhaps? Oh, I know; why don't you fuck our mail lady? That way you can be the one giving *her* a *package* for a change. *Won't* that be convenient for you? You can wait at the door naked, stick one in her, then send her on her way five minutes later. Because that's all it takes you, isn't it, Jack? You're a lousy lover who takes far more than he gives. No wonder you can't keep a mistress, let alone a wife."

"Maybe if you put out a little more often instead of being so focused on your career I wouldn't have had time to stray," Jack bellowed. My hand itched to slap his face.

"Then why the fuck did you marry me?"

"Because you wouldn't quit *pestering me!*"

Because you wouldn't quit pestering me. He married me to shut me up.

What the fuck?

My fists balled at my sides. I wanted blood. I wanted to scratch that smug look off his face and watch him bleed. But that would be too easy for a man like Jack; he'd use it as ammunition against me. Instead, I kept my cool and used my words instead, hitting him in the one place I knew would hurt. "Your dick isn't as big as I said it was. It isn't even average. In fact, I'd peg it as a little on the small side."

His face went so red, I expected steam to come out his ears.

"I think it's time to calm down now." Mr. Magoo interrupted before things could go any further. "Insults and yelling will not be tolerated." *Tolerated?*

"Who the fuck cares if he's insulted?" I spat. "Who the fuck cares how he feels? He did this to us. And you can't tell me that counselling and talking it over can do anything to make me forget that." I leaned over and picked up my bag. "Forget this shit. Forget you. I don't want to find a common ground with him. I don't even care about the fucking intervention order anymore. I just want this fucking bullshit"—I pointed straight at Jack —"out of my life." I turned and stormed out the door, slamming it behind me.

The moment I got outside, my skin felt too tight. *Nine.* I undid the top buttons of my blouse and fanned at my face with my hand, trying to breathe, to get some air. *Nine women.* I couldn't believe it, couldn't make the number sit right inside my mind. *Nine.* For the past ten years I'd been *sharing* Jack with *nine* other women. Had *they* known that? Had they all known what a *fool* I was? How *epically blind*?

Shaking my head, I choked back a sob and started walking down the street, getting faster and faster until I broke into a run. I ran all the way to ACU, all the way to the lecture hall I knew Bran would be in. Students were filing out of the door when I arrived, but there was only one I wanted to see. *Needed to see.*

I saw his head and shoulders first, rising above the other students. As soon as our eyes met, I pushed forward to get to him, flinging myself against his chest and into his open arms. "What happened?" he murmured against my hair, his hands rubbing the backs of my arms. "What's wrong?"

I shook my head, crying into his chest as he held me tight. I didn't want to talk, didn't want to admit my stupidity or think about Jack in any way. I just needed Bran to hold me.

When I didn't explain, I felt his sigh as his arms tightened their embrace. "It's OK, baby. I'll take care of you."

"Open." Bran held up a spoon of minestrone soup he'd ordered from room service.

Dutifully, I did his bidding, sitting in the centre of his bed wrapped in a big white robe, eating the tomato-based soup that was perhaps a little too salty. Still, it nourished my fatigued mind.

When I swallowed, Bran ran the backs of his fingers down the side of my cheek. "Want to tell me what all this was about?"

I shook my head. "I'd rather forget it ever happened."

His brow furrowed with concern as my eyes watered again. "Did someone hurt you? If they did I'll—" He made a fist and his knuckles cracked.

I placed my hand on his. "No. Well, not physically anyway. My pride has taken a beating, but that's really all."

"Your pride?"

I thought it over for a moment, trying to figure out a way to explain it without bursting into tears again. "It's just...am I enough for you?"

Eyeing me carefully, he set the bowl of soup to the side. "What do you mean?"

"Sexually. Am I enough for you?"

"Are you enough? Baby, you're more than enough. I can't fucking stop thinking about you, and when I think about you I want to fuck you. And I think that about *all the time.*"

"So, you don't wish I was more adventurous, or experienced?"

"No. Where is this coming from? Are you freaking out about the age thing again?"

"I don't know." I looked down at my hands and frowned. "Maybe."

With a heavy breath, he climbed into bed with me, curling his body around mine like a big spoon. Then he pressed a soft kiss against the back of my neck. "You are more than enough. To me, our age difference doesn't matter. I wish it didn't matter so much to you because there is no one—*no one*—on this earth I'd rather be with at any given moment."

Closing my eyes, I pulled his arm even tighter around me and snuggled against his warmth. I didn't know how true those words were. It wasn't that I didn't trust Bran, it was that Jack had lied to me for so long that words had lost their meaning. The only thing I felt I could believe were actions. "Just hold me," I whispered.

"Always," he replied, his lips pressing against my shoulder.

I knew I could probably tell him about Jack, lump my problems on him and perhaps he'd be able to sympathise with the position I was in, but that wasn't what we were to each other. We were sex. We were passion. We were a feeling. Having him near was all the comfort I needed. I didn't need to voice my problems for him to make me feel whole. I didn't want to colour our situation with the drama from my marriage. We worked the way we were. So instead of speaking any more useless words, I closed my eyes, drifting into a deep dreamless sleep.

24

THE MESSAGE CAME through with a photo of Bran and me leaving the university yesterday. His arm was around me, and I was pressed tightly against him. It was very intimate to look at, even for me. *How the hell did he get this?*

My hand went to my mouth.

Did he follow me?

Obviously taking my silence for the shock it was, Jack started typing again.

I looked at Bran's sleeping form, my heart squeezing a little because I was terrified. People were finding out. It didn't matter how well we fit together, at this stage of our lives we couldn't work. He was still at uni. I was in the middle of a marriage breakdown. I was his boss. He was *my* boss's *son*. My reason for years of sacrifice could be over the second this photo was delivered to the wrong hands. *Fuck.*

With my eyes closed, I blew out a calming breath, my eyes burning at the thought of letting him go. God, what had I been thinking running to him like that in the open?

Me: I'll be there

Slipping out of bed, I moved about the room as quietly as possible, pulling on my clothes but keeping my shoes off until I was on the other side of the door. Bran was still sleeping soundly, and I took a moment to drink him in. I could hear our clock ticking, and I honestly didn't want it to end. How was I going to go back to being alone when I'd experienced *him?* The idea made my insides ache.

Checking my appearance in the mirrored elevator, I pulled my brush from my bag and ran it through my hair. I didn't have a scrap of makeup on, but had to make do with a swipe of clear gloss on my lips and pinched cheeks. It's all the ride to the lobby allowed for.

Stepping through the doors, I headed out into the cool morning, my head down as I typed out an explanation to Bran.

Me: thanks for last night. gone home to get ready. See you at work

It was a boldfaced lie that sat heavy in my stomach, so

I switched my phone to silent and hid it away from view in my bag.

A few minutes later, I was sliding into a chair across from Jack. He'd already ordered coffee and there was a plate of fruit toast waiting as well. The sweet spices tickled my nose and made my stomach growl even though I didn't feel hungry.

"I followed you yesterday," he started. No hello. No how are you. Just straight to the point.

"I figured." To distract myself from reacting badly, I took a bite of the warm toast. "Thank you, by the way," I said, pointing to the food.

He nodded once, but kept his brown eyes hard as he studied me. "Who is he?"

"He's none of your business. Why did you follow me?"

"We said some really shitty things to each other yesterday, and I'd thought, maybe a breakthrough. You left upset. You ran. I was worried. But we didn't have a breakthrough at all, did we? He's why you've been so resistant to the therapy, right? This whole time I've been thinking we were working on our marriage and you were off banging some kid."

I laughed through my nose. "*You're* the reason I'm adverse to therapy. You and your harem of nine."

"At least I'm trying."

"To what? Make my life miserable? Congratulations. So far you've been a roaring success."

"To get *help*. I know I fucked up."

"You fucked up *nine* times." Picking up my coffee, I took a mouthful, closing my eyes to stop any tears. My heart felt torn to shreds by this man.

"I'm trying to better myself. I'm seeing Dr Montgomery on my own as well as with you." *Dr Montgomery? Who the hell is that? Oh, Mr. Magoo.* I'd never actually registered his real name. "He says that sex addiction is a real problem that can be fixed with counselling and honesty."

I almost spat coffee down my chin. "Sex *addiction*?" Laughter bounced in my chest. "You're not serious?"

"I'm deadly serious. The overwhelming need to seek sexual gratification is a real thing. I'm learning to control it, and if you'd just give me the chance, I know we could make this marriage of ours work."

"I gave you eleven years, Jack. I don't have any more for you. This isn't about what you want any more. It's about what I want."

"What *you* want? You're telling me this new guy is more important than fixing our marriage? What is he? The new love of your life?"

"He's none of your business."

"I'm your husband, Cora. If you're sleeping with some other guy, it's definitely my business."

Pushing the plate and the coffee away from me, I shook my head and looked away. "You have no right, Jack. You cheated on me, repeatedly, had me removed from *my own* home, ruined the state of my career, and forced me into counselling by dangling *only the hope* of righting some of that wrong in front of me. I keep telling you that I'm done. You've completely obliterated any love I had for you. There is no going back for us, Jack. Accept it and move the fuck on. I want nothing more from you than a divorce." I stood to leave, dropping a twenty on the table. "My attorney will be in touch."

"Brandon Sharp," he called after me, freezing me in my tracks.

"What did you just say?" I moved back to the table, keeping my voice low.

He grinned. "That's his name, isn't it? Son of the Director of Public Prosecutions. Your intern."

Pursing my lips, I slid back into my seat and clasped my hands in front of me. "Why all the questions if you already knew who he was?"

"Perhaps I was giving you the chance to come clean over your affair. Same way I came clean over mine."

I choked out a laugh at the audaciousness of his comment. "It hardly compares." *He only came clean because I caught him mid-fuck.*

"Let's see." He reached down beside him and pulled a folder from his bag, dropping it on the table in front of me. "You've been sneaking around with him for at least three months, maybe more, and no one knows about you." He flipped open the folder and spread a bunch of pictures in front of me. "Looks a lot like an affair to me. We've even got a few compromising positions in there. I can't imagine you've disclosed this relationship to your boss, *his dad*. I doubt he'd be as understanding as I am. Especially when the reason young Brandon was dragged back down here was because he was caught having an affair with one of his teachers."

"What?" I pushed the photos aside, finding the report that detailed my recent whereabouts as well as Bran's history. Sure enough, it was all there in black and white. He'd narrowly avoided a suspension and she was transferred to another university. *Did he have a predilection for older women?* I closed the file, not wanting any more information. I'd had all I could handle. "I can't believe you had me followed, Jack. Let me guess, another suggestion from your attorney?"

"He's very thorough." He took the file back and slid it into his bag.

"I'll bet. Exactly what are you planning to do with all that? Blackmail me into going back to you?"

"Well, your job *is* the most important thing in your life. All I'm asking is one more chance."

I opened my mouth to object, but I knew he was right. I had nothing to say to that comment. Absolutely *nothing*.

"Get rid of the kid. Someone that young can't be any more than a rebound anyway, and come back to counselling with me. Take it seriously this time, and I *promise* I'll revoke that order. You can even move back into the house."

Give up Bran. Save my career. Get my house back. Give Jack one more chance. It was a short list with massive consequences. Two things had been at the top of my goal list for months. But as I sat there, focussing on what he offered me, the cost far outweighed the reward. "I don't want to live in that house anymore," I said, my voice awfully quiet.

Jack smiled like he thought he was getting his way. "Then we'll sell, get something new. Just give us a real chance to work things out and your life can go back to what it was. I'll be the best husband you can imagine."

My breath stilled in my chest. The offer created an acrid taste in my mouth. For so long, I'd lived for my work. Jack wasn't wrong about that. Having lost that element of my life, I'd felt incomplete without it. Well, until Bran came into my life anyway. Ever since he came along, everything had felt a thousand times better. It actually made me realise how empty I'd felt when I was with Jack. We'd cohabited while living separate lives. With Bran, even though it was still new, we were more together than I ever felt with Jack. Bran wasn't a rebound. He was a realignment of my soul. My heart. My mind. And while I knew the idea of officially dating a man ten years my junior sounded crazy, I also knew I'd be crazy to give up what we had—especially at the behest of a manipulative arsehole like Jack. No. Fuck that. Fuck Jack. Bran was far more important to me than any of this bull-shit being held over my head. The only real question left was: *why the fuck am I still sitting here?*

"No," I said, my head shaking, my eyes locked on Jack's. "I won't give him up. Not for you. Not for anyone."

His expression morphed in surprise, his forehead creasing. "What about your job?"

I shrugged. "Fuck my job." I couldn't believe those words came out of my mouth. But I meant them. "And fuck you too, Jack. You were never going to revoke that order. I was a fool to ever believe you would." Picking up my bag, I stood to leave.

"You're seriously in love with this guy?" he scoffed, disbelief in his eyes.

Maybe...

I picked up my twenty and shoved it in my pocket. I considered it tax for him wasting my time. "I don't know, Jack. It's still new. But I do know one thing for certain. Brandon Sharp is a better man at twenty than you've ever been in your entire life." Spinning on my heel, I took off down the street. The next time I spoke to Jack, I hoped it was during our divorce proceedings.

25

I NEEDED OLIVIA. I needed to talk to her about Jack and the information bomb of a folder he had that he could detonate at any moment. I needed her usually calm brain to help me figure out what to do about it: should I tell the director before he could? Or did I sit on the information and hope Jack didn't use it against me? I was too involved and agitated to work it out on my own.

Unfortunately, my need for clarity would have to wait. For the past couple of months, Olivia's morning sickness had been in full force, and she'd taken reduced hours because of it. It was the first time since she'd contracted Bird flu in 2010 that she'd taken any sort of time off before the holiday period. Back then, she'd been dreadfully ill for almost two weeks and would only let me visit through the door so she didn't spread her germs. I'd bring her soup and pick up her medication then tell her about all the office happenings she was missing out on. It kept her in the loop.

This time was different though. Office gossip was of

no comfort; from six weeks onwards, she felt queasy from sun up to sun down. It had seemed to ease off a little now that she was in her second trimester, but she was still struggling with the effect pregnancy hormones were having on her body. She was tired and irritable. I really felt bad for her. Which was why I wasn't already on the phone to her whining about my own problems. She had enough of her own, and she needed her rest. Instead, I headed straight for my office and crossed my fingers in the hope that Jack wouldn't do anything until I'd figured my side of things out. I also crossed my toes—it had always worked for me as a kid.

Needing to keep my mind from fretting, I thought about Olivia and her growing belly. It was something I hadn't considered in my own desire to start a family. I'd kind of convinced myself that I'd breeze through pregnancy, work up until the kid was born, then hire a nanny so my career wouldn't be stalled at all. Like many of my previous outlooks on life, that too had been naïve. Babies changed everything—pregnancy changed everything. From the moment that test showed positive, life had completely changed for my best friend.

"Olivia isn't coming in today?" Bran asked, meeting me in my office with this morning's cases. "I heard some murmurings about an ultrasound around the coffee machine."

"Yes. She should be in after lunch. Paul is taking her to get their twenty-week scan done. They might find out the sex of the baby," I responded, smiling. I couldn't wait to shower that little bundle of theirs with pink or blue Wondersuits.

"She's letting him be more involved now? That's a

good thing, right?" Olivia had been incredibly resistant to any of Paul's attempts to take care of her, but as the morning sickness got the better of her, she started to come around. Based on her vague information, he was eagerly at her beck and call.

"I think he's wearing her down." I pressed my lips together in a small smile. It was an odd beginning, but it seemed they were making the most of it.

Bran checked over his shoulder before speaking again, making sure no one was listening. "Are *you* OK? I was worried when you were gone this morning."

"I'm fine. Like I said, I needed fresh clothes. But thanks for being there for me yesterday. It meant a lot."

He pressed the tips of his fingers against the wood of the table. "You can come to me any time. If you haven't guessed already, I kind of like taking care of you."

His words made me feel warm inside, because I knew they were sincere. He'd given me zero reason to doubt him. "Do you see yourself having kids some day?" I asked suddenly, the idea spending far too much time on my mind of late. With everything I stood to lose if our relationship got out, I needed to know exactly where he stood and how he saw his future playing out.

He shrugged. "Eventually, I guess. I'm not in any hurry though."

"I see." I wasn't sure if that answer disappointed me or not.

He lowered his head slightly, studying my expression. "Why? Do *you* want kids?"

"I do," I answered honestly. "When, I don't know. It's just that I'm thirty soon, and with what's happening with

Olivia, it's kind of on my mind. I'd always thought that by this point in my life I'd at least be planning them."

"It's definitely not out of the question for me. But there's time, right? The clock isn't ticking too hard?"

"What? Oh, no. It's not like I want them tomorrow, or anything, I'm just airing thoughts I guess. Wondering where you stand. Am I scaring you off now?" I smiled meekly, feeling a little silly for even bringing it up. Bran was still at uni. As if he was thinking about kids. This conversation was way over the top—we hadn't even fully defined our relationship yet. I was starting to regret my words. "Just forget I said anything," I added, waving my hands in the air dismissively.

"I'm not going anywhere, Cora." We stopped talking when someone walked past my open door. Once they were out of earshot, he took a breath and wrapped his knuckles on the table. "Will I see you tonight?"

I nodded. "I'm yours all long-weekend."

His expression turned wicked. "Four days. I'm looking forward to it."

"Me too," I whispered, biting at my lip. He made a slight growling sound then tore himself away, exiting my office to attend to his work.

The moment he left, I sat back in my chair and blew out a loaded breath. There was a lot that Bran and I needed to sort through. It had been four months and we weren't showing any signs of slowing down. If anything, we were growing closer, more serious. It was time for us to talk about what that meant for us as a couple. We couldn't continue hiding, couldn't keep avoiding important discussions by falling into bed together either. If he truly wasn't going anywhere, then it was time to ask the hard questions and come clean about our hidden truths. We'd been avoiding it for far too long.

Making a mental list inside my head, I decided that calling my divorce attorney should be at the top. I'd put it off because I didn't want to rock the boat until after I'd completed counselling with Jack, but now that was no longer happening, there was no point in wasting more time. I needed to quit hoping and start taking action to sort my life out on my own. Getting a divorce and ending any connection I had to Jack was my most pressing concern. I needed that part of my life over. And when I told Bran that I was married, I wanted to be able to show him the paperwork that proved it was over. I didn't want him to have any doubt in his mind about how important he was to me.

After a bit of begging to her secretary, my attorney agreed to squeeze me in during my lunch break. I was sitting eagerly across from her within a few hours, feeling as though I was finally, *finally,* starting to take back control.

"It's good that you've been to counselling," she told me. Her name was Katrina Mahoney. She was tall and thin with honey-blonde hair and an angular, but very pretty face. She looked to be late twenties, which meant she'd only been practicing unrestricted for a few years. But Olivia had assured me she had a stellar reputation, so that was enough for me. "It's actually a requirement for the disillusion of a marriage less than two years old. However, you need to prove that you've been separated for at least twelve months and one day. From my under-standing, you've been apart almost seven months?"

"That's right. And there's no way to speed up that process?"

With a smile, she shook her head. "There isn't, I'm afraid. But, it gives us time to get your affairs in order and open a dialogue with his attorney so that the eventual divorce proceedings go smoothly without either of you having to go to court. The fact you have no children will make things run even smoother. Is there anything else I should know?"

"He's, um...trying to blackmail me into giving him another chance. First he was using the intervention order to get me to go to counselling and now he's using surveillance photos of me and my..." I struggled to come up with a word to explain who Bran was to me. Explaining it in this situation made it feel so sordid when it wasn't.

"You're in a new relationship?" she asked, to which I nodded, relieved that she filled in the blank for me. "What exactly is your husband threatening you with?"

"See, that's the problem. He hasn't *overtly* threatened me. He's too smart for that. He's simply suggesting that *if* those pictures *got* into the wrong hands my job *could* be at stake."

"This new relationship is within your workplace?"

"Yes. He's my boss's son," I squeaked out, feeling my face go red from voicing it. "And my, um...intern." *What must she think of me?* As strongly as I felt towards Bran, I was under no illusion that others would understand the circumstances.

Although, her face showed no reaction. "I see. Well, I can't say I'm a stranger to complicated work relationships. I risked my job for a man once too."

Her candidness surprised me. "Was it worth it?"

Thinking for a moment, she smiled to herself. "Yes. Everything worked out exactly how it was supposed to."

"So you're still with the guy?"

She shook her head. "No. But it led me to my husband. I'm thankful for that."

"And did you lose your job?"

"Almost."

"So, what can I do in this situation?"

"You could look into charging him with attempted blackmail.You work in the right place to make that happen."

I shook my head. "The onus of proof is on me. There's no way a charge would stand because he could claim that it was just a miscommunication. Blackmail is really hard to try without hard evidence."

"I see. And if this gets out, is there a policy against dating within the workplace?"

"No. But there are the usual issues with me being in the position of power."

"Then, technically, if both parties are consenting adults, and you can prove that, it doesn't really have anything to do with your office."

"Normally, no. But, I believe I'm already in poor standing with the director because of the intervention order. He could cancel my contract for inappropriate conduct. Being the OPP there are morality clauses... I need to know if there's a way you can put an injunction on Jack to keep him from using the pictures. Something like that. Perhaps talk to his attorney and see if you can get him to back off?"

She nodded and made some notes on the file in front

of her. "I can't promise much because of the vagaries of the situation, but I'll see what I can do."

"Thank you." I released a hopeful breath, noticing the light bounce off the diamonds on her wedding finger. "How do you do this?" I asked, indicating her ring.

"Stay married or help others end theirs?"

"Both, I guess."

Folding her arms across her waist, she leaned forward slightly. "It works for us because we want it to—both of us, not just one. No relationship works without the other taking part. And I do this job because I've been in bad relationships before." Turning her head, she shifted her hair back, revealing a series of fine scars smattered all over her left side. "I hate the thought of a woman being trapped in a relationship she couldn't get out of, regardless of the reasons—violence, lovelessness, or in your situation, serial adultery and general nastiness. Everyone deserves to be happy in his or her life, and every person deserves his or her fair share of the life that relationship built. So I do what I can to make things as easy and as fair as possible."

"I just want that part of my life over," I said, feeling emotion push at the backs of my eyes. "I want him to leave me alone so I can move forward."

"I understand that. And I promise to call his attorney immediately to try and find a way to keep Jack from using that surveillance information."

"I really appreciate that. Thank you."

"Of course. I know this process can feel a lot like limbo at times. But there's only five months to go before we can file. The waiting will give you plenty time of time to think and reflect on all the things that went wrong so your new relationship will be healthier because of it."

"I already know exactly where I went wrong: I put all my hopes in the wrong man."

"Give me some good news," I said when I returned to the office and found Olivia standing outside her office with a group of women looking at her ultrasound pictures.

She grinned and showed me the printed image. "It's a very healthy baby girl."

"That's so wonderful," I said, throwing my arms around her neck. "How are you feeling?"

Touching her tiny bump of a stomach, she gestured for me to follow her into her office. "I'm feeling a lot better today," she said once we were alone. "It was amazing watching this living thing moving around inside me. She looks like a perfect little human already. I can barely feel her moving, but she moves *all the time*. You should have seen it." She looked genuinely happy as she gazed at the black and white pictures then pointed all the features out to me. "Paul cried when he saw her."

"Happy tears?" I struggled to make much sense of the image, but smiled along, feeling glad for her. "She's beautiful, Liv," I said, feeling slightly jealous of her happiness. Her life hadn't really been any less complicated than mine, but she'd managed to take everything in her stride. There wasn't much that could keep Olivia down.

"Where were you when I got in?" she asked, sticking one of the photos to the side of her computer screen with tape. "I wanted you to be the first to see everything but you were late back from lunch."

"Oh, I went to see that divorce lawyer."

Her eyes lit up. "Wonderful. So everything went fine?"

I didn't have the heart to ruin her buzz with the news of Jack's latest dickhead move, so I smiled and nodded. "Everything went perfect. It's open and shut."

"I'm so happy to hear that. Let me take you for a drink after work to celebrate."

"How about *I take you* out to look at pink baby clothes?" I suggested instead.

She grinned, looking much younger in her excitement. "Is it weird that I would really love that?"

I shook my head. "Not at all." Things were changing. A year ago, I'd never have dreamed I'd be talking to Olivia about her impending motherhood, while I headed for divorce court and struggled to come to terms with my feelings toward a younger man. It felt like the world was upside down.

WHEN I WALKED up to the front of my building, Bran was already waiting, leaning against the wall, and looking like sin on two legs.

"I thought you were never going to get here," he commented with a grin, taking me in his arms and kissing me until my toes curled. "Mmm. But that was worth waiting for."

"I stopped in at Olivia's to say hi to Paul and show him the outfits we bought for the baby."

"Did they find out the sex?"

"They did. It's a girl."

"Congratulations to them."

I pulled out my keys and opened the security door. "You could tell her that yourself, you know. It wouldn't be unusual since you work in the same office, but even without that, she sort of knows about us..." I dropped that tiny bomb, testing the waters before I felt comfortable telling him how big the leak of knowledge about our relationship had become.

"I'd find it odd if she didn't know. You are best friends, after all."

"She won't say anything to anyone."

He hit the button to call the lift. "I don't care who she tells."

"Maybe you should. It could change everything. Do you understand how serious the implications are for me?" Even with possible attorney intervention, there was no telling what Jack would do with that file. I half expected to go back to work next week to a cardboard box sitting on my desk and a notice of termination stuck to my computer screen. I knew I did the right thing telling him to shove his 'deal' up his arse, but I was still worried about the repercussions.

Bran's brow furrowed. "Who else knows about us?"

My husband. Opening my mouth to come clean, I pressed it closed again and shook my head. Now wasn't the right time to get into it. It was a massive discussion that had the ability to ruin our entire weekend together. Right now, I just wanted to fall into his arms and enjoy the simplicity of what we had for a little while longer. "No one. I'm being paranoid."

Grinning down at me, he hooked his index finger into

the top of my skirt and pulled so I collided against his chest. I immediately relaxed. Something about the contact made everything better. *Bran* made everything better. "Then relax. We have a four-day weekend ahead of us and I plan to spend every moment of that feasting on your flesh." He lowered his head into my neck.

"Never have I been happier for a horse race," I sighed as his tongue and teeth played against my tender skin. The Melbourne Cup long weekend would be a perfect break from prying eyes and routine stresses. It would give us uninterrupted time together, the opportunity to talk all this shit through and work out exactly what this was.

"I could fuck you right where you stand." A low growl rumbled in his throat, and he kissed me until the lift hit my floor. I was practically liquid by the time he came up for air.

"I don't want to say no, but the building body corporate might not appreciate the show." I pointed to the camera in the corner.

"They'd love the show." He chuckled as he grabbed my hand and pulled me off the lift.

Walking hand in hand to my apartment, I couldn't stop the thoughts of those prying eyes watching us. Some of the pictures Jack had shown me were taken through my windows. I hated that, hated that Jack's slimy reach had found its way into my own private space. I paused at the door and turned to face Bran.

"How about we get out of here for a few days?" The idea of leaving Melbourne for a period made my anxiety levels less uneven.

"And go where?"

"I don't know. Somewhere warm and sunny. We can

lie on the beach and have sex in the pool. Get drunk at a bar. Dance like no one's watching."

He quirked a magnificent eyebrow. "I could be persuaded."

"How about I make us some dinner and we can search for the perfect spot while we eat?"

He took the keys out of my hand and opened the door. "How about I fuck you first. Then cook while you relax in a bath, and *then* we can find somewhere last minute to go. I have it on good authority that the Gold Coast is a pretty nice place."

Asking him if he was planning on looking up his old flame while we were there was on the tip of my tongue, but I bit the comment back. He wasn't Jack and he hadn't given me any reason not to trust him. I wanted him to tell me about his past in his own time because it wasn't like I'd been forthcoming about mine. Besides, Brisbane and the Gold Coast weren't exactly neighbouring cities. I had nothing to worry about.

"You're too good to me," I said instead.

He kissed me on the nose. "What can I say? I like taking care of my woman."

26

"CAN I BURY YOU?" I asked Bran, squinting over to where he was lying back on his beach towel. He seemed so relaxed, digging his toes in the sand and soaking up the sun's rays on the sandy beach across the road from our hotel at Broadbeach. We'd flown to the Gold Coast early Saturday morning, and after barely emerging from our room for the next twenty-four hours, we decided to take advantage of the sun and surf.

Turning his head, Bran lifted his sunglasses just enough that I could see one of his eyes. "Bury me?"

I got on my knees and crawled a little closer to him. His eyes lowered to my chest. I was wearing the busty woman's version of a black string bikini. It had the same principles, but there was added support in the form of a double strap and tailored cup. The girls weren't going anywhere. "I want to hide you under the sand so those schoolgirls over there stop perving on your delectably perfect abs." I did a little side-eye move in their direc-tion. They'd been parading up and down the beach, flicking their blonde hair and shaking their young, golden-skinned, tiny arses, all in an attempt to get his attention.

His mouth kicked up on one side, but he didn't turn away from me. It made me realise something else I'd been missing for years. Bran was *completely* ignoring them. He only had eyes for me. Those girls were probably wondering what the hell a guy like Bran was doing with a woman like me. Or worse, they were speculating on whether I was his *mother*. I hoped to God I didn't look that ancient next to him. But, the fact he didn't look their way made me one very happy woman—especially after the bruising my ego had taken over the last few months from the knowledge of Jack's *nine* extra-curricular 'activities'.

"My abs are delectably perfect?" He chuckled, placing one hand against my thigh.

"Are you going to keep parroting what I say or let me bury you?"

Leaning back, he laced his fingers behind his head. "Knock yourself out."

As I pushed the sand against him, I could see him watching me with amusement. "You know, I should probably be the one hiding your body under the sand. With that arse of yours in the air like that and your tits barely staying hidden behind that scrap you call a bikini, I'm sure I'm not the only man looking."

I shrugged. "You're the only man who gets to touch," I said, dumping a pile of sand in the centre of his chest.

"No other woman gets to touch my delectable abs either," he teased.

"Better not," I replied, as I finished covering his legs

and stomach. He wriggled his toes and broke free, so I shot him a playful scowl then piled on more sand.

"You're as bad as my brother at this."

"You have a brother?" he asked, sounding surprised at the information. There was so much we still didn't know about each other.

"Uh-huh."

"Younger or older."

"Older."

"You close?"

I scrunched up my nose a little. "Not really. He lives in New Zealand with his wife and three kids. I see them every second Christmas."

"And you don't talk to him between then?"

"Sure, I do—sort of. I call him on his birthday and message him occasionally. But it's mostly Facebook stuff. He's a big online sharer; lots of bragging about my nieces and nephew. They're pretty adorable."

"See, I don't get that. All the time growing up, I wished for a sibling. Then here you are with one and you hardly ever talk."

I shrugged. "That's family for you, I suppose. Don't get me wrong. We love each other fiercely, but we do take each other for granted all the time."

"Maybe we should take a trip to see him some time in the next year. The skiing is good in New Zealand, right?"

A smile crept across my features. "You sure you want to make plans with me that far into the future?"

He lifted his brow. "Baby, we were having a discussion about kids yesterday."

"I was just trying to see if we were on the same page—

or at least in the same book. I'm not pressuring you for a commitment or anything."

"What if I want to be committed to you?"

Running my hand over the thick sand on his chest, I thought more on what a commitment between Bran and me would mean. "Then I think we need to talk about how that's going to work."

"I can quit the internship. All problems would be solved that way."

"I can't ask you to do that, Bran."

"I'm offering."

Taking a moment to look at him—really look at him —I considered the man who had pushed his way into my heart with his brutish and boyish ways. There were a lot of qualities I loved about Bran. I loved his strength, I loved his command. I loved his tenderness, and I also loved his vulnerability. When he cared, he cared with his whole being. I didn't need to know everything about him to see that. His actions told me everything I needed to know. I wanted so much with him.

"How about we table this discussion until later?" I suggested. "Right now, I want to enjoy the sun and finish burying you in the sand. Then, I want to go back to the hotel and have my wicked way with you." I bit my lip seductively.

"Sure. But you're going to have to help me shower and wash all this sand off."

"I'm counting on it. All that soap, my hands gliding over your skin...I'm getting excited just thinking about it."

"Oh baby. Me too. I think you might need to add a little extra sand at the crotch zone."

"Down boy." I smiled, patting the growing area. It was so easy to refocus this man's mind. I felt so *wanted* by him.

"I can't with your tits in my face like that."

Laughing, I swayed a little closer. He growled and snapped his teeth at the air, unable to reach without breaking out of the casing I was applying.

"This might help." I gathered the sand between my hands and set a mound of it on his chest, sculpting it in two large piles.

"What are you doing here?" He laughed, his chest bouncing, jostling my creations.

"You like my breasts so much, I thought I'd make you your own." I topped them off with two shells for nipples.

"Ohhh, I like these," he joked, cupping his hands around the new additions to his chest.

"Don't move! You're wrecking the whole thing." Laughing, I stood at his feet, holding my phone in preparation to take a photo.

He made a kiss face for the first shot, then I shifted angles to take a few more and instead captured shots of him erupting out of the sand and shaking it all off like a dog. I squealed as it landed against my skin and stuck to my sunscreen.

"Stop, you're getting it all over me!" I threw my phone inside my canvas bag to protect it from his onslaught.

"Then I should probably wash you off." Charging for me, he bent down and caught me at hip height, flinging me over his shoulder and running for the surf.

Squealing with laughter, I leaned down and slapped his arse, beating on each cheek like a set of drums.

"Oh, you're gonna get it." I squealed as I fell, landing in the water with a splash, the noisy rush roiling against my ears. When he pulled me to my feet, I was still laughing. The smile only dropping when he kissed me hard. Waves crashed against his back as his held me tight and vanquished my mouth. It felt like something out of a movie. It felt unreal. I was standing in the surf being devoured by the hottest man I had ever laid eyes on—out in the open, no hiding—and I felt happy. Carefree. It made me feel positive about our future. Bran made my world better.

"LET ME GUESS, you were the popular guy all the girls lusted after and the guys wanted to be friends with." Sitting back in my chair, I looked over the rim of my glass of red wine. The restaurant was full of chatting people. A pleasant hum of conversation flowed through the air. The entire room lit a soft yellow that mimicked the glow of candlelight. String instruments played music through hidden speakers, and waiters were eager to please without being obtrusive.

So far, it had been a perfect night. In another day, we'd be flying back to Melbourne. I honestly didn't want to leave. I felt warm, safe and healthy up here. My cheeks hurt from smiling so much. This weekend away was just what I needed to release my worries and gain some perspective about the future of Bran's and my relationship. We both wanted one—that much was certain. But so far, we hadn't done a lot of talking about the logistics. We were *talking*, a lot actually, learning things about each other we'd yet to explore. We spoke about growing up and going to school, the places we liked and books we'd read. Even though it was only surface knowledge, I realised how much I liked him as a person. Sexy Adonis aside. Each time one of us brought up a serious topic, the other steered the conversation along more playful avenues and we ended up naked. We were both as bad as each other, always avoiding facing just how complicated things really were between us. Depth over distance. It had worked for us so far, we'd allowed ourselves to fall for each other in a protected little bubble without really focusing on what was going to happen when that bubble burst. But, here we were. It was happening around us, and yet we continued to evade. Everything left unsaid was turning into a knot in my chest.

Toying with the stem of his wineglass with two long fingers, Bran smiled and shook his head. "I was the opposite at school. I was the guy everyone feared. I was always bigger than everyone else and looked a lot older. When my parents sent me to boarding school—"

"Your parents sent you to *boarding school?*" I honestly didn't think that was a thing anymore.

"Good ole Melbourne Grammar."

"Gosh. They would have been so close. Why didn't they let you commute? There are plenty of excellent private schools in Melbourne."

"Tradition. Generations of Sharp men went there, and they wanted me to undergo the full 'character building' experience. Besides, I wasn't there very long. I attended several different boarding schools around the country."

"Why was that? Were you a troublemaker?"

He grinned, focusing on his wine glass. "Because of my size, there was this rumour that I was perhaps a little simple in the head and had been held back as a result. A group of them tried to gang up on me and, I suppose you could say I taught them a lesson they wouldn't forget. Instead of suspending me, they accepted a donation from my father and transferred me to another school. Whispers followed... I was an angry kid. The pattern kept repeating. Eventually the rumours suggested I was more of a danger than anything else. From then on, most were very kind to me. But I could tell they were only behaving that way because they were afraid. So, I focused on my studies, kept mostly to myself." He smirked as he met my eyes.

"You had no friends?"

"I had friends. I just wasn't popular in the classic sense of the word. More...revered for the weight of my punch."

"Sounds like you've lived a very transient, if not lonely, life so far." My heart broke a little at the thought.

"It hasn't been so bad. I keep my possessions to a minimum so I don't mind moving around."

"Is that why you live in that hotel? Because you don't want to put down roots?"

He shrugged. "It's not that I don't want to put down roots, more that I haven't found a place I've connected with."

"You don't feel connected to *anything* now?" I blurted, my mind racing. *What did that mean?* That he was just biding his time with me until it was time to leave again? Had I been reading all of this wrong? The idea felt thick in my throat.

Smiling, he reached across the table and took my hand. "If you'd let me finish, the next two words out of my mouth would have been 'until now'. I can see myself building a life with you."

Building a life with me. Oh, how I'd longed for those words when I was young like him. They still felt amazing as they touched my ears with their gentle promise, but I couldn't help questioning them.

"Why me, Bran? There are thousands of girls closer to your age who don't have the life experience to have the many hang-ups I come with. Why choose me over them?"

He took a mouthful of wine then licked his lips before answering. "I'm not interested in girls. I never have been." Studying my expression, his eyes shone with desire.

"I see. Is this a thing for you?" I pointed between us. "Have you always preferred an older woman?" I was trying to get answers without giving away the fact I knew that there had been at least one other inappropriate age and power relationship in his past.

"I've always been mature for my age. I like a woman who is more mature as well."

"So, this started young?" My worries mounted. I didn't know how I felt about being another in a string of older female conquests. He wanted me *now*, but what happened when I was *too* old? Would he go find some other thirty-year-old to take my place? I picked up my fork and poked around at the remaining pasta on my plate, trying to force my fretting mind to quiet down. Jack had really done a number on me. I could jump from discussing the future to seeing it all crumple through my fingers in a matter of seconds. "Did you ever crush on one of your teachers?" I tried to keep my tone light and inquisitive.

He grinned. "Doesn't every boy at some point?"

Deflection. I knew that tactic well. "I suppose they do." Taking a moment to realign my questioning, I chewed on my pasta thoughtfully. "Did you ever act on one of those crushes though?" This was the moment where he could tell me about the woman in Brisbane. I almost didn't breathe while I waited for him to answer.

Turning away, he laughed. "That would have gotten me into trouble now, wouldn't it?" *Yes. Perhaps even sent to a catholic university in a different state and placed into an internship where your father thought he could keep an eye on you.* The words were on the tip of my tongue, but I didn't say them. I couldn't. If I did, I'd have to explain how I knew. And that would lead to a conversation about Jack. And that would be it, bubble popped. In a panic, I scrambled for something less confronting, yet still baiting to say. I wanted him to trust me with his indiscretions. How was I supposed to share my history with him if he wasn't going to do the same? How were we ever going to be any more than we were if we didn't open up to each other?

"Your colourful academic record tells me that trouble is your middle name. Let's not forget you had no issue slipping into a secret affair with me. Seems you enjoy pushing boundaries." I lifted my brow, my eyes locked squarely on his.

His jaw tightened slightly as he leaned a little closer, lowering his voice. "Calling this an affair implies that I'm sharing you, Cora. And we don't share, do we?"

I shook my head, suddenly feeling very alert and aware that this conversation had reached its end point. "No. We don't share."

Keeping his eyes on mine, heat simmering under the surface, he lifted his arm to call our waiter. "I'd like whatever chocolate cake you have wrapped up to go. Make sure you include a lot of cream."

"Yes, sir." The waiter retreated as fast as he appeared.

"We were talking."

He grinned lasciviously. "I've had enough talking. I'd rather remind you who you belong to while I lick chocolate and whipped cream off your body. Are you going to object?"

"No," I whispered, pressing my knees together. Opening up was going to have to wait. *Again.* Apparently, I had an extremely sweet tooth that needed to be fed.

27

"How do you do that thing with your tongue?" I asked, a grin stuck to my face after being the recipient to one of Bran's gifted wakeup calls.

We were in our giant, obscenely comfortable bed in a suite at the Sofitel. Sunshine filled the room and the scent of salt water filled the air. Our last morning in paradise.

"You mean this?" He stuck his tongue past his lips and vibrated it. It moved so fast it blurred.

I tried to copy but just ended up blowing raspberries. Laughing at my attempt, he pulled me closer then rolled so he was on top of me, kissing me languidly, using that tongue as a gentle force.

I hummed contentedly, my fingernails scraping against the smooth skin of his back, making him shiver and his flesh bump. I loved how big he was, how small he made me feel beneath his strength. I also loved that there was a slight vulnerability to him. It was as though he needed me as much as I needed him, and there was a real fear of having this fall apart and getting hurt as a result. It wasn't so much what he'd said that brought me to that conclusion. It was the way he looked at me, an emotion hidden in the backs of his eyes. I recognised it because I was feeling it too. There were things we weren't telling each other. Things that were bigger than the risk to my job and his standing within his family. And yet I felt claimed by him completely, taken in the most primal way possible. Despite the things we didn't know, I wanted to lose myself to the urge; to allow myself to be claimed and to claim him in return. The consequences were huge, but I didn't want to hide anymore.

For the first time in my adult life, my job was a distant second to the desires of my heart. Becoming a Crown Prosecutor wasn't the be all and end all of my legal career. The OPP wasn't the only facility in the country that could benefit from my skills. If being with Bran meant that I needed to get another job, then so be it. People altered their career goals for love all the time...

Love.

Is that what this was?

Searching Bran's eyes while also searching inside myself, I honestly didn't know. I'd thought I loved Jack all those years, but this felt completely different. It didn't compare. My relationship with Bran was...intense. From the moment we met and every day since, Bran and I have been a spark.

"I don't want us to be secret fuck buddies anymore," I whispered, my fingers playing with the hair at the nape of his neck.

A smile played at the edge of his lips. "You still thought that's what we were?"

"We haven't exactly defined it as anything else."

"Well, let me make one thing very clear." He bowed his head and playfully bit my collarbone. "You are one hundred per cent"—he took a hold of my breast, sucking to refresh the love bite he liked to keep there—"unequivocally"—he shifted and did the same to the other side —"irrefutably, mine."

I giggled, my hands going into his hair. "Is that so?"

"Mm-hmm." He took my mouth in his, breathing me in. He made me feel drunk and off balance. Like I didn't know which way was up. I always wanted more, loving and needing the way his arms kept me steady.

"I think that when we get back, we need to stop hiding," I whispered.

"I agree," he returned, running his nose alongside mine.

"There are people we should tell first. To try and lessen the damage. And I need to tell y—" My words were cut off as his mouth sealed over mine, his hands moving over my body arousing me. It was getting hard to focus.

"Shh," he whispered, his hand cupping between my legs. "There's only an hour till we have to check out. We'll figure out the rest later." The moment his fingers found their way inside, I quit thinking and surrendered to his delectable control.

When we arrived home, the cab dropped me off outside my apartment and waited while Bran said goodbye. We were spending a rare night apart while he caught up on his studies before exams.

We still hadn't had that conversation about telling his father about our relationship, or the one where I told him I was in the middle of a divorce. Each time I tried, he silenced me with a kiss or changed the subject. Admittedly, it was kind of odd. I knew why *I* didn't want to talk about Jack, but why was *he* so against any sort of conversation relating to his father? Adrian's reaction to our relationship was the top reason on the list of why we'd kept things quiet for so long. And honestly, I *wanted* to talk it all out. It was playing on my mind. The fact I hadn't mentioned Jack to him in the four months we'd been together was beginning to feel duplicitous. It was fine at the start, because I never thought we'd last this long or fall this deep. But now that we had...I needed to get it off my chest.

But how was he going to react?

I was afraid he'd flip out. And for that reason, I decided it best to wait. I would call my attorney the next morning and find out if she'd had any success quashing the use of the information gathered in that folder. At least if she'd managed that, it would give me until after Bran's exams to lay it all on the table. That seemed a less stressful timeline; I'd never forgive myself if he reacted badly then failed his semester. No. It really was best to wait...

"Tomorrow's your birthday, right?" he asked, leaning against the cab as he brushed my hair back from my face.

"How'd you know that?"

He grinned. "I have my ways."

"That memory of yours, huh?"

"That, and Nick was collecting money to get you something from all the juniors."

"Oh, did you put in?"

"Of course." He pressed a soft kiss to my lips and I sighed.

"The big three-oh. I was kind of hoping to pretend it wasn't happening."

"No. You should celebrate. Let me take you out to dinner." His fingers brushed lightly along my jawline.

I tilted my head a little to the side, my overactive mind still analysing every nuance of our relationship and questioning it. "How do you afford this stuff? The internship doesn't pay and I can't imagine your father being OK with you paying more than your fair share in Queensland..." The question had been playing on my mind for some time. He lived in a hotel and never seemed short of money when it came to living his life. I'd barely paid for food since we started seeing each other. Now, he was happily standing outside a cab with its meter running without any regard for the mounting price.

He laughed and ran his thumb lightly against my cheek. "You're really taking this girlfriend thing seriously, huh? Already questioning me." There wasn't an ounce of annoyance in his voice, and I had to admit to getting a little flutter in my stomach when he said the word 'girlfriend'. He seemed genuinely mirthful when he dropped a kiss on the end of my nose. "Relax, baby. I come from a long line of powerful men." The last sentence was said in a mocking voice that I assumed mimicked his father. "It means I'm a trust fund kid."

"I see. Then why did your father make you move back down here? Not that I'm complaining, we wouldn't have met otherwise. But, if you have your own money, why does he have any control over you?"

"I imagine you're an amazing solicitor. And you'll make an even better barrister."

"I'm being serious, Bran."

"So am I. You're the most amazing woman I've ever met."

"That doesn't answer my question." I folded my arms in front of me.

"I'm the beneficiary and he's the trustee. It's my money but he has control until I'm twenty-one. Is that enough information for you, counsellor?"

"I'm sorry. I've just been feeling funny about my boss inadvertently paying to date me. I'm trying the make sense of all this before we're public knowledge."

Pulling at my folded arms to loosen them, he took a hold of my hands. "Then you should have asked sooner. I won't lie to you, Cora. Lying is kind of a deal-breaker for me."

My heart kicked up a beat. I understood why he'd feel that way. Being in the dark side of a deceitful relationship had made me far less trusting than I normally was. What happened to him for it to be his number-one deal-breaker?

At the same time, the comment made me even more nervous over telling him about Jack. Would he consider *not* telling him something as a lie? Surely not.

I placed my hands on his chest and leaned in. "It's a deal-breaker for me too. Pick me up tomorrow at seven?" I already knew he wouldn't be in the office all day because of his exams.

He grinned, pulling me a little closer by gripping my arse. "I'm going to parade you around and show the whole city that you're mine, mine, mine."

"We're really going to do this in the open now?"

"Well, I'm not going to fuck you in the open. I'm far too selfish to share that experience with the rest of the world…"

Slapping him against the chest, I laughed. "I'm being serious. You don't want to wait until we've spoken to your father? Maybe I'll see him tomorrow and lay this on the table."

"*No,*" he said emphatically. "You do *not* want to do that. It's better if I talk to him myself."

"When?"

"After exams. Just, quit worrying, OK? Everything will be fine. I'm sure about us."

"OK," I said, releasing my breath. I wasn't comfortable prolonging things, but felt somewhat appeased knowing there was a plan in place.

He kissed me gently. "Now get out of here before I change my mind about having a University education and follow you upstairs."

"Till tomorrow then," I said biting my lip.

Using his thumb, he pulled it free, desire in his eyes. "Until tomorrow."

28

WALKING BACK into work after a long weekend was always a depressing endeavour, especially when that long weekend was spent lounging in the sunshine of the Gold Coast. I already wanted to go back.

"I'm so glad to be going back to work," Olivia said, practically rushing to hug the building. Her demeanour was so contrary to mine. "I'm so over agonising and telling Paul that I don't want to get married. That man doesn't seem to understand that it is no longer the 1950s, and I'm quite capable of having this kid on my own."

"Maybe he's in love with you," I suggested as we stepped through the entry doors.

"He thinks he is. But he's too young to know what he's talking about."

"He's older than Bran and Bran seems very clear about what he's feeling."

Her eyes went wide. "You two are getting serious?" she asked in a hushed tone. "Does he know about a certain someone with the name starting with J and ending in arse?"

"Not yet. We're going to get everything out in the open next week when his exams are over. He'll talk to the director and everything will be fine." I shrugged. "We're not technically doing anything wrong. We just have to be careful about how we come out."

"Jesus, Cora." She abruptly stopped walking and when I turned to face her, she had her hands folded across her chest and was shaking her head. "You know what? It's your birthday. I don't want to call you names and be responsible for ruining your day. So I'm going to reserve my comments about this for another day. Today, however, I'm going to take you out to lunch and feed you as many calories as I can. You look so gorgeous and tan that I can see you wasting away before my eyes."

"You should take a trip up to Queensland. It's so relaxing. Take Paul."

"Paul is *not* a relaxing man right now." Obviously not wanting to talk more about him, Olivia sighed and headed for the security door to swipe us in. "I'll see you at lunch," she said over her shoulder, and I smiled to myself as I waved her off.

I was only a few steps into my section of the office when the word 'Surprise' was yelled and a red velvet cupcake was thrust in my face, with my team of junior solicitors crowding around me.

Penny grinned. "Happy birthday! It's fresh from Cupcake Central. We got enough for our whole team."

"Oh, guys," I gushed, my hand on my chest. "You really didn't need to do this."

"Sure we did," Nick said, reaching out to add a candle. "You put a lot of time into making us better solicitors. The least we can do is something special for your birthday." Holding out a lighter, he lit the candle. "Make a wish, boss."

With a smile so wide it felt like it was touching my ears, I closed my eyes and wished for the impending phone call with my attorney to go my way. Then I blew out the candle to applause. In that moment, there was nothing more I wanted. As long as Jack stayed away, today would be perfect. I was greeted with cake, my best friend was taking me to lunch, and my boyfriend was taking me to dinner, and without a doubt, would also treat me to more than one mind-blowing orgasm. What more could I possibly ask for?

"Thank you so much, guys. You don't know how much this means to me," I said, making eye contact with each of them.

"Wait, there's more," Nick said, signalling to one of the other guys to hand him something. His eyes glinted mischievously as he held something behind his back. "Since thirty is such a huge milestone, we all pitched in to make you a gift basket to help you in your new phase of life."

Laughing because I had a fair idea what was about to happen, I held my hands out for the basket. Inside were all things stereotypical for old ladies: a fold-up walking stick, fold-up reading glasses, a tub of Metamucil, Digestive biscuits, hankies and a packet of boiled lollies that were all stuck together.

"Very funny," I said after going through it to the tune

of their snickers. "I'll treasure it always." I flicked out the walking stick and used it to hobble toward my office while they laughed. Once inside, I saw that they'd also gotten me a large bunch of native flowers. I called out thank you to them, then dropped the basket onto the visitor's chair, looking at it with a smile. I was glad my juniors felt comfortable having a joke with me; I spent so much time tearing apart their work that I often worried they hated me. Obviously not.

The message alert went off on my phone, and I dug it out of my bag, smiling even wider when I saw Bran's name.

Bran: Happy birthday, baby. Check your top drawer.

With my bottom lip between my teeth, I wandered around to my side of the desk and pulled the handle. Inside was all my usual desk supplies, but on top of that was a burgundy box with a gold trim.

Me: You got me jewellery?

Taking a seat, I set the box on the desk in front of me and ran my hand over the soft fabric casing. You could tell a lot about a man by the jewellery he bought you. Men who paid close attention to their woman's tastes could pick beautiful pieces time and time again. Then there were men who chose pieces they liked without taking her preferences into account at all. Which one was Bran?

Bran: Put it on. Take a picture. I want to see you.

Opening the box slowly, I saw that Bran was a mixture of both—he'd chosen something that had meaning to the both of us. He'd given me a beautiful pearl necklace. Each pearl was small and delicate, the strand just long enough to rest against my collarbone.

Clipping it on, I held my phone and posed for a picture, my fingers touching the fine strand lightly. I smiled to the camera a very private smile, encapsulating the meaning behind such a gift and the intensity of my feelings toward him. He could turn me on and have me quivering at the snap of his fingers.

Sending the picture through, I added the caption...

Me: Thank you. I love it

Bran: I love the thought of you working all day with my pearl necklace wrapped around that pretty neck of yours.

He was doing it again, making me wet, aching for release, and it was barely past nine.

Me: I'll wear it for you tonight. Just the necklace.

Bran: And the blue shoes

I smiled.

Me: Deal. Good luck in your exam

Bran: xx

Hugging my phone against my chest, I sighed then

touched the necklace again. I loved it, loved that it gave me dirty thoughts about Bran. That man did things to me that I never imagined enjoying. This day was already better than I'd expected. I couldn't wait to see him later.

29

"THIS WHOLE NOT DRINKING FOR nine months thing is really screwing with my social life," Olivia scoffed, closing her menu and handing it to the waiter. She'd ordered soda water with a lime wedge so she could pretend it was a vodka lime and soda.

"I can *not* drink if it makes you feel better. I don't mind," I offered.

"No. It's your birthday, you get to drink and have fun." She sighed. "Fun. Are all my fun days behind me now? Am I going to turn into one of those women?" She nodded toward a table where two women sat with small children: one in a pram and the other old enough to sit at the table and eat. They were trying to carry on a conversation while holding pieces of food out for their children to eat. The baby slapped at his mother's hands and sent the food toppling to the floor.

"I don't know that being them is a bad thing," I said with a shrug. The baby giggled then wrapped his chubby hand around his mother's finger, trying to put it in his mouth. It was pretty adorable. "Kids are cute."

"I know. They're fucking adorable." She made a noise that sounded like she was disgusted with herself. "You know, Paul downloaded this app on his phone; it shows all the stages of development. Right now, at almost twenty-one weeks, the baby is as long as a carrot and she already has eyebrows."

"Wow. That *is* adorable." I loved seeing her smiling about the idea of her baby, loved the sparkle in her eye.

"Paul is totally into research, knows more about this process than I do. He's a scientist, you know, works at some big lab in the eastern suburbs doing forensic chemistry. I could have done worse for a father; he could have been beautiful but stupid. Now *that* would have been a worry. I do not want a stupid kid."

I laughed and reassured her she was going to be the greatest mum on earth. Our drinks were placed in front of us then we ordered our meals.

"Enough about my life, tell me about yours. You spent the weekend away with Bran and decided it was time to bring the relationship out in the open?" Olivia leaned forward on her hands as she spoke. "Things are getting serious."

I narrowed my eyes. "Are you judging me?"

"Not at all. I'm genuinely interested. You've spent the last eleven years of your life with fork-tongued Jack-Arse and now you seem...happy."

"I am happy." I smiled, reaching forward to take a sip of my wine, the cool crisp taste washing over my tongue. "In the beginning, all I could see were problems—his age, the fact

I'm his boss, how *my boss* would react, what effect that would have on my career..." Placing my glass on the table, I shook my head. "But the last week or two, I've started to realise that none of that matters as much as I thought it did. There's always a workaround. Honestly, Liv, I have *never* felt this good, never felt this wanted. I don't want to let go of that."

Looking at me with wise, assessing eyes, she took a breath then sat up straight in her chair. "You really didn't listen to a single bit of my advice on the single life, did you?" she teased. "You seem to be attracted to long-term relationships like moths are to flames."

"Says the woman who is pregnant and on the verge of closing the deal with husband number three."

"I am *not* marrying Paul. I need to set my limit some-where. He can move in. But, marriage needs to stay on the no pile."

"He's moving in?" I smiled, something about the way she spoke told me she didn't really mean it. I esti-mated that she and Paul would either marry just before the baby was born or shortly after. He would win her over.

She waved her hand dismissively. "He was always at my place anyway. It's silly paying rent on his own place when I have enough room."

"When Jack and I split, I really couldn't perceive a time when I'd even consider wanting to get married again, but I don't know"—I lifted my glass to my lips—"it could happen."

"You think you'd say yes if Mr Buns-of-Steel asked you?"

"Not yet. We don't know each other well enough. Plus, Jack and I aren't even divorced yet, so—"

"How are things going with Jack-Arse? Any progress in counselling?"

"He admitted to sleeping with nine women during the course of our relationship."

Her mouth dropped open. "*Nine?* Wow. How could he ever think you'd be on board the reconciliation train after that bomb hit it?" *This is why I loved Olivia. She totally got me.*

"Exactly. That's why he was holding the intervention order over my head, and why he tried to blackmail me when that stopped working."

"Blackmail how?"

"His lawyer had some PI following me. There's photographic proof of Bran and me together."

Her expression stayed calm while she took a sip of her soda water. "I'm guessing Bran doesn't know about this? Are you planning on telling him?"

"Yes. As soon as his exams are over. I don't want to upset the balance before he finishes."

"And what are you going to do if Jack uses that information before then?"

"My attorney issued a stop order threatening legal action. When I spoke to her earlier, she said the folder was delivered to her office this morning and he'd agreed not to use any of that information against me."

She narrowed her eyes. "What's the catch? Does he want more of the estate now? More counselling sessions?"

I shrugged. "Nothing yet, but time will tell. That man always has an angle. Personally, I'd rather he went chasing after some other woman. I'm obviously not enough for him."

"Don't ever talk about yourself that way. You're more than enough for any man. Jack-Arse is *not* a man. He's a piece of shit. From now on, make sure you tell him you're recording every interaction with him. If he slips up again, we'll slap his wrists so hard that his hands won't be capable of holding on to his dick for a wank." Just as the last syllable left her mouth, our food arrived.

"Actually, recording things is a good idea. I'll be sure to do that," I said when we were alone again.

Pulling a corner off the grilled sandwich in front of her, Olivia twisted it between her fingers thoughtfully. "You don't think Jack would try to hurt Bran, do you? I mean, the guy went to great lengths to try to make you desperate enough to take him back. Now that none of that has worked, *and* he's been legally blocked from doing anything to you, I worry Bran might become his next target."

I picked up my fork and poked at the melted cheese layer of my chicken. "What could he possibly do to hurt Bran? If he gives any information to Adrian, he's also acting against me. I don't see what he could do that would subvert the stop order."

"I don't know. I just know Jack isn't one to give up when he hasn't gotten his way. Remember that time we booked a cruise and he threw a tantrum until you agreed not to go?"

"How could I forget." The cruise had been for three days of pampering to reward ourselves after winning a massive case. He'd made my life hell, accusing me of not caring about him enough and calling me selfish, until I decided the girl time wasn't worth it and cancelled.

"I'm sorry, honey," she said, reaching across the table

to give my arm a squeeze. "It's these hormones. They're making me horribly moody and when I'm moody, I get really cynical. I just worry about you in the middle of all this. But, I'll stop, it's your birthday. We can worry about this stuff tomorrow."

"It's OK." I smiled as I compiled a mouthful of crumbed chicken, salad and chips. "Just know that there's a plan in place, and I'm feeling happier than I've ever been."

"Then we should toast," she said, holding up her glass. "To young men and turning thirty, may all your days be better than the ones before."

"Thank you," I said, tapping my glass against hers.

"Happy birthday, you gorgeous human being."

"Is this party just for two, or can anyone join in?" A familiar soft rumble filled my ear, just before he came into view.

"Bran!" I stood up and wrapped my arms around his neck.

"Happy birthday, baby." His arms engulfed me as he kissed with abandon, putting on quite a display.

"My God, you two. Get a room. I feel like I'm watching something smutty." Olivia was waving her hand at her face when we broke apart then mouthed to me 'so hot' when Bran turned around to grab a spare chair.

"How are you, Olivia?" he asked as he sat down.

"A little warm right after that display," she teased, taking a sip of her water.

Bran chuckled then glanced at me, his eyes dropping to my neck. "Nice necklace," he murmured, leaning close.

"Thank you." I blushed, pulling at it with my index finger. "My boyfriend gave it to me."

"He has great taste."

"He does actually," Olivia put in. "It really suits you. Well done, Bran." She smiled at him approvingly. "Do you want me to call the waiter over so you can get something to eat? My treat."

He shook his head. "No. I actually ate on campus after my exam. I have another one in about thirty minutes so I can't stay long. I just wanted to come and wish the birthday girl a happy day." Turning to me, he smiled then slipped his arm around the back of my chair, his thumb gently brushing back and forth against my shoulder. It made my stomach flip-flop like I was a teenager and the cutest boy in school just said hello to me.

"Two in one day? That's got to be hard," Olivia said between mouthfuls.

Bran shrugged. "I'm kind of glad to get them out of the way."

"Didn't it make it hard to study?"

He shook his head. "If I don't know the material after taking classes for the last semester, then cramming at the last minute isn't going to help me. I re-read all of my notes last night to refresh it all and that was it."

She narrowed her eyes a little. "I see, you're one of *those* kids."

Bran laughed, seeming to understand what I did not. "Yes, I am."

"Who are *those kids*?" I asked.

"The ones with excellent recall. They absorb and retain information without needing it repeated. That's why he doesn't really study, right?"

Bran nodded. "That's right."

That explained a lot. He always seemed to remember

minor details about me, like he was the curator of the encyclopaedia of Cora Knowles or something.

"So, what? You have a photographic memory?"

He chuckled. "No. It's nothing like that. It's just that if I pay attention to something, I absorb it then and there. Like, when someone gives me their phone number, I don't have to repeat it over and over to commit it to memory. I just remember it straight away."

"What are your grades like?" Olivia asked.

"High distinctions, mostly."

"Mostly?"

"I've ah, been a little distracted lately." He grinned at me.

"And what do you get when it isn't a high distinction?"

"A distinction."

My eyes grew huge. I'd never done *that* well at uni. I got more credits than I was willing to admit. I had to study really hard to be more than an average student.

"A mind like that is quite a talent to have, Brandon. Especially in our field of expertise. I expect you'll be vying for your father's job before he's even ready to retire." By the smile on Olivia's face, I knew Bran had impressed her. There were few people in this world who sparked her interest, and I was one of them. She loved finding uncut gems and turning them to precious stones. "I'll tell you what, when you're finished with your legal training, if you're interested in working towards becoming a barrister, I'd love to have you on my team."

Bran pressed his lips together then smiled. "I thank you for the opportunity, but I'll have to respectfully decline. I don't plan on following in Adrian Sharp's footsteps at all."

That was a surprise. I'd assumed a career at the OPP was the goal...

Olivia tilted her head to the side, regarding him. "But your family has such a long history in the public services. Wasn't your great grandfather the attorney general at one point?" Olivia seemed to know more about Bran's history than I did. I also found it odd that he'd called his father by his given name.

"That's right." Bran nodded.

"Then don't you want to continue that tradition? I mean, you're doing the degree and getting the experience as if you are... Are you playing some sort of game here?" Olivia asked, never one to shy away from a direct question.

"No games." Bran grinned then checked his watch. "I should go." He leaned close and pressed a kiss against the side of my head. "I'll pick you up at seven. Enjoy your lunch, ladies."

"That boy is hiding something. I'd bet a whole case of wine on it," Olivia said watching him walk away.

I felt a sigh leave my chest as I watched him go. I wanted to disagree, but I'd been thinking the same. *What was he hiding? And why?*

There was a lot more to Bran than met the eye.

30

THERE HAD BEEN times over the past few months where I'd wondered who was the more mature out of Bran and me. He was always so calm and collected, and I was the one with the flushed cheeks and the stupid smile on my face. Getting ready for him to take me out for my birthday dinner was no different.

I'd arrived home from work at six then rushed to the shower, stripping away my clothes and counting every second to being with him again. Somehow, I had become dependent on seeing him. My chest felt tight until that moment our eyes met and his smouldered. Then I could breathe.

As I primped and preened, I knew it was crazy that I was feeling this way so soon after Jack. He'd shattered my heart and trust to pieces and I had basically run straight into the arms of another man. Bran had been a welcome distraction in the beginning. He'd made what could have been a very lonely time full of self-discovery as he provided an environment where I felt safe exploring the limits of my desires. While I hadn't thought it would become what it was now, I was beyond glad that it had. He made me feel like I was getting the chance to start my life over again.

When a knock sounded at the door, I rushed to push my heels on and answer, taking an extra moment to readjust the girls so my cleavage was nice and high.

"Hello, lover," I drawled, doing my best Carrie Bradshaw impersonation as I swung the door wide.

Bran's eyes zeroed in on my chest, and by the carnal look in his eyes, it was as if a lust cloud had descended upon his shoulders. "Oh baby, I don't think we're going out tonight. You look good enough to eat." He gripped me around the waist, fingers pressing in as he pulled me against him while simultaneously walking us both through the doorway, kicking it closed behind him. He was already hard. So, so hard.

"Tempting," I breathed, seriously contemplating giving this whole dinner in public thing a miss, too. "But, I was looking forward to all the jealous stares when I stepped out with you tonight." Plus, I'd gone to a lot of trouble to apply my makeup and do my hair, not to mention the drama I underwent choosing my dress then squeezing into it. No, this was going to last longer than the two minutes since he walked in the door.

"All eyes will be on you. You look fucking gorgeous in that dress." My dress was a deep purple and form-fitting, with wide shoulders and a low neckline. I felt sexy in it when I put it on, but I felt drop-dead gorgeous with his reaction to it.

I laughed at his compliment, wondering if he had *any*

idea just how good he looked in a suit. It was lady-kryptonite.

"Then we'll make quite a pair. Give me a second to grab my bag," I said, stepping away from him.

"We're getting dessert to go, by the way. I'm going to feed it to you naked after you've wrapped those shiny red lips of yours around my cock."

I stopped and looked at him over my shoulder, grinning. This man really enjoyed his sweets. "I thought it was *my* birthday."

"You love deep-throating my cock and you know it," he teased, his mouth kicking up at the side.

Running my tongue seductively over my lips, I made a tiny noise of pleasure. "Mmm, you're right. I do."

He moaned. "Baby, I can't be a gentleman if you do things like that."

"Since when have you been a gentleman?"

"You're right, I'm not." Taking two strides, his mouth crashed against mine, hands gripping skin and searching for the zip on my dress. Like a human battering ram, he forced me backwards, using his body to guide me until the backs of my legs hit the foot of my bed. I felt the material loosen around my torso then, with a swift pull, my dress was a puddle of satiny material on the floor.

"On your back," he commanded, his hand pressing against my chest before he pushed, and I fell back.

Laughing as my body bounced, and Bran landed on top of me, I grabbed his thick hair, my fingers caressing his scalp, calming the fire just a touch. "We're going to miss our reservation," I whispered, pulling gently so his lips aligned with mine.

"It'll keep." His tongue slid across the seam of my lips. "I need my entrée. *Now*."

"I'm just one big buffet to you." I laughed.

"And I'll never be full." Humming contentedly as his hands roamed my body, teasing and squeezing, I gave up the fight and surrendered to his magnificent touch, glad that when he touched me, it was as my boyfriend and not my dirty little secret.

Twenty minutes later I was standing in front of the mirror reapplying my lipstick while Bran took a very long time fastening the zipper on my dress, his fingers caressing my skin while his beguiling eyes focused on my lipstick application.

"The red suits you," he said, running his fingers down the length of my hair. He wound it around his hand and held it against the nape of my neck, his mouth close to my ear. "Red lips, high heels and your hair up tight—sexy as fuck."

"You sure you don't want me to wear a pair of spectacles as well? Complete the whole librarian fantasy for you?"

He released my hair and I felt it tumble down and loosen before sweeping across my back. "I wouldn't say no, but it's not librarians I'm into." Both of his hands slapped against my arse cheeks and squeezed. "I'm into curvy brunettes. One very particular curvy brunette." He squeezed a little tighter and I gasped. "Finish getting ready." He relaxed his grip and gently palmed my arse instead. "I'll call the restaurant."

I nodded, my eyes shining as I looked at him via the mirror. He was so beautiful, so intense. It was hard to believe he was so young. It was even harder to imagine how I was lucky enough that he was all mine.

When he left the room, I finished up then pressed my lips together, sighing contentedly. I couldn't remember a time when my birthday had been this wonderful.

31

"YOU'RE FREAKING OUT, aren't you?" Bran looked amused as he cut off a mouthful of steak, and slipped it past his lips. I could see the muscles in his jaw working as he chewed, grinning at me from his seat in the crowded San Telmo steakhouse. Walking through the door was like stepping from the streets of Melbourne and into Buenos Aires, with meat dry-ageing behind glass at the entrance, and a massive open kitchen complete with a dangerous-looking coal pit in the middle. It was a spectacular place, and for a woman who loved steak almost as much as she loved chocolate, it was the perfect choice for a birthday meal.

"I'm not freaking out. I just feel like people are looking at us," I replied, glancing around the restaurant.

"Of course they're looking. You know how gorgeous you look tonight."

His comment made me smile. "That's not why they're looking and you know it."

"Do I?" One of his eyes narrowed slightly, and I knew

he was going to make me voice my concerns out loud. I also knew he'd think I was being ridiculous. It was times like these I wish I had Olivia's confidence.

"It's obvious that I'm way older than you."

"No. It's obvious that that guy over there is way older than *his* date." I followed his gaze, noting that the couple he indicated could have been easily mistaken for father and daughter if it wasn't for the fact they were holding hands across the table. "*You* are being paranoid." He cut off some more eye fillet and held it out to me. "Just relax and enjoy yourself, the same way you did in the Gold Coast."

I took the morsel from his fork, the meat melting in my mouth as I chewed. My taste buds sang.

"It was different up there. No one knew us. Here, we're so used to sneaking around that it feels...I don't know, risky."

"Isn't this what we both agreed? Fuck the risks?"

I nodded. "It is, and I'm not getting cold feet, I'm just nervous about the repercussions and how this is going to work—how we'll be *perceived*. You have to admit that our situation is a little unusual. That over there"—I looked toward the couple he'd pointed out—"is somewhat normal. Turn the tables and it becomes a whole new thing. I mean, what happens when I'm fifty and I look it, and you're only forty and barely have creases around your eyes?"

He grinned.

"Why is that so funny?"

"I love that you're thinking long-term, baby."

"Well, I have to. I'm thirty now. This is the decade when young becomes old. When I start finding grey hairs and develop crow's feet, not to mention my fertility will take a dive. You're just at the beginning of your adulthood. And besides, ageing is different for men."

"I seriously don't give a fuck about any of that. I don't give a fuck what anyone thinks or feels when they look at us. I like you exactly as you are, and all I see when I look at you is the woman I love."

With the air stolen from my lungs, I stared at him, wide-eyed and blinking while I let his words sink in.

"You *love* me?"

He kept eating and nodded like it was any other conversation. "Yep." When he swallowed, he took a sip of wine and ran his tongue around his teeth.

"Since when?"

He shrugged. "Couple of months, I guess."

"You guess? Why didn't you tell me?"

"Because I knew you'd freak out like you are right now. But I figure you're already freaking out over stupid shit, I might as well give you something real to add to it."

"Well..." My cheeks felt hot as I tried to find the right words to say. *He loved me. My God, that felt wonderful.* This thing between us had been building and building behind the scenes, making it so we'd become the biggest priority in each other's lives. I even placed him above my career, and that was *huge* for me. But I was afraid of being hurt again, scared to embrace this new relationship when there was so much still to learn and sort through.

"Don't say it back," he said, his eyes growing serious. "Say it when you feel it, not as a response to me."

Knitting my brow, I nodded then piled food on my fork to fill my mouth so I didn't speak. Suddenly my mind was filled with every unspoken detail about me, things I should have told him way before the L word happened. Perhaps waiting until after his exams were over wasn't soon enough.

"Listen," he started, reaching across the table and covering my hand. "I get that you're worried about your job, and you're worried about our age difference and both of us wanting kids. And you're worried what all of it means now that we're making this relationship public knowledge. But I want you to know that I'm all in. I have never wanted a woman the way I want you. In the time we've been together, my feelings have done nothing but intensify. I need you in my life, Cora. All that other shit is just semantics to me."

With emotion pushing at my eyes I let out my breath. "Jesus, Bran. I love you too," I started, preparing myself to clear the air.

"You weren't supposed to say it yet." But he was smiling.

"Well, I wanted to. It's how I feel. However, I also feel there's still so much we need to talk about. *Before* we get any deeper."

He lifted my hand and pressed his lips to my knuckles. "It's too late, I'm centre-of-the-earth deep with you, baby."

My heart filled with the conviction in his words, and the honesty shining in his eyes. I wanted to be all in with him too. But I felt as though I was straddling two worlds. It felt so wrong to hide it from him now.

"There's something I need to tell you," I began, although only the first half of the sentence could be heard as the staff converged on our table, carrying a cake and singing happy birthday. "No, stop. I really need to say something." My words got lost in the sound as the entire restaurant joined in. Bran pulled out his phone to film the whole thing, and all I could do was laugh then look at Bran and smile.

"I love you. So much," I mouthed. I was ridiculously happy because of the effort this beautiful man had put in to make my night a special one, even though I simultaneously hated that our conversation had to wait. A few months ago, I thought I'd be commiserating my milestone, feeling hopeless and very alone. Yet here I was, in love with a man who not only said I was his world, but acted that way too. I felt truly blessed.

32

"LEAVE THE NECKLACE ON," Bran whispered, leaning against the doorway to my bedroom as I sat on the edge of the bed removing my earrings. The room was lit with soft lamplight, casting a gentle glow over his features.

"And the shoes?" I extended my leg to show him the electric-blue pumps he'd mentioned earlier.

"Fuck yeah. Those are staying on too."

"The hair?"

"Tie it up."

I smiled, twisting my locks into a bun. "And the rest?"

"Take it off, or I'll tear it off."

"Well then," I said, as I stood and reached my hand up the centre of my back, pulling at the zip to put on a bit of a show for him. "I suppose I'd better comply." Except the zipper stalled halfway and wouldn't budge. "Shit." I tugged and pulled, then looked over my shoulder at him, laughing. "I think I'm going to need a little help."

Coming up behind me, I felt his warm breath wash

over the back of my neck as his fingers stroked against my skin before he grabbed the zip and pulled. "It's stuck."

"Can you fix it?" I asked, my voice breathy because I was turned on from his touch.

"Of course." I felt his hands wrap around either side of the seam and pull. The slider popped and shot off into the room somewhere. I gasped as the fabric released. But he didn't stop there, he kept on pulling, the tearing of fabric, punctuating the quiet of the room as the dress fell from my body.

"That was one of my favourite dresses," I whispered as his fingers slid beneath the band of my bra and released the clasp.

He pressed his teeth against my shoulder. "I'll buy you one with a working zip."

Spinning me in his arms, he palmed my breasts. "Fuck, I love these."

I grinned. "So you keep telling me."

His eyes met mine, one side of his mouth curved upward. "I love you more though."

I wrapped my arms around his neck. "I like hearing you say that," I whispered against his mouth, swimming in need as his tongue sought entry, and his lips sealed over mine. Lifting my legs, I wrapped my thighs around his waist crossing my legs at the ankles.

Grabbing my arse, he stepped back and sat on the bed, making it so his hard cock was pressing against my core. I rocked my hips over his length, taking control of the kiss from my advantageous position.

Wanting skin against skin, I worked at the buttons on his shirt, pushing it off his shoulders until all I could feel was hard skin. "Have I told you how much I love *your* chest?" I whispered, pushing him back on the bed so I was straddling his waist.

"I recall something about delectable abs." He smiled, his hands resting against my hips.

Lowering down, I ran my tongue down the line between his pecs. "The whole thing is delectable."

Sliding off his lap, I lowered myself to the floor, resting on my knees in front of him. With my bottom lip pulled between my teeth, I smiled up at him and slid his belt open before working on his button and fly. "Lift," I instructed, holding the waist then pulling his pants and boxers down. His cock sprang free, standing proudly before me, the tip of it glistening. "Has anyone ever told you that you have a beautiful cock?" I asked, taking it in my hands and stroking its length.

He groaned softly, resting on his elbows so he could watch me. "No one that matters."

I grinned. "Good answer."

Flicking my tongue across the tip, I tasted his salt, could smell his skin. My desire pooled between my legs as I looked up and met his eyes, so dark and wanting.

"Suck it," he commanded.

Loving the way he took control, I slid my lips over his smooth head, using my tongue to tease the sensitive ridge. He hissed through his teeth, his fingers spearing into my hair and gripping from the roots. "Deeper."

With one hand wrapped around his base, I drew him deeper into my mouth, taking his mass as far as I possibly could. His hips moved as he began to lose himself, his other hand gripping my hair as he pushed a little deeper, fucked a little harder. My eyes watered and the roots of my hair stung, but the feeling of him coming undone in my mouth, the sounds of him hissing and trying to hold on was enough to drive me forward, sucking a little harder, swallowing a little deeper.

"Fuck, Cora," he hissed, his head dropping back. "I'm going to come in your mouth if you don't stop."

I didn't want to stop. I wrapped my free hand around his wrist and held on tight, keeping my head bobbing back and forth as he lay back and groaned. "*Fuck.*" A spurt of hot cum erupted from his tip, and I swallowed it down, pumping my hand up and down his length until I'd milked him dry. Slowly, he relaxed his fingers, releasing my hair, the ache of his grip throbbing gently. "Get the fuck up here," he demanded, reaching down and lifting me until I was beside him on the bed.

He sat back and pulled my panties down my legs and tossed them over his shoulder. Then he climbed over me, his hands wrapping around my wrists, pinning me down. His knees nudged open the space between my thighs. "I told myself I was going to be gentle with you tonight," he whispered, running his mouth across my cheek. "Told myself that tonight was special and we should be making love. But all I want to do is hold you down and fuck you until you bruise."

I gasped and opened my thighs even wider.

"You'd like that, would you? You like it hard?"

"I love it hard."

Adjusting his hips, he aligned himself with my opening, driving inside until our pelvic bones collided. Then he pulled back and did it again, each thrust a little deeper, a little harder, a little faster. I called out, my fists balled as he pressed my wrists into the mattress. Not being able to touch him as I watched his body enter mine was sweet torture. I could do nothing but surrender and moan.

"Bran." I spoke his name as my climax built, the only word I was capable of saying when he filled me so completely.

Releasing my wrists, his hands went to my hips as he tucked his knees beneath him, lifting me off the bed so his cock was hitting my insides at an angle that made my eyes lose focus and a guttural moan escape my throat.

"Ohhh."

"That's it, baby," he gasped, out of breath from his ferocious pumping. "Let it go. Squeeze my cock while you come."

"Ohhh." It was all I could say. The intensity of my burgeoning orgasm meant that my mind and my mouth could not connect.

"Let go," he urged, thrusting once more. Then it happened, my hands slapped down against his thighs and my fingernails bit into flesh as my entire body rocked, a long, low moan rolling out of my depths as he held me tight against his base, his cock pulsing within my walls.

The moment I could breathe, my hands went to my head and I let out a gasp. "Holy shit."

"Good?" He grinned, placing his hand on my chest then dragging it lightly down my body.

"Amazing."

Keeping himself inside me, he leaned down and touched his mouth to mine. "I love you, baby. Happy birthday."

Wrapping my arms around his shoulders, I whispered in return. "I love you, too." Then he kissed me, slow, gentle, controlled, the intensity of his emotion clear with each gentle stroke of his tongue. His hips shifted, his length languidly stroking at my insides, showing me the gentle love he'd intended. Each tender movement, every delicate touch, felt like it lit a spark on the ends of my nerves that travelled down and set my soul on fire. I loved him, knew that there was no living without him. He'd come into my life and taken over so completely, so wonderfully, that he'd completed me and made me whole. I was a better woman when I was with him.

We took our time, each deliberate movement held a promise of our future. When we finally reached our climax, the emotion of it brought tears to my eyes. Gasping for air, I held on tight, breathing him in, knowing that in him, I'd found my forever. Once everything was out in the open, I knew we'd still make it.

33

"I KIND OF like having him come in to work with us," Olivia mused, standing to the side with me while Bran lined up for our coffee.

"I quite like it too," I replied, having thoroughly enjoyed having his arms wrapped around me all morning. It was nice getting ready for work together and not having to arrive separately. After all the declarations of love the night before, Bran had decided that he didn't want to wait until after exams; he would talk to Adrian today. I was both nervous and excited by the prospect, because it meant with everything in the open, Jack couldn't hurt us. I just hoped I'd still have a job at the end of the day. But if it came down to it, I was willing to make the sacrifice and find a job in the private sector instead. Once Adrian knew, I felt we could truly move forward, and to do that, absolutely everything needed to be laid out on the table. We both deserved the truth and had earned that respect. Everything would be perfect after that.

Perfect. My eyes drank him in. The giant man who was all mine. *I loved him. He loved me.* I felt like I could burst.

"Well, the PDA is a little over the top," Olivia pointed out. "And we can't gossip quite as much. But, I do enjoy a man who fetches my coffee in the morning."

"Even though it's decaf?" I asked, earning me an eye-roll because she'd given up alcohol, coffee and cigarettes for the sake of the baby.

"Yes, even though it's—oh shit." Her eyes grew as she stared over my shoulder.

"What?" I asked, about to turn around when a voice I despised entered my ears.

"Happy birthday for yesterday, Cor."

Jack.

Fuck.

This is not happening. Not now. Not yet.

I touched my hand against my forehead and glanced over at Bran, who was thankfully busy paying for the coffee. This was not a meeting I wanted to happen before this day was through. I knew that if Bran found out about Jack this way, he'd feel like he was part of an affair. He would *hate* that. He would hate *me* for that. I couldn't let that happen.

My chest went tight as panic set in. I needed to get Jack out of there. I had no idea if he'd spotted Bran, and I hoped to God he hadn't come here looking to cause a scene.

"Thank you, Jack," I replied, facing him with a saccharine smile on my face, my heart beating wildly as my mind rushed to find a way to avoid the imminent catastrophe. "But we're right outside the Supreme Court here, do you think you can leave so I don't get accused of breaking *your* intervention order?"

"I'll tell them it was me," he argued.

"That fact doesn't matter to the courts, Jack," Olivia inserted. "You put the order in place, and from what I've heard, you keep breaking it and putting Cora in further risk of losing her legal license entirely. If you care about her at all, you'll turn around and walk away right now. In fact"—she dug around in her bag and pulled out her phone—"I'm going to record this entire conversation so there's proof of anything you say here."

"Recordings aren't admissible," he countered.

"They are if all parties are aware they're being record-ed." She held her phone out, showing the voice recorder function to prove her point.

Jack didn't seem fazed. "I can wish my wife a happy birthday if I want to, Olivia. Besides, I came here to give her a gift." Turning his attention back to me, he held up a large mustard-coloured envelope.

"What is this?" I asked, snatching it from his hand and tearing it open. I half expected it to be a summons of some sort, but you couldn't serve those yourself or they were invalid. I was at a loss.

He waited in front of me, a shit-eating grin on his face as he watched for my reaction. When I saw the words written in front of me, I almost couldn't believe it. "You had the order revoked?"

"There's no danger in talking to me anymore." He held out his hands, a supplicating gesture. "I'm a changed man, Cor. I'd do anything for you." Reaching up, he brushed the backs of his knuckles along my cheek. The movement was too intimate and caused me to flinch away while at the same time, Jack's hand was caught mid-air. The world felt as though it was moving in slow motion. Olivia's eyes went wide and she took a step back, grabbing my wrist to pull me along with her. At the same time, I turned, my stomach souring with the knowledge that something so horribly dreadful was playing out beside me.

"She's not yours to touch," Bran growled, his eyes dark and stormy as he stood over Jack.

Shit, shit, shit.

"Bran," I called out, wanting him to turn his attention to me so I could explain. But, the moment Jack's lips curved into a smile, my head started moving—shaking—because I knew what was about to happen.

And I couldn't stop it.

My boyfriend was about to meet my husband.

No no no no no no.

"Not sure who you think you are, mate, but since I'm her husband, I'm pretty sure that's exactly what I'm allowed to do."

Bran shifted backward, the words tipping him off centre like a hard kick in the gut. His eyes spoke volumes as they connected with mine. I could see hurt and betrayal. "Your *husband*?" The question left his mouth through gritted teeth.

Pleading with my eyes for him to understand, I opened my mouth to answer, to explain to him what was going on. But the words I needed didn't make it out of my throat when Jack took the opportunity to dig the heel in a little deeper.

"That's right, kid. You're nothing but her plaything on the side. Run along so the grownups can chat."

For a split second, Bran looked crushed, then a hurricane of fury stormed within his eyes, twisting his expression.

Oh God. "Bran! No!" I reached out futilely as his arm cocked back and his tightly coiled fist collided with the side of Jack's head, dropping him immediately.

"*Fuck,*" Bran yelled, picking Jack up and punching him again. His cheek split open and blood poured from the wound.

"Shit!" I dropped to my knees beside Jack, checking he was still breathing before I turned my attention back to Bran. "Are you *insane*?" He wasn't even there. "Bran! Where did he go?" I asked, my eyes darting around.

"He went that way," Olivia said, pointing up the street. I moved to run but stopped and looked back at Jack moaning on the ground.

"Should we call an ambulance?" I kind of had a duty of care to make sure he was OK.

Olivia pushed my shoulder. "Go after him," she urged. "I'll make sure Jack-Arse is OK."

"Thank you," I gasped, turning tail to run down the street after Bran. Due to his size, he wasn't hard to spot. But he was walking so fast, and running in heels wasn't the easiest thing to do. When he turned the corner, I almost lost him, but was thankful when a set of lights slowed his pace as he waited for the pedestrian walk sign to stop the peak-hour traffic.

"Bran. Wait. *Please.*" I sucked in air between words—I wasn't fit enough to be running through the streets—my hand gripping the back of his arm.

He shook my hand free, giving me a cold stare. "I don't date married women." Then the light changed and he crossed with the crowd, weaving through people to place obstacles between us.

Following as close as I could, I bumped into bodies and tripped over uneven pavement until I fell into step beside him again.

"You don't understand. We're not together anymore. I'm getting a divorce."

He didn't slow his step at all, causing me to jog in order to keep up. "Is he aware of that?"

"Yes! We've been over for months."

He stopped and whirled around to face me. "Then why the fuck am I finding out about him when he's touching your face like he's about to fucking *kiss* you?"

"I wasn't going to let him," I shot back.

"He shouldn't be touching you. There shouldn't be a fucking husband at all, Cora," he bellowed. "I *don't share*. Another man thinking he has the fucking right to touch the skin that I claimed as mine is a *huge fucking problem*."

He moved to storm off, but I grabbed his arm with both hands and held on for dear life. "Please, Bran. Just listen to me. It's a misunderstanding we can sort out. Let's go somewhere and talk."

"A misunderstanding?" There was a slight sneer pulling at the corner of his mouth, making me uncomfortable.

"Yes!"

He lowered his face so it was just above mine, almost too close for me to be able to focus on his features. "Are you married, Cora?"

"I'm separated."

"It's a yes or no question."

"*I'm separated.*"

"Yes, or no."

Looking up at him, my eyes burned as I clenched my jaw tight and forced out the answer he wanted. "Yes."

"Then I understand completely."

When he took one step away from me, blind panic gripped my heart and I launched myself in his direction, wrapping my entire body around his middle. Had I been in my right mind, I'd have seen it for the ridiculous and childishly desperate move it was, but I had this horrible feeling that if I let him walk away, I may never see him again.

"Let go, Cora," he said, his voice calm but hard as he stood in place.

I shook my head, my face pressed against his broad back. "Not until you talk to me."

"There's nothing to say."

"Maybe not for you, but I at least deserve the opportunity to explain."

I felt his chest fill then release. Then his hands wrapped around my forearms and he prised my grip loose. I fought against him, crying when I felt my grip loosen, yelling *no* when he held me at arm's length.

"Please," I begged, crying openly, knowing that the passers-by probably saw me as a mad woman.

His jaw ticked and his eyes stormed—like the sky before hail—as he glared at my pitiful form. Then his hand wrapped around my arm. With a grunt, he tugged me in the opposite direction and started walking with purposeful strides.

"Where are we going?" I had a moment where I feared a repeat of the stripper performance and planted my feet.

"You want to talk. Let's talk," he shot over his shoulder, pulling me under an awning and through a set of double glass doors. On the wall, the words, 'Best Western Atlantis'. *A hotel?*

Stalking toward the front desk, he pulled his wallet from his inside jacket pocket and flicked his credit card at the receptionist. "I need a room," he grunted.

The girl's face creased with concern as her eyes moved to me, taking in my tear-stained face and the strong grip of his hand wrapped around my arm. "Are you all right, ma'am?"

Straightening, I tried to look as calm as I could despite the state of my mind. "I'm fine. We just need a room, please." I smiled to try and reassure her, but her wary eyes just moved between Bran and me.

"Now," Bran added.

"Do you have a reservation?"

"No. But any will do. We won't be there for long."

"We don't rent rooms by the hour, sir."

Bran took a calming breath then relaxed his grip on my arm. "I'm not asking for you to charge me for an hour, I'm simply asking for any room that's available right now. I'll pay for a week if that's what you'd like. As long as you can give me a key so we can have a little privacy, I'll pay you anything you want."

"Do you want a room for a full week?"

He smiled, even though his eyes closed in frustration. "No. I just want whatever is available right now. You can charge me whatever you want."

"It'll be for a minimum of one night's stay."

"That's fine." He pointed to the credit card he'd already given her, and they went through the process of booking a room. The moment the key card was placed in his hand, his grip on my arm tightened and he pulled me toward the lifts.

Unlike the last times we were in a hotel together, there was no sexual tension filling the small space, no excitement, no desire. There was tension, sure, but it was the angry, world-destroying kind. This was what I hadn't wanted. Bran, at his core, was a caveman. I loved that about him, loved the way that animalistic aggression made me feel. Truthfully, every time opportunities to talk were blocked, I'd been secretly relieved. And that, combined with knowingly deceiving him, was what had me so agitated now. And terrified. I loved this man, and the idea of hurting him tore at my heart.

I should have told him sooner...

The moment we entered the room, he released my arm, the absence of his grip a relief and a disappointment simultaneously. It ached where his hand had been, the throbbing syncing with my frightened heartbeat. *This can't be the end.*

Standing with my back against the closed door, I watched him walk into the room, removing his jacket and loosening his tie. He threw it on the end of one of the two queen-sized beds dominating the room, then stalked toward the small window that overlooked another large building, his hands tucked into his pockets, his back facing me.

"Speak," he commanded.

"I'm so sorry you found out that way," I started moving farther into the room. "I was going to tell you. I just—"

"*When*?" he bellowed, turning to face me.

I jumped at the timbre of his voice, closing my eyes for a moment to try and find my bearings. "Tonight. I've been trying to tell you. I even tried to tell you last night, but...we got interrupted... Then it didn't seem the right time."

"Any time over the past few months would have been a perfect time to tell me."

"I didn't tell you in the beginning because I didn't know how serious we were. This was just supposed to be a fling—a dirty little secret. Those were *your* words."

"So this is my fault now?"

"No. It's not your fault at all. I'm just trying to explain. We hooked up *three months* after Jack and I split. Our marriage was *over*."

"That's his name? Jack?"

I nodded. "I caught him fucking some woman he worked with."

"He's the cheater? So, what was I? Your revenge fuck?"

"No! I don't know. Maybe in the beginning. That very first night, I suppose I was out there trying to get back at him. But then I met you, and it wasn't like that at all. It was all about you and this crazy connection we have."

"Why didn't you tell me after we started seeing each other?"

"Because I thought it would go away."

"Your marriage?"

"No. Our connection. You're so young and beautiful, and well...I'm not either of those things anymore. I thought you'd get bored with me and find someone who was more suited to you—someone your age and your equal."

His eyes flashed and his jaw clenched just before he shook his head. "That's a bullshit statement."

"It's how I felt, Bran. I didn't know what you saw in me. I didn't know that that feeling was only going to grow and intensify. I'd never met someone like you before, never felt this strong about someone. I'd only ever dated Jack. I came to you completely clueless."

"But you didn't come to me as a single woman."

"Technically, no. But you never shared me—I promise you that. The moment I walked out on him was the end of our relationship. We were broken up when you and I met. The moment our one year of separation is up, we'll be divorced. I have an attorney working on it. Call her if you want." I reached for my bag to grab my phone but dropped the whole thing on the floor when he advanced on me.

Taking a hold of my upper arms, his touch seared my skin as he met my eyes, studying me intently like he could see the lies and truth in my irises. "Those times when you came to me upset, it was because of him, right?"

My eyes stinging from the memory, I nodded. "I came to you because I needed *you*. You made everything feel right again."

"Those were the times you should have told me what was going on." He released his hold. "Instead, you hid the truth, kept the knowledge of your marriage up here." He tapped a finger to my forehead. "While you wormed your way into here"—he tapped against his chest above his heart—"with *lies*."

I shook my head. "I didn't lie," I whispered, feeling my tears fall and glide down my cheeks.

"Then why are you crying?"

My mouth opened then closed, wordless. He was right. Omitting the truth is the same as lying. I should have been honest from the start, should have told him so many times before we got to this moment. With a shake of his head, he stepped away. He looked...disgusted. Then he turned to the window, raking his fingers through his hair.

"I think you should go," he said, his voice cold and unfeeling.

"No, Bran. Please. Please understand. It's you. It's only you."

"How often did you see him?"

"Excuse me?"

He turned to face me. "While we've been dating, how many times did you see your husband?"

"I..." I knew the number, knew the amount of times I went somewhere without telling him. I'd convinced myself that I was protecting him when really I was just protecting myself from the truth. Bran and I were having an affair. I was a married woman and he was the lover I hid from the world.

"How many times?" he repeated through his teeth.

"Every second Wednesday, sometimes more..."

"What were you doing with him?"

"I never slept with him," I said quickly.

"Answer the question." There was something about the way he spoke, something that was resonating deep inside my bones. He was asking me the things I'd been asking Jack—the questions of a person who felt betrayed by the person they loved.

Closing my eyes, I took a deep breath. He deserved

the truth. Full disclosure. "I met him for lunch just after you and I began seeing each other. That legal trouble I told you about? He took an intervention order out against me after I knocked him unconscious the day I found him mid-coitus with the accountant from his work. I hit him over the head with my laptop and an ambulance was called when he wouldn't wake up. That was the reason I met him. I wanted him to revoke the order so I could work as a solicitor advocate again. He used the order to make me go to marriage counselling with him. Every fortnight on Wednesday afternoon, we met at our counsellor's office and discussed what went wrong in our relationship—namely his *nine* affairs over the course of eleven years. I quit going when I realised he had no intention of revoking the order. That time I met you after class crying? That was when I found out how *many* women there had been. I told him I was done with all of his bullshit. I'd rather spend a year working as the junior advisor than spend another moment in his company, another moment where I felt as though I was deceiving you. The next morning, he messaged me asking who you were. So I left while you were still sleeping and met him at a café where he showed me a surveillance folder with pictures of you and me together. He wanted to use it to blackmail me into leaving you and giving him another chance. It had information about you and that woman you dated in Queensland—the one you almost got kicked out of school over." Bran's jaw tightened. "Yeah, I knew about that. But I let you keep your past a secret. I figured we'd have plenty of time to dig through the dirt in each other's past, because I told him to shove his blackmail plot up his arse. I'd rather lose my job than lose you. It was the moment I realised that you were more important to me than anything else in my life. It was the moment I realised I was in love with you."

"You love me," he stated, leaning his body weight against the windowsill.

"You know I do. More than my job, more than my dignity, more than myself."

"Just not enough for the truth."

My heart stilled. This wasn't working. "I'm telling you now."

"Now is too late."

I moved closer to him. I could feel the tension radiating off his body as I reached for him hesitantly, but I pushed through my nerves, placing my hand against the curve of his shoulder. He shook me off.

"Please, Bran. Don't do this to us." I touched his hand, taking it in both of mine, and for a moment, I thought it might be OK as he stared at our joined fingers. I lifted his palm and pressed it against my cheek, kissing its centre. "Please. I love you so much. Don't let this be it."

The apple of his throat bobbed before he spoke. This time, his voice was much softer, his gaze more intense as he stared at his hand held in mine. "Have you wondered why I don't look like my father?"

The moment the words left his lips, my heart fell and I released his hand, slumping my weight against the wall beside him. "He's not your dad," I whispered, suddenly understanding exactly why he'd reacted so vehemently to today's revelations, why he was so dead-set against lying.

"My mother had a penchant for sleeping with the help."

"That isn't what this is," I assured him, trying to take

his hand again. I needed him to understand that. "You are so much more to me than—"

"Than a dirty fuck?"

I shook my head. "*No.* That was *not* what I was going to say."

"My entire life, I've been forced to be a part of a lie, forced to pretend I'm a Sharp and act as though I'm my father's real son while being constantly reminded what a disappointment I am to the name. But it's not *my name.* I don't even know what my name is." My heart went out to him, living with a secret that felt that huge must have been horrible for him. "I made a mistake when I agreed to be your secret too. I did it because I wanted you, wanted you so much that I was willing to do whatever it took to have you—as long as you were *mine.* But even that was a lie, because like me, you bear the name of another man. You were never mine to take. You're still *his.*"

"I don't belong to Jack. I never gave myself to him like I have to you." Lifting his hand, I placed it against my chest, holding it over my heart. "You own me, Bran. Body, mind and soul. I'm yours."

He wouldn't look at me, kept his eyes downcast and his hand limp and unparticipating in the touch. But his chest heaved with the struggle to stay that way. Even angry, I knew he still wanted me, craved me in the same way I craved him. I couldn't let this end here, couldn't let him push me away when what we had surpassed any sort of feeling known to exist. Love was a feeling, something that grew until it wrapped around you in a blanket of comfortable warmth. But this, this thing I had with Bran, it was even more than that. It was an urge, an instinct, a *necessity.* If one had to live without the other, I feared we'd become like a flower without sun, withering away.

Taking a sobering breath, he removed his hand. "And still, you were sneaking off to work on your relationship with another man."

"No. I went to counselling to get rid of the intervention order."

"But he thought you might, right? A man doesn't sit in a counsellor's office or touch the side of his estranged wife's face if he doesn't think he's getting somewhere."

"I kept telling him no," I whispered, knowing that the very fact that I kept showing up had offered him hope. "I'm sorry, Bran."

He turned away. "I can't trust you anymore."

A sob escaped my lips as I covered my face, trying to regain control over my emotions. Then I stepped closer to him, pressing my face against the shirt on his back, breathing him in. "Please understand. I'm yours, Bran. I'm yours."

He turned to face me, searching my eyes as I lifted my hand and touched his cheek, running the tips of my fingers over his skin. "I'm yours," I repeated, tilting my head upward, my lips brushing lightly along his jaw. I could hear his breathing changing, feel the quiver of his desire beneath his skin. Slowly, his hand returned to my chest, flattened out, then pressed against my flesh. My breathing hitched and I pressed my lips against his chin, urging him to bow his head and meet me part way. "I love you, Bran. You're all that matters to me. Please understand."

His hand twitched, moving upward, but seeming to fight the urge. Sweeping fingers caressed the skin on my neck, moving into my hair, before pressing against my scalp and dragging back down until his hand rested once again on my chest and the base of my neck. Then he pushed me backward, my body landing against the wall with a thud.

With his eyes closed, he leaned in close, inhaling deeply, his body shuddering with barely controlled restraint. His arms moved so they caged me in, his forearms against the wall, hands holding either side of my head as his forehead pressed against mine. All I could hear was his ragged breathing. All I could feel was his heat and the emotion vibrating the air between us.

"I understand that you *lied*."

I choked out a sob. "Bran, please."

His breath hissed out between his teeth, heat radiating off his body. "Do you feel this?" he grunted, pushing his hips against me, his erection throbbing against my stomach.

"Yes," I gasped, my chest heaving.

"It's what you do to me. I want you. So much it makes my blood burn, so much that I want to fuck you even when I can't stand looking at you. But you hid the truth from me, Cora. And I. Can't. Fucking. Stand. *Liars*."

Pushing against the wall, his body left mine at a speed that felt like a blast of ice washing over me. "No," I cried, my hands grabbing his chest, fingers holding fabric, seeking skin. "Bran, *please*." I wanted to deny that I'd ever lied to him, wanted to tell him that nothing about us was ever a lie. But it all was, right from the very beginning. I even lied about how I felt towards him, told myself it was only a fling when I knew full well that what we had was so much more.

His hands wrapped around mine, our gazes finally matching up. "Do you have any idea what it's like to be in love with you, Cora?"

I shook my head.

"It's like water. I want to swim in it, feel like I could drown in it, but it slips straight through my fingers when I try to hold it in my hands."

"What does that mean?" I whispered, my voice shaking as my fists held on a little tighter.

"That it's stupid to try and hold on to something I can't have." With a swift flick of his wrists, he knocked my hands free and turned away, swiping his jacket off the bed, leaving.

A wave of desolation slammed into my chest, I was powerless. "Would it have made a difference if I'd told you in the beginning?" I called out before he reached the door.

Pausing, he didn't turn to face me, just spoke facing the door. "Probably. I never would have touched you if I'd known." Then he left. And I didn't run after him, didn't even cry out his name. I simply sunk to the floor and put my head in my hands, tears streaming down my cheeks.

34

Me: If being honest from the beginning means that we never would have been, then I'm afraid I'm not sorry at all. I'd rather spend the rest of my life missing you than never having known what you were to me.

Sent.
Received.
Read.

Me: Actually, no, I am sorry for withholding the truth from you. It was wrong of me to keep half of my life a secret from you. It wasn't that I was hiding it. It was just me being selfish because I didn't want to be sad around you. I didn't want to lump my stupid thirty-year-old problems on your twenty-year-old shoulders.

Sent.
Received.
Read.

Me: Please don't leave me because I fucked up. I love you.

Sent.
Received.
Read.

I WROTE that last text out and deleted it more times than I could count. No matter how I worded it, it came out a little pathetic. In the end, I sent it anyway, because I was pathetic, and I wasn't going to give up. I understood he was hurt. I hadn't been straight with him. And while, yes, *technically,* our relationship could be considered an affair, the fact that I was already separated without hope of reconciliation meant that my marriage was unequivocally over when we met. And that *had* to count for something. Surely he wasn't going to throw away what we had because of a technicality? It was stupid and he was being pigheaded. This wasn't over.

I'd spent half the day in that hotel room, crying my eyes out over the disaster we'd become, texting him in the hope he'd return and take it all back. But the fact he was reading my texts and not responding just made me cry a little harder. When Olivia called looking for me, she could barely understand a word I was saying. I had to text her my location, and when she showed up and listened to my tail of woe, she pulled me off the floor and told me to wash my face and get my shit together.

"We don't fall apart over men, Cora," she'd said, holding me in front of the mirror. "You are smart, beautiful and trusting. There is *nothing* wrong with you, *nothing* you need to apologise for. Do you know about every one of his past relationships? No, you don't. Why? Because they have nothing to fucking do with what was going on between the two of you. If that boy wants to play in the pool with the big kids then he needs to grow the fuck up, realise people over twenty have some baggage, and get on with things. And you, you are a thirty-year-old woman crying on the floor in a hotel room that doesn't even have a mini bar. I can't even begin to tell you what's wrong with this picture."

Somehow, she'd turned me from a crying mess, to a woman resolute in knowing what she wanted out of life. I wanted Bran, and I wasn't going to give up on him. He filled me, heart and soul, and there wasn't a single thing in my life that meant more to me than he did. Things that had previously been my focus had lost their allure. I wasn't just a solicitor advocate. I was a women first. A woman in love who had wronged someone dear because of my stupidity. I wouldn't allow it to be our end. I fucked up. But I refused to accept that my fuck-up should be categorised with his mother's inability to keep her legs together throughout her marriage. That wasn't me. He needed to understand that.

There was no sleep for me that night. I sat up alone, drinking wine and staring at my phone while trying to figure out what I was going to do to convince Bran to give me another chance—there may have also been a hefty dose of self-pitying tears added into the mix too. But by the time the sun started to rise, I felt as though I had a plan.

It took a little longer to get ready for work than it normally did, given my eyes were red and swollen with two dark crescent-shaped divots sucking against my sockets. It was a neon sign advertising my lack of sleep and poor emotional state. "Fuck it," I muttered, dropping my concealer into my make-up bag. The basic cover-up job would have to do.

I'd filled Olivia in on my plan on the way to work. She listened quietly and nodded, telling me that she'd support me in any way she could. Just knowing that helped to steel my emotions so I could get through this.

Skipping our usual coffee, we walked into work. Nerves were swirling about in my stomach, but I had a game plan. I would hand the paperwork in to prove my intervention order had been revoked, while also admitting to my relationship with Bran. Then I'd accept whatever consequences came my way. It wasn't every day you marched up to your boss and told him you were in love with his son. The idea made my knees wobble.

"You're going to be fine," Olivia said, giving my arm a friendly squeeze as she held her card against the lock on the entry door.

Taking a deep breath, I gave her a shaky smile then stepped over the threshold of the foyer to the office. Instantly, the hair on the back of my neck stood on end. I could have sworn people were looking right at me and whispering.

"What's going on?" I whispered to Olivia who shook her head, quietly surveying the room.

"I have absolutely no fucking clue. But something..."

"Cora. My office please," Adrian Sharp called out, his tone clipped.

"Oh shit. Do you think he already knows?" I asked, grabbing her by the arm. This wasn't how the morning was supposed to work.

"Maybe it's about the intervention order? Maybe it has nothing to do with Bran at all."

"Ugh. I feel sick. Wish me luck?"

"You won't need it." She gave me an encouraging smile as I pointed my feet toward the director's office and held my head high, ready to face whatever penalties that would befall me.

"I'm glad you called me in, sir. There are a few things I needed to talk to you about," I said, trying to stay ahead of the eight ball. There was very little going on in my life that could have made my boss angry with me, so I wanted to start off with an impression of transparency.

He wasn't interested in letting me speak, however, and slapped today's newspaper on his desk in front of me. "Have you seen today's headlines? My name seems to have made it in there."

"Your name?" I frowned, stepping closer to his desk to look at the article in question. The moment I saw the front page, the bold print sent my heart plummeting. 'SON OF DPP EMBROILED IN ILLICIT AFFAIR.' The byline belonged to none other than Jack Knowles.

"That son of a bitch," I muttered, reading the details that painted Bran as a predatory homewrecker, and me— labelled as a 'nameless solicitor from the OPP' to cover his arse against a lawsuit over the stop order—as a clue-less and confused woman who'd allowed herself to be lured away from a doting husband. Accompanying the article were two photos. One of me leaving the restaurant with Bran last night, and despite the black bar across my eyes, it was obviously me to all who knew me. In the other photo, it showed Jack and me on our wedding day —black bars included. I looked far happier in the photo with Bran. "I see Jack doesn't mention his own name in the article, or his serial philandering at any point. How objective of him." I threw the paper back on the desk and folded my arms. "I suppose I'm fired now?"

Taking his seat, the director shook his head. "My son has a habit of doing these things. He goes after women in positions of power and leaves a trail of carnage in his wake. It started in high school and continued through to university. I'd hoped you were too smart to fall prey to his charms, especially after the troubles with your husband, but I suppose my faith was misplaced. I'm disappointed, I'm not going to pretend otherwise, but as always in these circumstances, I'll do what I can to assuage the damage. As you can see"—he gestured toward the article—"I can't always get ahead of these situations before they hit. This is going to hurt your reputation, Cora. Especially following the damage the intervention order did, but you're good at what you do, and I've no doubt that given another twelve months supervising the trainees, you'll be ready to return to the solicitor pool and resume your original career path." Letting out his breath, he leaned forward in his seat, clasping his hands in front of him. "As for Brandon, I've already made arrangements for him to finish his studies and internship in Sydney, so you needn't worry about any awkwardness where he's concerned. However, your estranged husband doesn't seem to feel the same way."

"He's angry, yes. But I honestly don't care about Jack. I'm more concerned about Bran. Sending him away isn't going to help anybody—least of all him. I need you to understand, sir. What was happening between Bran and me...it isn't how that article paints it. We met before he started working here. After Jack and I had split. Neither of us knew who the other was at the start of things, so neither one of us preyed upon the other or played any games. We were simply two people attracted to each other in a less than ideal situation—which is why we hid it until we were sure it meant something. But in the end... it still got messy. Really messy. But I'm not sorry for falling in love with your son, sir, and I'm not planning on walking away from him to save face either. He's angry with me too, but I'm going to fix all of this, I promise you. I only have your son's best interests at heart."

"I don't think you understand my son, Cora."

"No, Adrian, I don't think *you* understand your son. He didn't prey on me because I'm in a position of power. Your son simply prefers a more mature woman. We met outside this office, and we fell in love, plain and simple."

Adrian eyed me for a moment, one hand toying with a pen on the desk. "You *love* my son?" He said it as though the idea was a little crazy, and maybe it was, but I wasn't going to act like it was any less than the truth for the sake of my dignity.

"I do, sir. Yes." I held his gaze.

"And he feels the same way?" *He did...* A burst of nerves jittered about in my stomach as I hoped with all my might that his words still held true.

"He's said as much, but he's angry over all of this." I gestured to the paper. "I was and still am understandably angry at my husband for his multiple affairs, and I chose not to speak about him to Bran. Bran was shocked when he found out about Jack. I dare say he felt more than a little betrayed."

"I can sympathise with both of you," he said, sitting back in his chair, rocking it slightly as he regarded me. I could see the emotion behind his eyes, knowing he'd experienced infidelity himself and been hurt by it. I could see his understanding, and I could also see his concern for his son. I hurt him. "My son is a risk-taker, Cora. As much as it would pain him to admit, he's very much driven by his emotions, much like his mother. They like things they shouldn't, and their actions tend to get them into trouble. Normally, as a man in my position, I'm able to keep the worst of it from public record. But *normally*, I'm approached before things get this far. Money seems to close a lot of open windows. Other times, my connections allow me to open certain doors that other parties are happy to walk through and disappear from my son's life. It's generally a good indicator as to how serious those relationships really were. This time, however, it seems things are different. You're telling me you love Brandon and won't walk away from him. And it seems Jack isn't interested in either money or opportunity, or he would have come to me with this before printing, and *before* pressing assault charges."

"Jack did *what*?"

"The police report came to us late yesterday after-noon, seeking advice before charging Brandon for the assault that occurred yesterday morning outside the court. But there wasn't much I could do. Jack was pushing hard. He has witnesses, a medical report, not to mention it was all caught on CCTV. I had no choice but to let the charges go ahead."

"You're prosecuting him?"

He nodded. "His bail hearing is today. I can't save him this time. I can't stop them linking you to this, or your name from being dragged through the mud. But, I can guarantee that you'll still have a job at the end of all this." *What?*

"And what price do I have to pay for that guarantee?"

Adrian smiled and shook his head. "I'm not blackmailing you, Cora. I'm simply placing my hope in you now. Brandon has refused any sort of legal counsel. Jack is intent on creating a scandal out of this, and frankly, damage control is all I can do. But *you* might be able to do something—talk some sense into one of them, or both of them, anything you can think of—because you're the one at the centre of all of this. Seems these men are lashing out because of their feelings for you."

"Lucky me." I picked up the paper and stared at the article. "I'll go talk some sense into him."

"Which one? Jack or Brandon?"

"Both. I need Jack to back off and drop these charges, but I'm honestly not sure how I'm supposed to do that. All he's interested in is lashing out because I won't let him control my life anymore."

"He's adept at hitting you where it hurts most. Your career and your previously impeccable standing in the public eye. It doesn't take a mastermind to see that woman in the pictures is you. Perhaps it's time you went after whatever is most important to him."

Putting the paper back on the desk, I shook my head. "The only thing he gives a shit about is the dick between his legs. Pardon my language," I said, holding up my hands so he forgave my verbal slip.

"Jack is an unapologetic, self-righteous prick. The legal community and press associated with the courts is a fairly small community; I'd heard rumours about him, but I'd always hoped they weren't true."

"Seems everyone knew about his proclivities before I did."

"We never want to see the negative side of the people we love."

"Loved. The e-d is key in this situation. I'm just glad he didn't end up giving me some nasty—"

I grabbed for my handbag, searching for my phone.

"Is everything all right?"

I grinned, nodding as I dialled. "I just figured it out."

With my phone pressed to my ear, the director sat silent as I waited for the call to connect. It only took a couple of rings.

"Cor." Jack's voice sounded delighted when he answered. *Arsehole.*

"What the fuck have you done this time, you miserable excuse for a human being?" I demanded, my teeth jammed together.

"You read my article. I thought the photos of you came out nice. They certainly captured your good side."

"I swear to you, Jack, quit messing with my life, or I'll pay to have billboards put up all over the country with your face on them. The caption will read: 'Genital warts can affect anyone. Don't take the risk.' You'll *never* get laid again."

The director's hand went up to cover his mouth, stifling a laugh.

Jack chuckled on the other end of the line. "You wouldn't dare. I could sue you for slander."

"And take what? You've already taken everything, already ruined my life. Take away everything a woman holds dear and she becomes a monster like none you've ever seen. So, keep pushing, Jack. Keep pushing me and *find out.* I will follow you around and hand out pamphlets. I will whisper in the ears of every woman you go near, 'Don't touch him, he has VD.' If you don't undo this I will make your life a living hell. *That* is a promise." Not waiting for a reply, I ended the call and shoved my phone in my bag.

Adrian chuckled and shook his head. "Remind me never to get on your bad side."

I smiled and prepared to leave. "Now, exactly where is Bran?"

35

"BRANDON SHARP. I'm his legal counsel."

The desk sergeant checked the paperwork in front of her. "He's waived his right to legal counsel."

"I was employed by his father. I need to confer with my client before his bail hearing."

"Mr Sharp is a grown man; his father doesn't get to override his legal decisions."

"Even when his father is the Director of Public Prosecutions?"

"His father is *Adrian* Sharp?"

"You weren't aware? It's all over the front page of today's newspaper. You can call him if you want. I have him in my contacts list." I held out my mobile phone.

"That won't be necessary. I'll let you through. But, Ms Knowles, if your client chooses to pass on you as his counsel, you'll need to respect his wishes, DPP or no DPP. Understood?"

"Understood." She buzzed me through, and I was taken to a windowless interview room to wait for him to be brought in. I sat on one of the two chairs provided, tapping my fingers against the worn table in agitation. Each second ticked by like four.

It felt like an age, but ten minutes later, the door opened and a constable I'd known for years nodded in greeting before gesturing for Bran to enter. "You have fifteen minutes," he said. He'd been one of the officers present when I removed my belongings from the home I'd shared with Jack. He had kind eyes and liked to keep his opinions to himself.

"Can you make it thirty?" I asked, needing as much time as I possibly could.

Bran paused in the doorway at the sound of my voice, his eyes meeting mine. His jaw clenched. "Actually, we won't need any time at all," he said. "It's a bail hearing; I'm fine without counsel."

Constable Reeves gave me a withering look and went to close the door again.

"Wait!" I called out, leaping to my feet. "Let me help you, Bran. A criminal conviction could completely ruin your legal career."

"I honestly don't give a fuck."

"You might not, but I do. I care what happens to you. Please, Bran. I'm at the centre of this mess. Let me help you fix this."

With a heavy sigh, he nodded his head and stepped through the door.

"Half an hour," the constable said, giving me a friendly smile before closing the door and leaving us alone in the tiny room with poor lighting.

"I don't see how you think you're going to help me, there's irrefutable evidence to back up the assault charges. Plus, I did it."

"I'm working on it. Just, *please* sit down." I reached across the table and tapped my hand lightly against the cool surface. "We need to talk."

He did as I asked, another sigh escaping his chest as his hands raked through his hair. He looked tired, the naked overhead bulb casting a thick layer of shadow over his under-eye area. He obviously hadn't slept either. He was still wearing the same clothes I saw him in yesterday, minus the tie, and his hair stuck up all over the place. There was a light smattering of stubble over his cheeks and jaw; it made a scraping sound when he ran his hands over his face.

"I thought I made myself clear yesterday; I wasn't interested in seeing you again."

His words made my heart squeeze with pain, but I kept my cool. Nothing would be accomplished if I started getting upset. "Yeah, you did. But I remember someone telling me a few months ago that this wasn't over when I tried to push him away. So, I guess I'm repaying the favour."

He shook his head, his arms folded across his chest as he stared at the wall to his right.

"You know, I've spent the last twenty-four hours thinking a lot about the things you said, and the thing that stuck with me most was that you wouldn't have touched me if you'd known I was married."

"I don't fuck married women."

"I get that. You've got principles, and it's part of what I love about you. You have this brutishly masculine way about you. But at the same time, you're sweet and vulnerable and you care for me like no one ever has."

His jaw flexed and relaxed, his eyes stayed turned away.

"But, I have to think, what if Jack and I had been in a de facto marriage? You see, for most of our relationship, that's what it was. We got married last year—turns out he only did it to shut me up—but still, if that hadn't happened and I'd simply walked out on an eleven-year relationship under the same circumstances, would you have had a problem then?"

He shook his head, and for a moment, he glanced at me. The eye contact caused my stomach to flip. Those eyes, those beautiful green eyes. They held my heart and mirrored my soul. "I suppose not," he admitted.

"Why not?" I responded, shifting my head to try and keep our gazes locked. I needed him to look at me, see how much I was hurting without him too. "We'd still have the same problems we do now. Jack still would have taken out the intervention order, I'd still own property with him, he'd still be trying to ruin me with some fucked-up notion that it would get me to give him a second chance... Why does a slip of paper change the way you feel about me?"

"It doesn't change how I feel about you. It changes *us.* I respect the vows made between a man and a woman for that piece of paper to come into being. It's a contract, one that binds you together in sickness, health, good and bad. How can you be completely with me, when you're still legally connected to another man?"

Pressing my lips together, I nodded slowly, searching his eyes and seeing hurt and confusion. I hated that I'd caused that.

"I was eighteen when Jack and I started dating. Do you know how old you were then?"

He frowned then shrugged.

He knew, he simply didn't want to voice it.

"You were an eight-year-old boy. I was old enough to drink and vote, old enough to drive and make every decision any other adult could, and you were a boy in third grade. A decade is a lifetime, Bran. I think it's incredibly naïve of you to expect that I could come to you as a thirty-year-old woman without any sort of baggage. People often marry in their twenties, and sadly, they often get divorced too. To end our relationship because I don't qualify for a divorce yet is just shooting us both in the foot. If I know my marriage is over, and Jack knows our marriage is over, then why can't you and I be together? It doesn't make any sense to me."

"You're missing the point, Cora. We are over because of the secrecy. You've been going to marriage counselling this whole fucking time, secretly working on a marriage you claim to be over. That means you were either lying to your husband, or were lying to me. People don't do counselling for almost three months when they aren't interested in reconciling."

"Ordinarily I'd agree with you. But during the first session, I was told that if I walked out that door, the order would remain for the full twelve months. I was advised that the sessions were court ordered. To breach that court order was to guarantee the continuance of the intervention order. There was never any thought of reconciliation on my behalf."

"And yet, Wednesdays were the one day I couldn't expect to see you, they were also times you were quiet or upset. Not once did you trust me enough to let me inside your head. You kept it all hidden, told me you were mine, and kept that *very* important detail from me. Maybe if you'd explained that from the beginning, I would have understood. Maybe, if you'd trusted me enough to spare me the shock of finding some guy laying his hands on you in public, I could have been prepared."

"I thought you said you wouldn't have touched me if you'd known I was married."

He released a heavy sigh. "On that first night, if I'd seen you wearing a ring, or if you'd mentioned your breakup when we spoke at the bar, no, I wouldn't have touched you at all. But after that...*fuck, Cora*, after that first taste of you, I was addicted. You could have told me you were a monster in human skin and I still would have wanted you."

We stared at each other across the table, the silence in the room buzzing around us. I wanted to leap across the table, sit on his lap, and wrap myself around him, breathing in that intoxicating scent that was so unequivocally him.

"Your father knows about us," I whispered.

"I'm fairly sure the whole of Melbourne knows. You must be in a panic over everyone looking at you and thinking you're a cougar."

I ignored the jibe. "He said that this is what you do. That you have a thing for women in a position of power."

He dropped his gaze, running his fingers through his hair roughly, messing it even further. "I told you I've always been attracted to older women. There were times when those women were teachers, and sure, I got a kick out of seducing them, but it wasn't a thing I did on purpose."

"There seems to be a bit of a pattern of behaviour here. Wasn't the woman before me a university lecturer?"

He swiped a hand across his face. "Yes. She was. But it was just something I did because I was young and stupid and hormonal. If you're interested in knowing, I fucked some of my friends' mothers too, simply because I could."

I hated hearing this. He was far more experienced than I was, even at ten years my junior, and it sounded like he slept around without much thought of the consequences.

"Your friends' *mothers*?"

"*Single* mothers," he clarified, taking a sobering breath. *Jesus, how many women has this man ploughed through?* The thought made me feel sick. Could *I* look past that? If he could sleep with all these women then claim it didn't mean anything, and he did it 'just because he could', what was stopping him from doing it again? *Just because he could.* It felt like a cold hand slapping my face.

Wouldn't I be the naïve one to continue something with someone capable of acting on impulses simply because he can?

"You're talking like this behaviour happened years ago, but it was only *months* before you and me. I'm honestly starting to wonder if maybe your father is right. Maybe this *is* just something you do. Now that you and I are out in the open, will you lose interest and take off like you did with the others? Will I just be another older woman left in your wake, a mess for your father to clean up?"

"That's bullshit, and you know it," he snapped. "*None

of that shit has a thing to do with my interest in you. I met you having no idea you were about to be my boss. The nightclub was dark, and I didn't even know you were older than me. I wanted you because of the way you moved on that dance floor. There wasn't a single thing about my desire for you that was for kicks."

"You didn't get a kick out of seducing me?"

His eyes darkened as he waited a beat to answer. "I didn't seduce you, Cora. I reached out and *took* you."

Yes, he did, which was what made this all so much harder. "And yet you're leaving me, just like all the others. Are you even capable of long-term, Bran?" He'd made me feel like I was the centre of his world, but now that he was turning his back on me, I wondered if he did that with his other women too.

His lips pursed as his breathing grew heavy through his nose. He was getting pissed off. Good. I was pissed off too. He was being pigheaded.

"*I. don't. leave,*" he roared. "*I'm* the one who keeps getting fucked over. *I'm* the one forced to relocate while they all just walk the fuck away, not giving a shit about me and my feelings. You'll do the same. My father will pay you off or fast-track your career, and you'll walk away, just like the rest. *No one fights for me!*"

"What the fuck do you call *this*?" I shouted, my finger pointing at my chest. "I forced my way in here, made a fool of myself on the street yesterday, all because *I'm in love with you*, Bran. You're not even trying!" My pitch rose and angry tears sprung from my eyes. I stood and turned away, my hands covering my face as I took a few deep breaths. This was getting out of hand, and I needed to stay calm.

There was a knock, and Constable Reeves opened the door. "Time's up," he said, looking between us with wary eyes.

I wiped my hand over my face and put on a bright smile. "Can we have five more minutes? Please?" The moment his eyes met mine, his features softened with understanding. He nodded then left the room.

When I turned back, Bran's face was angled away from me, his leg bouncing under the table.

"Why didn't you just tell me why you were pulled out of school?" I asked, trying to understand why his secrets were less damning than mine.

"Because you'd think I was some sort of pervert with a fetish for older woman," he stated, his arms folded tightly across his chest.

"Are you?"

Meeting my eyes, he stared at me for a moment, hurt. "*No,*" he said angrily. "Fuck you for even asking that."

"Can you blame me? You're sitting there judging me for hiding my past when you've done exactly the same thing. Except when you do it, it's all OK."

"It hardly compares." He laughed, the sound anything but jovial.

"Hardly?" *Hello, pot. I'd like to introduce you to kettle.* "Are you even listening to what you're saying?" Just like when a witness was caught out on the stand, I noted the way his gaze shifted to the side, giving away his thoughts. He just realised he was being a hypocrite, but wasn't willing to admit it out loud. "*I* hid my past relationship from *you* because I worried about how *you'd* react."

"You hid a *marriage.*" The last word came out strained, punching me in the heart.

"I know," I whispered. "And I'm sorry that I hurt you. I'm sorry that your mother messed up and that it's coloured your life. But this isn't the same. I had left my marriage both physically and emotionally. I came to you with an open heart."

His hands flew to his face, fists balled against his eyes. "God, you don't *understand*," he forced out, emotion and tension coating his words.

I sat down and reached across the table, placing my hand over his forearm. "Then explain it to me so I do."

He lowered his hands and blew the air of his lungs, his eyes red-rimmed and patchy. "Jesus, Cora, I feel like a fucking pussy," he grunted, wiping angrily at his eyes.

"Talk to me, Bran. It's just you and me, no pussies around." I placed my hand on his. He looked at our fingers for a moment, moving his against mine, then he sat back and raked at his hair again.

"I just...I feel like I'm always on borrowed time. I have been sent away more times than I can count. I guess I was either in the way, unwanted, or an embarrassment, I don't know. When my parents split, I thought it would all stop, that Mum would take me with her and I wouldn't have to live this lie anymore. But she left without looking back and I remained the bastard son that no one wanted."

There it was, that vulnerability I'd seen. My heart ached for him, knowing that he'd spent his whole life feeling that way. It seemed he was forever waiting for the proverbial ball to drop. His whole life, he'd been taught that when things blew up, you packed up and moved off.

"You don't have to leave this time, Bran," I assured him, my hand still reached out even though he wasn't taking it.

"With you," he continued, not responding to me. "I felt...different, like I'd finally found my home. It's stupid because we've only known each other a short time, but being with you felt *right*." He frowned and shook his head. "Discovering you're married... It made everything between us feel like a lie. You turned me into the *other* guy, and I had no fucking clue. Do you understand that? I've had enough lies and secrets to last a lifetime, Cora. I can't breathe anymore because of them."

The door opened again, interrupting us at worst possible time. "I'm sorry," Constable Reeves said. "We need the room."

"It's OK," I assured him even though it wasn't, and I was close to tears. I swallowed them down. "We can talk after the hearing."

"There won't actually be a hearing. The complainant called in. He's dropped the charges. I would have told you earlier, but..." He shrugged, not needing to explain that he knew we were dealing with something rather personal.

Bran released an audibly relieved sigh, while I smiled, glad that for once, Jack managed to do the right thing— even if I did have to almost break his arm. Actually, his *dick*.

"This was you?" he asked as we stood to follow the constable out.

I nodded. "I hope that's OK. I made a few threats to get him to back off."

"Of course." He caught my hand just as we stepped into the hall, then stopped me by dropping his weight against the wall. His exhaustion aged him under the harsh fluorescent lighting. When he looked into my eyes,

I saw his torn emotions: anger, sadness, and more surprisingly desire. I could barely breathe wondering what that meant.

"We should go. They don't like us hanging around the halls." My voice came out as a whisper. I wanted so much to lean into him, to hold his palm to my cheek and kiss along his arm until our lips met. I wanted to take him home and tangle our bodies for hours on end, closing the world out until we'd somehow merged into one. But I did none of that. Instead, I stood there, silent, hoping he wouldn't turn my heart away while also knowing that was exactly what he was going to do. The realisation was a bitter pill to swallow.

"Listen to me for a second," he started, his eyes dropping to focus on our hands.

I closed my eyes, not wanting to hear the words that were about to come out of his mouth. "Don't," I whispered.

"Cora." His hands shifted and he caught my head in his hands, pressing his forehead against mine. My tears started falling and I shook my head.

"Let's just go," I gasped, sniffling as I tried to pull back and urge him to come with me. "Come home with me. We can talk all night."

His head moved side to side. "I can't. I'm sorry."

"You're sorry?" I sniffed, my throat closing. I was out of energy. Out of arguments. I'd laid my case in front of him, and he, as the judge and jury in this instance, refused to consider the plea. I pulled back, wanting to get angry, but all I could do was cry pitifully.

"I'm trying here," he whispered, his voice hoarse. "I really am. It means a hell of a lot that you came down here, that you're fighting for me to stay. But, I don't know if I can. I'm fighting against something that's controlled so much of my thoughts for years. I can't just forget the lies that brought us to this point."

My hands wrapped around his wrists and I pushed my body against his, our foreheads grinding. I wanted him to let go. He was breaking my heart. "You could try harder." My words forced their way out between my teeth.

"I just need some time. I need to think. I need to get my head straight." Still holding on to me, he lifted his head, pressing a hard kiss against my forehead as I fought against him.

"Ms Knowles and Mr Sharp." The desk sergeant's curt voice broke through just as Bran released me. I pressed my palms against my eyes.

"I'm sorry," I told her.

"Perhaps you can finish this...moment outside when Mr Sharp has collected his belongings," she suggested.

"It's fine. We're done. There's nothing left to say." I stepped out of his reach.

Why were the men who claimed to love me so willing to hurt me?

"Cora," Bran called softly.

"You know what, you keep saying that our age doesn't matter, but it does. If you were just a tiny bit older, you'd have the maturity to understand that I'm not your mother."

"I haven't thought that for a second," he shot back.

"Then quit punishing me for something she did!" *I'm so fucking over not being what someone really wants. Being punished for someone else's issues.* I was beyond done with that shit.

The desk sergeant inflated her chest, her eyes wild as I stormed past her. "Leave," she insisted.

"I'm going!"

With a clear focus on the exit, I didn't pause once until I was on the street, sucking in great gulps of air, trying to calm down. He wouldn't listen, wouldn't understand what he was giving up. He was angry at a woman who wasn't even me. I tried—maybe I failed—but all I could do now was wait and hope that his love for me would open his eyes, because if it didn't, I honestly didn't know what I was going to do. The day before, he'd likened loving me to water because water couldn't be held.

But his analogy was wrong. Water was necessary to life. Living things simply couldn't exist without it.

36

"I CAN'T BELIEVE we didn't do this sooner," Olivia said a few hours later when I'd finally settled down. We'd been on the phone since I got home from the station after my failed attempt to reconcile with Bran. She was sitting on her balcony, eating pretzels, and I was sitting on the roof of my apartment building near the pool, drinking wine straight out of the bottle and eating a family bag of Kettle Chips to myself in a bid to ingest my feelings. My emotional go-to was normally chocolate, but I was too upset for chocolate. In fact, I was a total mess.

At the start of the phone call, I'd subjected Olivia to more blubbering over Bran in between mouthfuls and crunches. She'd offered to come over and sit with me, but when I refused, she told me to get my binoculars and go to the roof. The idea had been just crazy enough that it got me to compose myself and explain exactly what happened.

"Ugh. Relationships. They're too fucking painful," she commented. "Feelings are the devil."

"I think I hate love," I sighed. "I should have listened to you."

She laughed. "No, you shouldn't. What the fuck do I know? I'm pregnant to a twenty-six-year-old scientist who has become my live-in lover and won't stop proposing to me."

"Sounds like a nightmare." I smiled, holding my binoculars to my eyes so I could see her. She was stretched out on a chaise lounge with her feet crossed at the ankles and her hand resting on her growing belly. I felt a pang of longing in my gut.

"You have no idea," she commented, just as the sliding door opened and Paul came out handing her something in a glass.

"Did Paul just make you a milkshake?" I asked, laughter in my voice as I watched her try to shoo him away. He didn't listen, just sat at the base of her chair and started massaging her feet.

"It's so I get enough calcium. This man is a hoverer, always making sure I'm OK, that I have something to eat or drink, that I'm not working too hard. It's exhausting."

I heard his voice, faint in the background. "You love it." Then she smiled and teased him with her foot. It was nice to see her looking happy despite her objections.

"A man to dote on you? It sounds *and looks* like torture," I deadpanned, taking a sip of wine. I was beginning to feel lightheaded and probably needed to go to bed before I got so drunk that I fell into the pool and drowned a sad and lonely rejected woman. At least I'd go knowing Olivia was taken care of... "I'm going to bed."

"No. Don't go. I can get rid of him so we can man-bash some more." I watched her kick her feet to shoo him away. The whole situation made me laugh, which was a pretty amazing feat since I was feeling more than a little numb at this point.

"It's fine. I honestly don't think I can talk anymore. I'm beat."

"What are you going to do about Bran?"

I shrugged. "There isn't much else I can do. He knows how I feel. I can't force him to forgive me or to feel the same way."

"Of course he feels the same way. He loves you."

"Yeah. But does he love me enough to put his pride and insecurities aside?"

"Of course he does. He'll be knocking on your door before you know it."

"I don't know." I sighed, thinking about all the years I spent thinking Jack loved me. All that got me was a bag of trust issues and a battered ego. "Why aren't I enough?" I sobbed, my tears forcing their way to the surface again.

"Oh honey, you *are* enough. You're more than any man on this planet deserves. I tell you what, if he doesn't come to his senses soon, I'll get Paul to head over and rough him up. He knows taekwondo. You can do that, can't you, babe?" The last part was obviously directed at Paul.

"I don't know," he said, his voice quiet in the background. "That guy she's with is pretty big, and taekwondo is more a sport than a fighting style—"

"You'll be fine," Olivia assured him. "He'll do it," she directed at me.

Sitting up, I brushed the crumbs off my chest and chuckled. I could always count on Olivia to pull me out of a funk.

"That won't be necessary. But thank you, Liv. You always make me feel better."

"Right back at you, gorgeous. Rest well."

"OK. Tell Paul he's off the hook and doesn't have to fight Bran."

"Nah, I'll let him sweat. See you tomorrow?"

"Maybe. I'll call you in the morning."

With that, I disconnected the line and collected my things, feeling a little drunker upon standing than I'd thought I was sitting down. Taking a few unsteady steps, I found my footing and headed for the elevator bay, a great sigh escaping from my chest. The last several months had been emotionally tough. I lost my husband, my career trajectory, my *house,* and now it felt like I'd lost my heart too.

Lying in bed, despite my exhaustion, I struggled to find sleep. For a good half hour, I also struggled with the idea of calling Bran. I wanted to hear his voice, wanted to whisper sweet words into his ear and convince him to come back to me. But it wasn't that easy. I couldn't nag him into being mine. He needed to make that choice for himself.

With a sigh, I opened our text conversation and scrolled through it, pausing on the photos we'd sent to each other. God, I wanted him. And I needed him even more than that.

Before I could stop myself, my thumbs were moving over the touchpad.

Me: loving you is also like water

I hit send then watched until the screen said delivered. It clicked to read almost immediately. Then the dots started bouncing, causing my heart to bounce into my throat with it.

Bran: ???

Me: Because you're a huge part of me, and I don't know how I ever lived without you

THE DOTS BOUNCED THEN STOPPED, bounced then stopped. Until finally, they bounced and a message turned up on my screen.

Bran: For the record, I don't think you're like my mother

Me: Good. Because that would be weird

Bran: lol. It would...

Bran: Goodnight, Cora

I was being dismissed. I wanted to keep texting him, wanted to keep the lines of communication open just a little longer, but clearly he didn't. That stung a little.

Me: Goodnight xx

I watched the screen until it clicked to read, then I shut off my phone and held it against my chest, holding him close to my impossibly hopeful heart as I drifted into a fitful sleep.

"I WANT to thank you for what you did for Brandon yesterday." Adrian stepped into my office not long after I sat down behind my desk. "Looks like your words of...*encouragement* made an impression on Jack's motives." A smile teased the corners of his mouth. It amused me to see my boss fighting a smile. He wasn't the most jovial character I'd ever met, forever the serious and important head of a government agency.

"I only wish I'd used that line against him sooner. Might have saved my career from the shit pile it's currently sitting on."

Smiling at my colourful language, he reached up and adjusted his tie, clearing his throat before he spoke again. "I actually wanted to speak to you about that. How do you feel about returning to your old position? With the intervention order gone, I can pull some strings to get you into the barrister's course for the next intake. From what I hear, we'll be a barrister short in the next few months."

"What about my reputation? Isn't it damaged right now? Would I even get past the initial bar interview?"

"You let me worry about that. You really saved the day yesterday, and it's the least I can do to show my appreciation. However, I also think that this might go a long way to mitigating the damage Jack's article caused." He pulled a folded piece of newspaper from his jacket and handed it to me.

The headline read "COURT REPORTER FIRED AMIDST DEFAMATION ALLEGATIONS"

"What is this?" I asked, eagerly reading the article clipped from today's paper.

"Well, I got thinking after you left my office yesterday. Having been in a similar situation myself, I know what it's like when you realise everyone knew about your partner's infidelities but you. So I contacted a woman at the paper I know and trust. Turns out, he'd pursued her last year, but she'd had no qualms in turning him down. She'd known he was married, and is more than happy to colour Jack for the philandering scumbag he is."

I grinned, hugging the article to my chest. "I want to frame this. I never thought someone else's demise would make me this happy, but it does. I don't even need a Christmas bonus this year. This is better than cash."

Adrian chuckled. "I'll remember that."

"No. Don't . I like cash too." I smiled. So did he, but he added a nod, and for a moment we just existed in a semi-uncomfortable silence. This was all a little weird. Adrian and I didn't often chat.

He took a breath then gestured to the article. "If he gives you any more trouble, let me know. Any person important to Brandon is important to me too."

"Thank you," I whispered, feeling a little sad despite the sentiment. It was strange to hear those words come out of his mouth. Not only had I been under the impression that there was animosity between Adrian and Bran, but I also wasn't sure if I was still that important someone to Bran.

"Is everything all right?" he asked, noting my shift in demeanour.

"I hope so," I said on an exhale. "Time will tell, I suppose. But if I may, sir, can I ask you something?"

"Shoot."

"I was under the impression that you and Bran weren't on good terms."

He nodded once, sliding his hands into his pockets. "I

see. Well, our relationship is...complicated. But he'll always be my son, despite anything he may have told you." When he spoke the words, he kept his eyes level with mine, showing his sincerity.

"You might want to let him know that," I suggested, my voice quiet even though I was trying to be bold.

With a thoughtful nod, he stepped toward the door, perhaps needing this awkward exchange to be over. "Thank you, Cora," he said. Then he left, leaving me alone, feeling hollow, while my heart missed Bran a little more with every beat.

37

WORK DRAGGED at a snail's pace, although the moment it ended, I wished there was more for me to do. The idea of going home to an empty apartment felt so much worse. There was nothing but memories there. If the worst-case scenario presented itself and Bran walked away from our relationship, I took small solace in the fact I could start barrister's training soon, knowing that the study for the bar exam alone would take up so much time I'd be too busy to mope. Still, the idea of that didn't seem anywhere near as appealing as it would have six months ago.

After parting ways with Olivia at her apartment building, I declined staying at hers for dinner—seeing her happily arguing with Paul would have been a little too much for my aching heart to witness—then dragged my feet along the concrete until I reached the steps of my building. I released an annoyed sigh upon seeing that someone had left the security door propped open using a rock from the outside garden. With a shake of my head, I picked up the piece of marbled stone and threw it back where it belonged. *How could someone be so careless?* Absolutely anyone could walk into the building that way. What was the point in having security access if people were going to use a rock to circumvent it?

When the lift opened on my floor, I poked my head out to make sure no random strangers were loitering in the hallway preparing to accost unsuspecting women. Seeing the coast was clear, I dug in my bag for my keys then headed toward my apartment. The scent of Indian food tickled at my nostrils, making my stomach growl. I realised that I'd barely eaten a thing all day. That's how I knew I was lovesick for Bran. There wasn't a single food group that seemed appealing at lunchtime today. I was going to lose my curves.

When I rounded the corner, the scent became stronger and the moment I spotted my door, I stopped in my tracks.

"What are you doing here?" I gasped, staring at Bran as if he might be an apparition that my hopeful mind had conjured up. He was standing against my door wearing a pair of jeans and a long-sleeved T-shirt with the sleeves pushed up, a bag of food dangling from his fingers—just like that first night.

"Thought you might be hungry," he said, smiling slightly. "Then perhaps, we could finish that talk?"

Taking a deep breath, I nodded my head and readied my keys to unlock the door. Except my hands were shaking so much that I struggled to get it in the slot. "I'm sorry," I whispered when his big hand covered mine and he took over.

"Don't be," he replied. "There's nothing left to apologise for."

When he pushed open the door, I looked up at him. "Do you really mean that?"

He nodded. "Let's go inside."

With my heart beating so fast I could hear it in my ears, I dropped my bag on the floor next to the couch then followed Bran to the kitchen where he was taking bowls from the cabinet.

"I missed you so much these past couple of days," I started, knowing it seemed stupid because it was only a short time. But I needed to say it because two days' worth of fighting felt like an eternity when you were afraid of losing someone.

"Me too," he said, carrying everything to my small table. "Eat," he instructed, holding out my chair. We sat and ate in silence, stealing glances at each other that were filled with the many difficult words we weren't saying. I wanted to smile and relax because he was back, and I felt sure he was going to stay. But still, I feared that the moment we started talking, we'd also start fighting again.

"Come here," he said when we'd finished and he'd pushed his bowl to the side. I did as instructed and he turned in his chair to face me as I came around the table. His eyes flashed with a confused passion as they moved over my body. I reached out and placed a timid hand against his broad shoulder, my whole body sighing at the contact. We belonged together.

"Shit," he grunted, his arms shooting out and wrapping around my waist as he pulled me against him, his face buried against my stomach. "I don't know how to do this." The words were muffled, but I could feel him moving, his mouth pressing kisses against my stomach through my blouse as he rocked his face against me.

Keeping one hand around my waist, he moved the other one down over my skirt, gripping the curve between my arse and thigh.

"Don't know how to do what?" I whispered.

"How to be OK with the fact you're still married. I've spent my whole life angry at my mother for cheating, and I know this isn't the same thing, but it still feels messed up in my head. I mean, why did she do it? Why couldn't she just stay faithful, or at the very least be somewhat caring towards her only son?" He shook his head, thinking. "I *don't* think you're like her. I'm just...I'm angry, and I'm triggered."

"I'm angry too, Bran. I can't even begin to guess at your mother's motives—I don't even understand Jack's motives for chasing after so many women behind my back. I can only imagine that they do it because they're selfish, and perhaps they're looking for something they aren't getting in their own relationships, or maybe they're just unhappy with themselves and somehow masking it all with sex. *I don't know.* I'll never know because that's not how I think. The only thing I do know is that when I met you, my relationship was over. I'm a one-man woman. And I know it was a mistake to not explain those circumstances to you sooner."

He lifted his head and looked at me, his eyes shining. "I'm angry with you for hiding what you did."

"I know. There's no excuse. I should have told you." We were talking in whispers, afraid the sound might break this fragile shell holding us together.

"The idea of not having you makes me lose my mind."

"You have me. You've had me from the moment you spoke to me at that bar. I'm yours."

His eyes searched mine, looking for the truth in my words. Then his hands tightened against my arse and he pulled me even closer, inhaling my scent. "*God*. I want to believe that so much."

I pressed my lips together, my brow knitting as I shifted my hands to his cheeks and urged him to look at me.

"It's the truth, Bran." I stared at him for a long time, filling my eyes with all the sincerity I had inside me, trying to get him to understand that he was the only man who mattered. In his, I could see how vulnerable he was, how afraid he was of the pain I could potentially cause him. For a man like Bran, staying was hard. He'd spent his life being pushed away from his problems, and had never been taught *how* to stay. How to resolve things. His decision to show up here tonight was monumental to me.

"I don't know what to do." His eyes widened. He was looking to me for answers. I knew what I wanted. I wanted him to stay and be mine. But I couldn't force that. He needed to make that choice on his own.

"Do whatever you feel is right in here." I put my hand against his chest, over his heart, the solid thump of his body's life hitting against my hand. "Why did you come here tonight?"

He covered my hand with his then closed his eyes. "Because I can't stop feeling like this. I have this urge to run but then my feet won't point in any direction but towards you."

"Doesn't that tell you something?"'

Releasing me, he let out his breath and sat back in his chair, raking his hand across his face. "You know, I tried to go. I packed my things, checked out of the hotel. I even booked a flight to Sydney."

"You were going to leave me?" The idea of it socked me in the stomach like a balled-up fist.

He shook his head. "*Tried*. I thought...I don't know. Maybe it would have been for the best. Give you the time to get your life sorted out while I finished uni. When I'm twenty-one my trust fund opens up, and I don't have to answer to my father anymore. I thought that maybe some time apart would put all this in perspective. Maybe we'd forget about each other; maybe our feelings would grow and this mess could be behind us. We could start fresh."

"You really thought going to Sydney would *help*?" I asked, shocked that the idea was still on the table.

"No. I booked the shuttle to take me to the airport, and when it arrived, I couldn't leave. I took my stuff back into the hotel, then came here instead."

Relief undid the knot in my stomach. I reached out for the edge of the table, leaning against it to steady myself. "Jesus," I gasped, my hand pressing against my chest. Bran reached out and took a hold of it, rising so he stood in front of me.

"I don't think I can exist without you."

"You think I could without you?" My voice shook, my eyes on the verge of overflowing.

He swallowed hard then shook his head. "No," he whispered.

"Then you're staying?" I asked, my chest hurting as I awaited his answer. I had to hear him say it to be sure.

"Jesus, Cora, of course I'm staying. I fucking *love* you."

"Oh, Bran." He caught me as I threw myself against him, absolute relief flooding my system. "I love you too.

So much. Please don't ever even think of leaving me again. I couldn't stand it."

With a dimpled smile, he pulled back slightly, his hands sliding into the side of my hair. "I'm not going anywhere, baby. My home is right here, with you. Just... no more hiding things, OK?"

Nodding, I pushed softly against his chest. "Same goes for you."

"Agreed."

"God, you just scared the absolute shit out of me with all that Sydney talk."

He grinned. "Then let me make it up to you." He brushed the tip of his nose against mine, his hands cradling my head as he teased me by briefly touching his mouth against my lips then pulling back to smile. "I love you," he whispered, the words washing over my skin like floating feathers. I basked in the feeling, closing my eyes. Then his mouth captured mine, soft at first then with increased fervour as his hand slid to the nape of neck, fingers gently soothing as I melted against him, starved from the lack of recent contact. As I fisted his shirt and pulled him closer, his hands dropped to my hips and his fingers bit into my skin.

When he lifted me and carried me to the bedroom, my world felt right again. I had no doubt in my mind that it was in his arms I belonged. I was his, he was mine, and I would never let go. Never Again.

EPILOGUE

One year later...

"I'D LIKE you all to raise your glass," Olivia said from her position on the stage. It had been months since she'd commanded a room, having opted to take twelve months' maternity leave to tackle motherhood instead of her never-ending caseload at the OPP. She was settling into it well, falling head-over-heels for the tiny bundle of pink skin and dark curls she gave birth to only seven months ago; a little girl they named Monique. Paul had proven to be an amazing father, always willing to do his share of changing, bathing and feeding. It had been a slow process, but Olivia had opened her heart and her home to another man—their wedding was in the process of being organised for next spring. I had no idea if it would stick this time, but for now, she was swearing the third time was the charm.

"We've all come together tonight to wish one very

special lady a happy third twenty-ninth birthday," she continued when she had everyone's attention.

"Thirty-first!" I called out. "I'm owning all my years." The room chuckled.

Olivia waved her hand in the air. "Either way, we have many things to celebrate. Not only did she make it through one hell of a divorce this year—that's right, we got the bastard to sign on the dotted line." The room cheered. The process of my divorce had been a long, drawn-out headache. Jack had fought me every step of the way, trying to extract more than his fair share from the marital assets. His arseholery knew no bounds. But in the end, my attorney had been a gun, beating them back to a seventy-thirty split my way. Since I earned more and therefore contributed more financially as well as domestically, there wasn't a lot they could do. Jack now lived in a tiny apartment in the western suburbs, working for an even tinier newspaper, the only newspaper to employ him after he effectively sabotaged his own career printing that article about Bran. *Oh, the irony.* I felt it was more than he deserved, but was mostly relieved the whole ordeal was over. The cheque for my portion of our assets had already cleared in my bank account, and Bran and I had already put a deposit on a house of our own. I was now a free woman. Well, free, but very much taken...

"But," Olivia continued, holding her hands up to quiet everyone down. "Our dear friend, Cora, also had an amazing year professionally. After many years of hard work, she's a barrister working directly for the DPP now." Another cheer went up. I was starting to get very red in the face from all the attention.

"Thank you," I called out, covering my cheeks with

my hands. They were starting to hurt from smiling so much.

"And to reign in that trifecta, she also met the love of her life, that giant thing sitting beside her, Brandon Sharp." She pointed to where we were sitting, and Brandon lifted his hands above his head, causing the room to once again erupt in applause; he'd won over more than just my heart during the sixteen months we'd been together—yes, I was still counting. "Those of you who knew Cora before will know how great young Brandon has been for her. Love knows no age limit, people—I'm a living testament to that." She looked to where Paul was sitting with Monique bouncing on his knee and waved. "Anyway, enough about me. Back to the birthday girl and her beau, Bran, who I'd like to hand the mic to."

Everyone clapped as Olivia held out the microphone and Bran stood. "What's going on?" I asked, catching him by the arm. I had no idea he was planning on speaking tonight. Not that I knew much about the night at all. It had all been an elaborate plan designed by both Olivia and Bran in order to surprise me with a combined birthday and happy divorce party. Once upon a time, any sort of secret whispering from those closest to me would have sent me into a panic. But birthday surprises were the exception, with this one being particularly exciting since we were celebrating my freedom and the beginning of my new journey in life. *Our* new journey. Personally, I was excited about all the presents on the table, because despite my thirty-one years, I was still a little kid at heart.

"You'll see," Bran said with a wink, heading to the stage.

With my heart thudding in my chest and my hands clasped in front of me, I watched the man I loved more than anything in this world stand in front of a roomful of everyone we both collectively knew. There were school friends, parents, extended family members and colleagues. Even my brother and his family had come. I wondered how Bran and Olivia had managed to pull this off without my finding out, but their careful planning had been well worth it. I'd walked into the hotel thinking Bran and I were having a quiet dinner and was met with a chorus of surprise.

"A year ago today, Cora and I had our first official date. Before that, we'd been quietly falling for each other behind the scenes, and if you believe the newspapers, we were embroiled in a scandalous affair where I purposely led her astray."

"More likely saved her from that cheating scumbag of an ex-husband!" That voice was my mother. She would never forgive Jack for the way he'd treated me. I smiled her way and blew her a kiss. She smiled and waved excitedly. She was a gorgeous woman.

"That's right, I'm the hero of this story," Bran said, winking at my mother, who incidentally, thought he was the most dashing specimen of the male species she'd ever met. The first time she met him, I thought she was going to faint. I was sure she'd steal him off me if given half a chance.

"The anti-hero," Adrian called out, a proud smile on his face as he looked at his son.

"Thanks, Dad." Bran chuckled. Over the past year, there had been a lot of growth in their personal relationship with Bran learning to understand that despite his original parentage, Adrian Sharp was his father. He wasn't an overly affectionate man and felt that being hard on his son growing up would turn him into a stronger man. It was a bit of a messed up way of parenting, because it created a lot of animosity between them. But it was something they were working through, and as Bran came to the end of his undergraduate degree, you could see the dynamic between them shifting—especially since Bran had decided to follow his father's footsteps after all by entering the OPP's Legal Traineeship Program.

"If we could quit the heckling for just a moment, I'd like to talk about the centre of my world." Bran flashed his trademark dimpled smile and melted the hearts of almost everyone in the room, including my own. "Cora, baby, will you come up here for a moment, please?"

I touched my hand to my chest, feeling nervous. What was he planning and why did I need to stand beside him? But I rose to the collective applause going around the room and took his hand while he helped me onto the stage.

"Some of you might not know this," he said, turning toward our audience. "But Cora actually pulled a Cinderella act on me after the first night we met. Instead of leaving her shoe, she left something a little more...intimate for me to find."

"Don't you dare," I gasped, slapping him playfully on the chest. It wasn't that big a deal, but our parents were in the room, *and* his grandparents. None of them needed to know I'd left my underwear for him to find. I literally heard his grandmother asking, "What did she leave?"

"Relax," he said in my ear, planting a kiss against the side of my head before he continued.

"Anyway, I searched high and low, holding the item in my pocket in the hopes of finding her again, and when I was nearly ready to give up, I found her in the last place I was expecting—the Office of Public Prosecutions where she was to be my boss for the duration of my internship. That's when things got really complicated. But, we couldn't say no to each other. Despite all the obstacles life tried to throw our way, we made it through and came out the other end stronger than we were before." His hand tightened a little around mine. "And from there, things just got better and better. I couldn't possibly imagine going through a day without having her in it." Turning to face me, he reached into his jacket pocket and pulled out a small pale blue box.

"What are you doing?" I asked, my voice a nervous whisper as I realised exactly what was going on.

He grinned and lowered himself to the floor, taking one knee before opening the box to reveal a beautiful Tiffany's solitaire. "Baby, from the moment we met, I knew there was something special about you, something I couldn't walk away from. Your name is the sound my heart makes each time it beats, because I've never been happier than with every new day you've been in my life. And, now that you're a free woman, I'd like to catch you up and make you mine. Will you marry me?"

I stuck my hand out and nodded my head emphatically. "Yes!" I forced out. "Do you even have to ask?"

My hand shook as he slid the ring onto my finger then stood to wrap me in his embrace. The room erupted into cheers and applause as he kissed me and spun me around. "I love you so much, Bran," I whispered against his lips.

"I love you too, baby. Now and forever."

He kissed me again, and I knew that in that moment, I was right where I needed to be. Everything I'd been through in life had been designed to lead me right there, to the very moment when my soulmate asked me to be his for the rest of our lives. I'd never considered that I'd want to be owned by someone, but that was before I met a man like Brandon Sharp. At first he took me, then he claimed me, and now he would make sure I was always his. The idea seemed like absolute perfection to me.

THE END

www.lillianaanderson.com

Our Lives Entwined

For information on upcoming releases visit

<u>www.lillianaanderson.com/preorders</u>

ACKNOWLEDGMENTS

AS ALWAYS, there are people to be thanked! Many sets of eyes go in to the creation of each of my books and I am very grateful to every person who takes time out of their lives to help me.

To **Julie Chippindale** and **Mary Sart,** thank you so much for beta reading and giving me excellent feedback to work with. I can't tell you how much I appreciate your sage advice. To my editor, **Marion Archer** of Making Manuscripts, I thank you for your detailed guidance during the first draft and your keen editing eyes on the second. **Helena Cullen** and **Margaret Neal,** thank you for helping to proof the final copy.

To my team of sharers, you're all so wonderful. I don't ask you to do what you do, but you see something I post and share it far and wide. I'm eternally grateful. Thank you all so much. I love you all!

To every blogger and reviewer who has an ARC or has signed up to post about my book – I thank you too. You are the first step to announcing my work to the world. No author can do this without you xoxox

Also, a big thank you to my husband for putting up with my bitching and moaning and his unending support and encouragement.

Thank you to my kids for being so patient while I stare at a computer screen and finish typing out a thought. I love that you all come and sit with me while I work just to spend a bit of extra time with mummy!

And of course – thank you to all of my readers. You are the most important of all. Without you, I would be writing to the crickets.

Mwah! xoxox

ABOUT THE AUTHOR

Bestselling Author of the Beautiful Series, Drawn and 47 Things, Lilliana has always loved to read and write, considering it the best form of escapism that the world has to offer.

Australian born and bred, she writes New Adult Romance revolving around her authentically Aussie characters with all the quirks you'd expect from those born Down Under.

Lilliana feels that the world should see Australia for more than just it's outback and tries to show characters in a city and suburban setting.

When she isn't writing, she wears the hat of 'wife and mother' to her husband and five children.

Before Lilliana turned to writing, she worked in a variety of industries and studied humanities and communications before transferring to commerce/law at university.

Originally from Sydney's Western suburbs, she currently lives a fairly quiet life in suburban Melbourne.

For more information on Lilliana and her work:

www.lillianaanderson.com
info@lillianaanderson.com